Deborah Simmons

MY LORD DE BURGH
"…a luminous novel about a journey toward
a celebration of self, and a love story not to be missed."
—*Romantic Times*

THE GENTLEMAN THIEF
"Ms. Simmons has a delightful flair for comedy."
—*Romantic Times*

Deborah Hale

THE WEDDING WAGER
"…this delightful, well-paced historical
will leave readers smiling and satisfied."
—*Library Journal*

A GENTLEMAN OF SUBSTANCE
"This exceptional Regency-era romance
includes all the best aspects of that genre….
Deborah Hale has outdone herself…."
—*Romantic Times*

Nicola Cornick

THE VIRTUOUS CYPRIAN
"…this delightful tale of a masquerade gone awry
will delight ardent Regency readers."
—*Romantic Times*

THE LARKSWOOD LEGACY
"…a suspenseful yet tenderhearted tale of love…"
—*Romantic Times*

THE LOVE MATCH
Harlequin Historical #599—March 2002

**DON'T MISS THESE OTHER
TITLES AVAILABLE NOW:**

DEBORAH SIMMONS

DEBORAH HALE

NICOLA CORNICK

THE LOVE MATCH

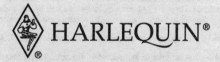

HARLEQUIN®

TORONTO • NEW YORK • LONDON
AMSTERDAM • PARIS • SYDNEY • HAMBURG
STOCKHOLM • ATHENS • TOKYO • MILAN • MADRID
PRAGUE • WARSAW • BUDAPEST • AUCKLAND

ISBN 0-373-29199-X

THE LOVE MATCH

Copyright © 2002 by Harlequin Books S.A.

The publisher acknowledges the copyright holders
of the individual works as follows:

THE NOTORIOUS DUKE
Copyright © 2002 by Deborah Siegenthal

CUPID GOES TO GRETNA
Copyright © 2002 by Deborah M. Hale

THE RAKE'S BRIDE
Copyright © 2002 by Nicola Cornick
First North American Publication 2002

This edition published by arrangement with Harlequin Books S.A.

® and TM are trademarks of the publisher. Trademarks indicated with
® are registered in the United States Patent and Trademark Office, the
Canadian Trade Marks Office and in other countries.

Visit us at www.eHarlequin.com

Printed in U.S.A.

DEBORAH SIMMONS

Deborah Simmons is the author of twenty historical romances and novellas. A former journalist, she turned to fiction when a longtime love of historical romance prompted her to write her first book, published in 1989. She lives in rural Ohio with her husband, two children, two cats and a stray dog that stayed. Readers can visit her Web site at www.deborahsimmons.com or write to her at P.O. Box 274, Ontario, Ohio 44862. For reply, a SASE is appreciated.

Please address questions and book requests to:
Harlequin Reader Service
U.S.: 3010 Walden Ave., P.O. Box 1325, Buffalo, NY 14269
Canadian: P.O. Box 609, Fort Erie, Ont. L2A 5X3

THE NOTORIOUS DUKE

Deborah Simmons

For Mary Muth,
dear friend to three generations of my family, with love

Chapter One

Brighton was a bore. Or so Pagan mused as he watched the usual phalanx of wealthy, pampered visitors promenade along the Steyne. He had followed Prinny here, but even the Prince Regent's elegant, and sometimes debauched, gatherings at the Pavilion were beginning to pall. What had been amusing during other visits now only seemed elaborate nonsense, as did so much else these days.

Even though Pagan told himself his growing ennui had absolutely nothing to do with the approach of his birthday, nonetheless he found himself wondering about his options at this juncture in his life. And yet what else would he do? He was no gentleman farmer to bury himself in the country nor was he a politician to waste his time jawing in the House of Lords. So he continued with the usual rounds of gambling and drinking and increasingly tedious social engagements with increasingly tedious companions, such as the one lounging beside him.

As if Pagan's thoughts had stirred him to speech, Hazard Maitland leaned forward to display a very white set of teeth in an ingratiating grin that was so predictable, Pagan had to stifle a yawn.

"Give over, Pagan. You're having me on. You can't actually mean to let Ramsey overturn your old-time driving the New Road without a protest. You've a reputation to uphold," Hazard said. He paused, leaning back in a casual pose, before issuing the expected challenge. "I'll bet you can't best his record by more than a quarter hour."

Hazard hadn't received his nickname without cause. He was always making outrageous wagers and finding himself in dun territory more often than not. Having lost quite a bit at the E.O. Table last night, the man obviously wanted to recoup his losses, but Pagan didn't feel inclined to humor him this afternoon. If Hazard wanted money he had only to ask for it, instead of cloaking his need in dares and false bravado. It was just the sort of posturing that Pagan had once found amusing, but that entertained him no longer.

"Well, if you're too lazy or hen-hearted..." Hazard ventured.

Pagan laughed, unmoved by the taunt. "Racing the New Road is for young pups, just like taking the reins of the mail coach or ogling women from the bow window of White's."

"Young pups? Oh, you still have a case of the blue devils over your upcoming birthday!" Hazard accused.

Pagan didn't bother to respond to that. He did his best to not think about turning thirty—an age he had once viewed as ancient. Just because he didn't want to risk his neck making a fool out of himself did not make him *old.* Or hen-hearted. Or even excessively sensible. "I've raced the New Road before, and it has become tiresome," he drawled with a finality he hoped would put an end to the subject.

Turning his attention away from his companion, Pagan

again surveyed the elegant crowd, his gaze finding and resting on a group of women who appeared to be harassing passersby. Now that was something you didn't see every day on the Steyne, he mused, his interest caught. They appeared to be passing out leaflets, perhaps of a political nature? No. Ladies—*especially* ladies of quality such as these—Pagan noted with a quick glance at their clothing, didn't pass out those kinds of tracts. Religious? Pagan imagined the look on Prinny's face should he inform the Prince that the Methodists were invading Brighton. The notion amused him, and he had to admit that they *looked* like Methodists. One was a whey-faced creature and the other a hatchet-jawed matron that appeared most forbidding.

Then Pagan caught a glimpse of the third member of the party, and he decided he might have to reconsider his church affiliation. Mahogany-colored curls peeked from beneath a beribboned straw bonnet and glinted in the sun, dancing about a heart-shaped face. Creamy skin held a hint of pink on smooth cheeks, a small detail that bespoke a refreshingly careless attitude toward hats. Dark brows arched over thick-lashed eyes whose color escaped him, and Pagan spent a good minute speculating on the shade. Now why couldn't Hazard have picked something intriguing like that to bet on?

But a swift check revealed that Hazard wasn't even watching the women, which proved just how tedious he was, Pagan decided as he returned his attention to the little charmer. At least one other member of the male population had noticed the dark-haired beauty, however, for a florid fellow stopped to take the leaflet from her gloved hands with a flourish. Indeed, he seemed quite smitten—until he read what she had given him.

"A New and Ambitious School for Young Ladies!

Pah!'' he said. ''Waste of good money to send females to school! What are you trying to do, raise a bunch of bluestockings? Schooling for women!'' With a loud snort of disapproval, he unceremoniously dropped the missive onto the street.

He might have been through with the lovely one, but she definitely was not finished with him. ''How dare you, sir?'' she cried. Obviously, not as charming as she looked, she rounded on him with a fierce expression that revealed a stubborn chin Pagan had neglected to notice before. ''How do you condone such boorish behavior? Perhaps with your own ignorance? Perhaps it is *your* mind that needs improving with a good dose of Mary Astell or Catherine Macaulay!''

Ah, a *female philosopher,* Pagan thought to himself as the older woman stepped forward to rein in the fiery beauty. *Too bad she was wasting all that bright young passion on education,* he mused with the disappointment of a connoisseur. He continued his surveillance long enough to make sure that the rebuked gentleman went on his way without further incident, then, having lost all interest in the exchange, he turned back to find Hazard eyeing him with new speculation.

''Pagan, you're terminally bored, and you know it. Why don't you take one of my dares and inject a little excitement into your life?'' Hazard challenged.

Pagan sighed. If he was terminally bored, Hazard was contributing to his decline. ''Perhaps if they involved something more fascinating than risking my best grays on a bad stretch of road, I might consider it,'' Pagan drawled.

''Just so! Racing's sadly flat. Old hat. I was thinking of something more along the lines of your particular specialty…''

"Hallo!" Just then a landau passed in front of them in which two ladies, one of them the wife of a Most Famous Personage, leaned forward to wave dainty handkerchiefs in Pagan's direction. He gave them a lazy nod of acknowledgment. The wife was his for the asking, should he rouse himself to the effort, while the other lady…well, she had proved to be quite inventive. Pagan smiled in fond memory.

"They say there isn't a woman alive who doesn't want you," Hazard remarked, whistling through his teeth as the carriage continued down the road. Pagan shrugged. Women were one of the few pleasures that had not palled for him, though he had become more discriminating lately. It had nothing to do with his *age,* but was simply a matter of an acquired taste, Pagan told himself.

"But I'd wager there must be someone, somewhere, who doesn't care for the cut of your cloth," Hazard said, his voice rising suspiciously. "In fact, I'll put my money on it. What say you?"

Pagan turned his head to fix his companion with a desultory gaze. Had he missed something in Hazard's babbling?

Hazard grinned, a little too eagerly. "I'll make a bet with you that I know *one female* you can't charm into your bed, or at least your good graces."

Against all sense, Pagan found himself intrigued. There was nothing he enjoyed more than a good pursuit, though few enough women gave him that challenge these days. Besides, he had a reputation to uphold, one far more important to him than taking the New Road at the fastest pace. And if he declined, Hazard was certain to pester him about some sort of gamble until he either succumbed or fled. At least this one roused his interest.

He straightened and pushed away from the brick

building he had been leaning against. "Very well, but she'll have to be of our own class and of a reasonable age," Hazard cautioned. He wasn't going to be tricked into wasting his considerable skills on some turbaned ancient or unsavory shop girl.

"Of course!" Hazard answered readily. *A bit too readily,* Pagan realized. What female did he propose to be immune, a devotee of Sappho? A devoted wife? Pagan smiled, a bit smugly, for he could count such women among his conquests. He began to wonder just what Hazard was going to do when he lost yet another wager. Perhaps the experience would be good for him. *Humbling.*

"Well, who shall it be?" Pagan asked with a certain arrogance. After all, his standing with the ladies was unassailable and had been since he was barely out of boyhood. Not even the eminent approach of the dreaded birthday could affect his well-known prowess. He lifted his brows, but Hazard seemed rather confident, as well.

"I name Miss Scholastica Hornsby," he said with a suspiciously triumphant grin.

"Who?" Pagan asked, unable to place the name or even countenance it. *Scholastica.* What kind of a name was that?

"That young lady right there," Hazard said, lifting a hand to point to someone nearby, and with a rather ominous sensation of dread, Pagan turned to see the object of his bet was none other than the dark-haired beauty who was still handing out leaflets and now prattling on loudly about *A Vindication of the Rights of Women.*

Pagan sank back against the building with a groan. Too late he realized that he had let his vanity run away with him, or perhaps that impending birthday nudge him too easily into proving his virility. Usually awake on all suits, he had walked right into Hazard's trap, and to be trapped by someone of Hazard's limited wit...well, that was ignominious indeed.

He should have set more specific guidelines, especially a minimum age, since this girl looked to be barely out of the schoolroom. Normally, Pagan avoided such types like the plague. He liked women with a certain amount of elegance, experience and confidence. Chits such as this one didn't have any experience or confidence, unless they were spoiled brats, which was even worse.

And as far as elegance, there was nothing remotely stylish about standing on the street exhorting the masses to a need for better female schooling. Before accepting this bet, Pagan might have established a minimum of sense, as well! The thought made him lurch forward in horror as he recognized just who this *Scholastica* might be: one of Cubby Hornsby's brood.

Related to the Duke of Carlyle, presumably on the wrong side of the blanket, Cubby vied with Henry Cope, the Green Man, as one of Brighton's resident eccentrics. Cope dressed, ate, and presumably breathed, only green, while Cubby was a philosopher, his rambling estate on the edge of town filled with so-called geniuses and modern thinkers, including several female "colleagues" and various children of indeterminate parentage. This poor girl, having been reared in that environment, was probably short a sheet, just like Cubby and the rest of his household.

Angrily, Pagan turned to his companion in protest, but Hazard stopped him with a wicked grin. "You didn't think it would be easy, did you?" he taunted.

Pagan's eyes narrowed as he considered loosing some teeth in that white smile of Hazard's. Of course, he could

call off the wager, pay Hazard his money and laugh off
the whole thing, but *something* was at stake: his pride,
his reputation, or simply his ability to meet a challenge.
Of course, none of it had a thing to do with the dreaded
birthday.

So, drawing a deep breath, Pagan effected a shrug and
turned to assess his prey.

"Don't look at him!" The admonishment from Miss
Rawlings made Scholastica glance up in surprise.

"Who?" Scholastica asked, though she suspected the
older woman referred to one of the two gentlemen who
had been lounging against a building nearby for some
time. Idlers, no doubt, but so far they had not interfered
with Scholastica's efforts to promote Miss Crossthwaithe's School for Young Ladies. They did not re-
semble footpads, nor did she imagine such men would
dare accost women here in the heart of Brighton's fashionable district. So why wasn't she allowed to view
them? Scholastica, who never took well to decrees, quite
naturally turned her head toward the forbidden fellows,
but before she could get a good look, Miss Rawlings
seized her arm in a fierce grip and swung her back
around.

"Don't stare!" the older woman hissed.

"Oh, no!" Now it was Matilda who whispered
fiercely, bristling in her most forbidding teacher manner.
"He's coming this way!"

"*Who?*" Scholastica demanded in more determined
accents. Unless this fellow was the devil incarnate, she
could not understand why she was not allowed a glimpse
of him. And not one to be denied without good cause,
as all those who knew were aware, she simply threw off

Miss Rawlings's hold and whirled around to face…the Notorious Duke.

Scholastica felt her jaw drop open, for in Miss Rawlings's opinion, he probably *was* the devil incarnate. How he got his name, Pagan, Scholastica hesitated to speculate, but there was no mistaking that tall, superbly dressed form. She had seen him from a distance before among the elegant throng that surrounded the Prince Regent. The Duke of Penhurst was a rich, powerful and sinfully handsome rake and just the sort of wicked character who wouldn't have the slightest interest in education for women, unless it was the kind provided in the city's brothels.

"Perhaps it's time we went home, girls," Miss Rawlings said, but she made no movement to leave, and in fact, seemed rooted to the spot, her eyes fixed upon the oncoming nobleman as though held in some kind of thrall. Scholastica felt no such enchantment. After all, the man was a dissipated character, probably as old as Cubby, and not worthy of their regard. Although she could not imagine what on earth he could possibly want of her, Scholastica held her ground and lifted her chin, clutching the leaflets before her like armor, just in case the snake would strike.

"Good afternoon, ladies," he said, bowing low, and Scholastica realized something immediately. Namely, *he wasn't that old.* Indeed, he looked to be in the prime of life, and she could see all too easily how he charmed his hapless victims. He was as dark and beautiful as an archangel, his voice deep and smooth as some rich confection. Indeed, he was altogether beguiling. And wicked. And dangerous.

And Scholastica would have none of it.

"Your Grace," she said with a dip of a curtsy.

"Ah, you have the better of me, for I know only that you have been diligently presenting these to the populace of our fair Brighton," he said. Bowing slightly, he reached for a leaflet, but Scholastica still gripped them before her like a shield. "May I?" he asked, lifting his dark brows. He tugged, and rather than precipitate a struggle, Scholastica finally let one go, albeit reluctantly.

"Thank you," he said, his elegant lips curving slightly as though she had amused him.

"I hardly think you would be interested, Your Grace," Matilda noted in a rather surly tone, apparently unaffected by the duke's rather formidable looks. Meanwhile, Miss Rawlings obviously had failed to heed her own warnings, for she seemed struck dumb by his magnificence.

He heeded neither one, but leaned close to Scholastica, almost indecently so, his attention focused solely upon her in a way she found most unnerving, as, no doubt, was his intention. "And would you be Miss Crossthwaithe?" he asked, glancing down at the paper.

For a moment Scholastica could not muster an answer, having discovered that his lashes were nearly as long and thick as her own. Then, as he lifted them, she saw the glint in those dark eyes and recovered herself. How appalling that she should suddenly be struck by the most base of feminine weaknesses! But she was not without her fortitude, and she called upon it now to still the ridiculous race of her pulse.

"No. This is Miss Crossthwaithe," she said, pulling Matilda forward. "Why? Have you an interest in female schooling?"

"I doubt that," Matilda snapped, donning her sourest expression. "I intend to educate my girls for other uses than your own!" she said in a tone that might be suitable when tapping an errant boy upon the knuckles, but was not appropriate for a duke of the realm.

Indeed, the Notorious Duke cocked his head slightly, a graceful motion that left no doubt of his arrogance, and Scholastica held her breath. "I'm sorry. I don't believe I heard you," he said, obviously offering Matilda the benefit of the doubt.

"He's getting old, you know," a dry voice noted, and Scholastica turned to see the other lounging gentleman had joined them, as well. He, too, leaned close. "Birthday coming up. Very sensitive," he whispered loudly, as if sharing a confidence.

The duke ignored the man as though he hadn't spoken, and Scholastica wondered if perhaps he *were* hard-of-hearing. "Well, I am told the ocean air can do wonders for the problems of aging," she said with an air of encouragement.

He cocked his head toward her, with that same arrogant tilt, while his friend laughed uproariously, and she wasn't sure what to think. He certainly did seem sensitive about his age, though Scholastic wouldn't have put him past thirty, and of course he was so handsome, who would possibly care how old he was? But he was a rake, and no doubt vain about his looks and everything to do with himself.

Scholastica reminded herself that here was a man who had devoted his life to dissipation, instead of using his money and position for the improvement of society. In the face of that realization, Scholastica's good sense deserted her, as it sometimes did, and she had the sudden urge to give him a good set-down.

"They're promoting a school for women," the other gentleman said a bit too loudly, as though continuing his jest. "Not something of interest to the Duke of Penhurst, I'd say."

Unwittingly, he gave Scholastica her opportunity. "Oh, I wouldn't say that," she noted, giving the duke a bright smile. "Perhaps Your Grace can recommend the school for your children or grandchildren!"

This time there was no mistaking the nobleman's expression. Beneath the veneer of politesse, there was a flicker of something dangerous, as if Scholastica had roused a sleeping beast, casually lethal in its intent.

Even the dazed Miss Rawlings must have seen it, for she suddenly moved, insinuating herself between the two younger ladies and the two gentlemen. "We really should be going along home now, girls," she said, reaching out to take Scholastica's arm and pluck her from the wolf's clutches. However, Scholastica had to admit that the man hardly looked like a rake right now, his handsome face having been stripped of its languid pose.

Indeed, the last glimpse she had of the Notorious Duke, he was eyeing her with no little enmity.

Chapter Two

All the way back to her home, Scholastica was rewarded with the glowing praise of her companions for
her handling of the "intrusion," as Miss Rawlings so
tactfully put it. Perversely enough, it was Matilda who
spoke most vehemently against the duke, while Miss
Rawlings appeared to have undergone a conversion, or
at least a swaying of her usually firm opinions.

But even as she accepted their kudos, Scholastica had
to admit to a bit of disappointment. After all, it wasn't
every day that she met such an infamous personage, and
yet their encounter had been very brief indeed. Too brief,
it struck her now. If she had not felt so compelled to jeer
at him, Scholastica realized, she might have continued
their encounter a little longer. Just for her own edifica-
tion, of course, and not because she was beguiled by a
pair of broad shoulders and a voice like warm chocolate.

Parting with her two companions at the gate to the
estate, Scholastica proceeded to make her way into the
house and upstairs with no little chagrin. Although she
could not claim to have been unaffected by the duke's
looks and manner, far more interesting to her had been

the stimulating nature of their exchange. Against all reasoning, she had enjoyed sparring with him.

And it was that pleasure that made her regret her sharp tongue as she prepared to change for supper. If truth be told, she was becoming a little bored with the same old acquaintances, though she would never admit as much out loud. Cubby was so proud of his eclectic household, of what he called the potpourri of ideas that ebbed and flowed around him, but the fact of the matter was that very few new and original thoughts were exchanged at his gatherings.

His guests all held the same "radical" notions, although after the trouble in France, people had turned away from seeking seminal societal change toward more cerebral philosophies. But it was Cubby who led the group, Cubby's generosity that financed any publishing, Cubby who invited the attendees or the long-term guests. And they all tried to please him or they weren't asked to return, an especial consideration for those often-impoverished writers and thinkers who were glad of a good meal. It was a cynical view, perhaps, but as she grew older, Scholastica began to believe the salons were less an exchange than a parroting of Cubby's latest version of enlightenment.

The Notorious Duke, Scholastica suspected, wouldn't parrot anyone. He was a law unto himself, if rumor was to be believed, indifferent to anyone's influence or opinion, except for the Prince Regent himself perhaps. He was certainly different than anyone else she had ever met. And, as one taught to appreciate individualism, Scholastica now wished she had had the opportunity to explore his character a little more, although from his reputation that might not be a good idea. All too easily, she recalled just how that deep voice had spread over her like melting wax and how those dark eyes had caught and held her own.

Scholastica shivered. It was probably just as well that she would never see him again, for she counted herself well above the sort of feckless females who swooned over a handsome face. Never in her life had she stooped so low as to curry a man's favor, and she would not do so now. Let the other, lesser, ladies of Brighton flock to the Notorious Duke, witlessly begging for his attention, but not Scholastica. She had more important things to occupy her.

At least, that's what she told herself as she hurried down the steps to supper, late again, seemingly because she had lapsed into an overlong reminiscence of her afternoon's encounter. Well, no more! She was going to put Pagan Penhurst from her mind, once and for all, she decided, only to pause, her hand on the heavy carved rail as she gaped like a hayseed. In this instance, she could be excused for staring, she decided, for at the bottom of the stair stood none other than the very object of her thoughts, the Notorious Duke himself.

Scholastica blinked, certain for a moment that she had conjured him from her ruminations, yet surely no memory could do justice to the actual man: tall, dark-haired and dark-eyed, with a masculine power that brooding poets like Byron would never have and fops like Brummel could only aspire to.

He was talking to Cubby, but seeming to have sensed her regard, he turned his head slightly, and his gaze met hers. Too directly. And far too intimately. Indeed, it was as though no one and nothing stood between them, as if they two were the only residents of the house, the town, and, indeed, the world. And then, just as though he could read her thoughts, his lips tipped slightly, sensually, in a kind of knowing curve that set her back up. For that smug smile told her quite clearly that he thought her one of those witless females who melted at his feet and leaped into his bed. Stiffening her spine and lifting her chin, Scholastic stepped down, determined to show him that she was different.

"Ah, Scholastica, dear!" Cubby greeted her with his usual jovial excess, though Scholastica could only manage a stiff nod.

He turned back toward the Notorious Duke with a good-natured grin. "Your Grace, my daughter Scholastica. A gem, isn't she?"

Without waiting for verification, Cubby continued with the introductions. "Scholastica, this is the Duke of Penhurst, a frequent visitor to Brighton, are you not, Your Grace?" Cubby asked.

"Quite so, though I've never had the pleasure of attending one of your lively gatherings," the duke answered.

"An error I am most happy to rectify," Cubby said with a hearty chuckle.

"Miss Scholastica, a pleasure indeed," the duke purred as he nodded slowly, his gaze never leaving her face. Steeling herself against the allure of those dark eyes, Scholastica was tempted to stick out her tongue, but since Cubby was looking on genially, she restrained herself.

"May I take you in to supper?" the duke asked, presenting his arm as though her assent was a forgone conclusion. The arrogant man needed to be brought down a peg, Scholastica thought, and she was just the one to do it! Unfortunately, she could hardly refuse, much to her disappointment, but when she thought of what dining with the Hornsbys was like, her spirits rose. In a quarter hour, the elegant nobleman would probably be running screaming from the room. Smiling a bit devilishly, Scholastica nodded in seeming agreement.

In actuality, she couldn't wait to see the Notorious Duke lose a bit of that confident composure. It shouldn't take long. Neither cook nor housekeeper ever knew how many would be sitting down to eat and since Cubby could never keep very good help, the menu was usually questionable, as well. Quite a few of Scholastica's ten half siblings were in attendance, as were several other current residents of the household, including a poetess of middling talent and a fiery orator. In addition, some young men who frequented the gatherings, arguing laboriously among themselves, were availing themselves of open invitations.

Surely the duke had never seen the like before, Scholastica thought with glee. Perhaps he would be so discomposed as to never return! However, when she slanted a glance at his handsome face, he seemed completely at ease even as he led her to table against the strict order of etiquette. Undoubtedly, the man could do whatever he pleased and presumably did, even as to choosing whom to escort.

He took a seat beside her with supreme grace, and Scholastica had the grim suspicion that he would be just as confident and in command anywhere. And although she waited for the noise, the odd variety of food, the erratic service and the long, tangled arguments about literature and philosophy to drive him mad, he did not even fidget, assuming a relaxed yet elegant pose, as though he were slightly bored.

Scholastica couldn't tell if the posture was real or simply part of his persona as a nobleman and rake, but despite his seeming languor, she could feel him watching her intently, rather like a hawk eyeing a squeaking morsel. Whether those dark eyes held genuine admiration or the pique of a man spurned, she didn't know. Either way, she was determined to ignore him.

However, as the evening wore on, and the man beside her made no move to speak with her, Scholastica found herself becoming the one piqued. As usual, most of the other young men at the table vied for her attention, and she gave it willingly, perhaps showing more partiality than was her wont, but the Notorious Duke was not one of those seeking her favor. Indeed, he said nothing, only occasionally adding a word to the general conversation or whispering something she couldn't quite catch to the lady on his left, the middling poetess, who was hardly the sort to catch his interest.

Why had he come? Scholastica wondered as she became more and more vexed at his behavior. And just what was he doing here? As the last of the fruit and biscuits was set out, she was tempted to ask him outright—or to pinch him to see if he were real. She was beginning to think him only a figment of an imagination desperate for stimulation.

"Plum?" The sound of his deep voice after his long inattention so startled her that Scholastica swung 'round in surprise. And the sight of him, so very handsome and relaxed, while she had worked herself into quite a state—most unusual, mind you!—set her to bedevil him.

"Oh, Your Grace, are you still here? I thought you expired during the first course, or at the very least, fell asleep. That sometimes happens to the aged, you know," she confided, determined to prick his enormous vanity right where she knew it was most sensitive. He eyed her with some surprise, and although she had hoped to disturb his excessive composure a bit, Scholastica was totally unprepared for his laughter. Like all else about him, it was smooth and sensual and so compelling that she was hard-pressed not to swoon.

"Oh, I'm still here, and alive, and awake on all suits," he said, leaning far too close. "Care to test me, darling?"

The intimacy of his stance, his voice, and his words made her flush, and for once in her life, Scholastica wished fervently for the useless fans that other ladies found indispensable. Now, she could certainly use one, for the air around her seemed to heat to an alarming degree quite suddenly. Indeed, she might have used her hand or her napkin to create a welcome breeze, but, thankfully, Pagan Penhurst leaned back just then, resuming his place with easy grace, as though nothing had happened.

The change was accomplished so quickly that Scholastica blinked in amazement, wondering if she had imagined his transformation from bored lounger to predator ready to pounce upon her. And yet, she had the eerie sensation that he was only barely leashed, and could, at any moment, strike, inducing heat and confusion and witless longing in his prey. But, surely, *she* was not his prey.

Flattering as it might be to assume his presence here had to do with her, Scholastica could not really believe it. Although rumors abounded whenever the Notorious Duke visited Brighton, they usually involved some married noblewoman or, less often, an infamous member of the demimonde. Pagan Penhurst would hardly spend his time pursuing green girls of Scholastica's ilk. Would he?

"I wonder that you were so eager to attend one of Cubby's evenings when you contribute so little, Your

Grace," Scholastica commented in an effort to discover his intentions.

His lips curved in that all-too-knowing smile. "Oh, I assure you that I have found something of interest here," he said.

Scholastica frowned at that supreme arrogance. "One wonders, too, Your Grace, just what you did to deserve a sobriquet like Pagan," she said pointedly. Several noblemen had nicknames, especially those of ill repute, such as Hellgate and Cripplegate, and Pagan certainly suggested a life of depravity.

"I was born," he said. At Scholastica's startled look, he smiled, a most beguiling and intimate curve of his mouth. "That's my name."

"Oh," Scholastica whispered. Since aristocratic gentlemen were usually known by their titles, the use of his given name was unusual. "No doubt you have managed to live up to it," she noted, but the Notorious Duke only laughed, robbing her of any verbal victory.

Becoming aware, once more, of the conversation ebbing and flowing around them, Scholastica decided it was time that she made her own views extremely clear, lest this man actually think her fair game in whatever sport he was engaging in.

"So, I assume by your presence here, after our encounter this afternoon, that you have an interest in the education of women that you wish to pursue further?" she asked.

He shrugged, a movement of masculine elegance no doubt intended to make her forget the course of their dialogue, and very nearly successful. Scholastica blinked at those wide shoulders, covered in such a tight midnight-blue coat as to be indecent, and nearly lost her train of thought. She drew a deep breath. "But don't you think women would better serve as wives, if they could hold a discourse with their husbands, engaging their wits, not only their eyes?''

"You needn't work so hard to convince me, darling," he said, leaning close once more. "I can't abide stupid people of either gender." He answered her smoothly, with a flash of white teeth, and Scholastica was so taken with his manner that she was a moment digesting his words. But when she did, she stared at him in surprise. He was telling the truth, she knew, and yet it was so simply put that all the declamation of the room's philosophers seemed silly in comparison.

Still, Scholastica wasn't about to concede just yet. "And how do you reconcile that attitude with your reputation as the Notorious Duke?'' she asked, daring to voice the question that was uppermost in her own mind.

He surveyed her from under those thick lashes, but Scholastica had the fortitude to withstand that liquid gaze. For a while anyway. He smiled. "Notorious? I hardly think so. Notorious for what?'' he asked, though Scholastica suspected he knew full well.

But if he wanted plain speaking, she was more than ready to oblige. "From what I understand, you are most known, not for any accomplishments in politics or science or letters,'' Scholastica said, her reprimand implicit. "But as a ruthless seducer of women.''

He lifted one dark brow. "Ruthless? Hardly. Only those few who call themselves my enemies would deem me ruthless. As for the other...'' He paused to shrug negligently once more, and Scholastica struggled to maintain her composure. "I like women, and, by my own good fortune, they like me, so I would protest that we enjoy each other. Shouldn't the seeking out of pleasure be the privilege of both genders?''

Of course, such a philosophy was often part of the arguments for equality for women, including those voiced by Cubby himself, but neither he nor any of those men could be called a ruthless seducer. "Yes, but doesn't a rake prey on women simply for his own satisfaction?" Scholastica asked.

The duke smiled once more, his full lips curving into the kind of grin that could only be described as wicked, and again she felt the heat in the room rise as he leaned close. "My darling Scholastica, if you imagine that any of my women were left unsatisfied, you are laboring under a misapprehension," he whispered, his voice full of promise, and Scholastica felt her cheeks color, for his reputation claimed no less.

When he took her hand, she nearly jumped as half-formed fears of him leading her off to some private spot to prove his point made her wary, for her own prickly fortitude seemed to be deserting her in the face of his relentless charm. But he only lifted one dark brow, as if in amusement, then escorted her to the withdrawing room. Scholastica let loose a long breath of relief. Or at least that's what she told herself.

Around her, the same old arguments raged, and Scholastica expected the duke to lounge back and assume his pose of boredom. But, as usual, he surprised her. He actually joined in, fending off the speeches of most of her father's luminaries with razor-sharp wit and reasoning, and making several of them appear doltish in their thinking. Cubby roared with laughter at his murmured comments, while the poetess hung on to his every word, apparently struck dumb by his magnificence, just as Miss Rawlings had been.

And in the face of his supreme confidence and grace and eloquence, Scholastica's retinue, as she privately called them, looked like callow boys in comparison. Most of them *were* callow boys, she realized. They were too earnest and puling and posturing. They came to the house, claiming interest in the discussions and arguing for the vindication of the rights of all people, but it hadn't taken Scholastica long to become cynical about their behavior. Although they professed to treat everyone equally, she had quickly deduced that Matilda and Miss Rawlings and other women of a certain age or appearance received far less attention than she did. It was to be expected, she supposed, even of the most free-thinking male, but it was their pretense that so annoyed her.

With Pagan there was no such pretense. Indeed, Scholastica couldn't imagine him doing or saying anything that he did not believe. Right or wrong, he was true to himself. And she couldn't help admiring him for that. His confidence, which so annoyed her when he leaned close, now seemed nothing more than justified. There was something shockingly appealing about a man of such experience and elegance and wit, and with a kind of sad irony, Scholastica realized that he had spoiled her now, for how could she ever look the same upon any of her father's so-called geniuses? Pagan Penhurst, rake and rogue and duke of the realm, was far more intelligent and insightful than any of them.

Although by the end of the evening Scholastica had grudgingly admitted to herself her admiration for the man, she was no closer to discovering the reason for his presence. Was his appearance here her punishment for disturbing his peace this afternoon, for taunting him about his age, or was there more to it than that? Because of the constant press of guests about them, Scholastica couldn't speak as freely as she might have, had they been alone. The very thought made her shiver, for she knew that a private conversation with the Notorious Duke was not a good idea, even as she longed for a chance to find out what on earth the man was about.

And when he took his leave, he was just as mysterious about his motivations. Indeed, Scholastica was beginning to think their earlier meeting nothing more than a coincidence when he bowed low over her hand. "Such a pleasure to meet you," he purred, his eyes holding some deep, dark promise. "Shall I call upon you tomorrow afternoon?"

"Oh, please don't bestir yourself," Scholastica replied, fighting against the girlish giddiness that seized her. The duke only laughed, a low, musical rumble that made her heart palpitate unnervingly. And then he was gone before she could marshal her wits to deny him further, if indeed she could.

For Scholastica was finding it harder and harder to remember just why Pagan Penhurst was the enemy.

She was caught, as neatly as a fish to bait, Pagan thought as he strolled down the crescent toward Cubby's town house. Oh, she might be thrashing on the hook, a bit less than willing, unlike most of his ladies, but just a couple swift jerks on the line and she should be in his lap. At the thought, hunger rose up in him, surprising in its intensity, and Pagan caught a swift breath.

That is the last thing I need, he reminded himself firmly. Against all odds the object of Hazard's wager had turned out to be interesting. Confident? She had the wherewithal of someone twice her age and experience. Elegant? How had he ever thought her not so? Even when spouting female rhetoric, she held herself with a beauty and grace that defied her antecedents, or perhaps defined them. She was, after all, related to a duke.

Pagan smiled. He never would have believed that he could possibly have enjoyed an evening spent at one of Cubby Hornsby's sham salons, but she had entertained him beyond anything with her wit and her beauty and her *passion.* He frowned. Unfortunately, it was best not to dwell on that particular aspect of Miss Scholastica, or her innocent yet provocative appeal. No matter how much his body clamored for more, he was not in the habit of seducing genteel young virgins. He enjoyed his reputation as a connoisseur of women; he did not care to be known as a cradle-robbing cad.

Besides, the pleasure was in the pursuit, he told himself, and in proving wrong a certain friend, who had dwelled far too much on his upcoming birthday. His age, despite Miss Scholastica's little barbs, obviously had not affected his talents one bit, for he sensed the little philosopher's capitulation was eminent. The bet would soon be won. But not *too* soon. Pagan was enjoying himself for the first time in weeks, maybe months, and he had no intention of putting an end to it just yet.

Today he was would take her for a drive, which ought to be enough, should he see Hazard, to win the wager, but Pagan was after more. He would not be contented with Miss Scholastica's idle attention or an afternoon's flirtation. He wanted, indeed, he *demanded,* that she succumb totally. She must be *his,* he decided with such ferocity that it startled him. He shook his head and tried to shrug off the feeling, so wholly unlike his usual attitude, attentive yet just a bit distanced. He had never liked the messiness of emotional ties, which was one reason he rarely stayed long with his lovers. Better to enjoy, like a connoisseur of fine wines, the taste and the bouquet, to appreciate and admire the uniqueness, rather than to drink oneself into insensibility.

However, Pagan couldn't help but note that Miss Scholastica would tempt a man to overindulge. Again, Pagan was startled by the sudden, fierce burst of possessiveness that seized him, startled enough to be wary. Perhaps it was best he could not pursue this wager to the obvious conclusion. He would see to it that Scholastica was his for the taking—and then walk away. She would be his to pluck, like a rose unbloomed.

Unfortunately, someday someone else would have the pleasure of seeing the blossom unfold, a realization that did not sit well with Pagan. Purely for competitive reasons, of course. He frowned, wondering why the devil that fool Hazard had to pick someone young and untouched and related, however obliquely, to the Duke of Carlisle. And he swore under his breath even as he reached her doorstep.

No one answered the bell at Cubby's residence. No doubt, the butler was deep in argument with the footman about the education of women, Pagan thought with no little impatience. Opening the door himself, he was met by a harried-looking maid, who curtsied quickly and informed him that he was to wait in the morning room for Miss Scholastica. And so he was led past a variety of debating young people—didn't they ever tire of working their mouths?—to a small room that was messy but blessedly devoid of inhabitants.

Although it seemed that most of the pieces of furniture were covered with items of some sort, at last Pagan found a vacant seat. He sat gingerly on the edge of a rather threadbare chair only to find himself staring at some choice reading material, namely *Letter to the Women of England on the Injustice of Mental Subordi-*

nation and the ubiquitous *A Vindication of the Rights of Women.*

Had the devilish Scholastica arranged this little display for his benefit? Pagan wondered. A slow smile of appreciation spread across his face as he leaned back and propped up his booted feet to wait for her, anticipation running hot in his normally cool veins.

Chapter Three

An hour later Pagan was no longer wondering. He was quite certain that the minx was deliberately delaying him, while trying to force her views down his throat. Did she think that locking him up in a room with these books would make him read them? Pagan might have laughed, if he weren't flush with unaccustomed impatience. Of course, he ought simply to walk out. His women knew that to keep him waiting was to lose his favor, that he countenanced no ploys of any kind. Unfortunately, Scholastica was not one of his women...yet.

And so the pursuit kept him where he was, determined more than ever to take her driving with him, whatever charming protests she might manufacture. Perhaps she hoped to be rid of him with all this nonsense? The idea was so novel that it gave Pagan pause. Imagine, a female actually courting his disfavor! He shook his head in disbelief, but there was no denying that he was kicking his heels with growing annoyance. And Scholastica seemed too intelligent to believe he would embrace her philosophies after but a few minutes idle reading.

Against his will, Pagan grinned. He could envision what Society would say if he started championing female education. Picking up the volume of *Vindication,* he considered penning notes in the margins to little Scholastica's attention, but decided against it. After all, it had been quite a while since he'd read the book.

Glancing at the mantel clock once more, Pagan wondered whether he ought not make his way upstairs and beard her in her room, but the sudden, swift leap of his pulse made him hesitate. He was no boy to be ruled by his passions, and yet, somehow, he didn't quite trust himself to be alone with her in her boudoir. He replaced the volume before him, annoyed to discover his hand was trembling, a wholly unfamiliar reaction that he could only put down to the ultimate frustration of his pursuit.

And then, just as Pagan stood, she appeared in the doorway, as fresh and lovely as the new bloom to which he likened her, but with an expression he had never seen in any flower. He smiled, and a host of emotions flickered across her open visage. Admiration, which he took as his due. Temptation, which he acknowledged, as well. But also a wariness that spurred him to move toward her swiftly, before her considerable wit could disarm him. Reaching behind her, he closed the doors once more, leaving them alone.

And then he kissed her, just to prove that he could.

Her back was to the white-painted portal, her face to him, upturned and gilded with surprise. He lifted a hand to tilt her head and lowered his own, brushing his lips against hers in just the faintest of exploration. Heat rushed through him, firing his blood as though he were much deeper into the game. To his consternation, his fingers shook again, and to still them he took her mouth more firmly, first one lip and then the other in a delicious foray that threatened his composure.

And then he stroked her with his tongue, teasing the

edges of her mouth until she opened for him with a soft sound that made him hard with want, and he leaned into her, pressing his body against hers as he tasted the rich flavor of her mouth, fresh and yet seductive. She was such a feast for the senses that he found it difficult to maintain control, to ply her with his usual practiced skill. When he felt the first touch of her tongue against his own as she sought him out, her delicate hands against the material of his coat, he loosed a groan, so affected that he could barely muster the wits to call a halt.

It was absurd really, ludicrous for a seasoned seducer of his talents and experience to come the slightest bit undone by a mere kiss from a young miss with a tart tongue, and yet when Pagan finally managed to pull away, his breath was coming shockingly swift and harsh. And only the most ruthless implementation of controls prevented him from returning for more.

Pagan closed his eyes, as if to shut out temptation, but then he only saw himself taking her against the door, her lemon-yellow skirts bunched about her waist, her slender legs wrapped around him as he stroked, deep and slow and... He whirled around, disoriented by thoughts better suited to a pimply-faced boy and swore under his breath. Lifting a hand to his forehead, he was chagrined to find a bead of sweat. He wiped it away and drew in a deep breath, searching for the composure that rarely had the audacity to desert him.

Then, only then, after seeking and finding it and cloaking himself in it, did Pagan turn to face her again. "Shall we go for a drive?" he asked smoothly as he bowed. And without waiting for an answer, he reached around her and opened the door, a rake glad of his reprieve. It was both laughable and lamentable.

And though he played at his usual charming self,

throughout the drive Pagan kept his distance, suddenly wary of this seemingly innocent young thing with the ability to affect him so powerfully. He was used to being in control at all times, and he didn't like the sensation that it was slipping away from him, let alone into the hands of a girl barely out of the schoolroom.

Itchy in his own skin, Pagan kept glancing at his companion to see if she had grown horns or some other emblem of her demonic command. But every time he looked, she appeared wholly benign, intelligent, amusing, and attractive, yet hardly the sort of woman who could lure a man beyond all endurance.

Pagan shook his head in confusion. He had been enticed by the most beautiful, sophisticated women in the country, and the Continent, as well, some more intelligent, most more sensual, and plenty with more luscious curves. And every single one dressed more provocatively than Scholastica, who totally disregarded the fashion for low-cut gowns, presumably as a nod to her theories on women's rights. Her colorful dress was pretty, but covered all except the lower parts of her slender arms. So why did he keep staring as if to catch a glimpse of that which was hidden?

She laughed, a fresh and musical sound, at some comment of his, and Pagan decided he had known no lady with a sharper wit or more amusing sense of humor. But since when had that become a prerequisite to passion? Yet, somehow when he looked at her, he saw laughter and sin and delight all rolled into one. Perhaps that was it, Pagan thought as he began to sweat again. She made such a nice, neat little package of *everything*. Why hadn't he seen it before? And when would he cease marveling at it?

By the time he deposited her once more at the door

of Cubby's rambling household, Pagan felt something akin to panic pressing in on him, and he was only too glad to rid himself of Miss Scholastica Hornsby and her bright smile and teasing eyes. Eyes the color of caramel. Sweet and rich and... He reached up a hand to mop his forehead again. Obviously he was losing his mind. He wondered vaguely if dementia set in around thirty.

As if he weren't having enough problems, whom should he see on his tortured walk home but the instigator of his incipient misery: Hazard Maitland, smiling and fit and looking particularly smug for a man about to lose a bet.

"Ho, there, Pagan! I was looking for you. I do believe you've been avoiding me," Hazard scolded with a smirk. "Care to pay up on our little wager?"

"No, for it's you who owe me money," Pagan answered. "Indeed, if you had been out and about just a few moments ago, you would have seen me taking Miss Scholastica Hornsby for a drive."

Hazard laughed. "So you say! Well, I guess I'll have to take your word upon it, eh? But I'm afraid that just driving the girl down the Steyne is not enough. Why, she could have been forced to join you by Cubby or one of her elders," he said.

Elders? "She is not a child," Pagan noted, his voice low and menacing.

Hazard lifted his quizzing glass, an annoying affectation at the best of times, and fixed it upon Pagan, just as if he had said something fascinating. "As you say," he murmured with a shrug.

"Plenty of young ladies her age are already married. With children," Pagan said.

"And just how old is the chit?" Hazard asked, looking bug-eyed through that blasted glass.

Pagan had no idea. "Old enough," he muttered. *But old enough for what?*

Hazard continued to peer at him in a most peculiar fashion. "Well, if you feel you are making some sort of progress with the girl, then perhaps I should inform her of your true nature," he suggested.

Scholastica already had a fairly good notion of his true nature, or at least as much of it as anyone, but Pagan took exception to Hazard's threat. "You're the one who made the wager. The least you can do is not interfere," he said through gritted teeth.

"Oh, very well," Hazard said with a sigh. "But I'm not giving you forever, you know, and if you even dream of collecting any money, I shall have to have something a bit more indicative of the lady's devotion than a ride 'round the park."

Pagan frowned, ill liking the sound of that. "I won't have a scandal," he warned.

Hazard whistled through his teeth. "My, my, aren't we getting particular in our old age!"

Ignoring the barb, Pagan reached out to move the quizzing glass from his line of vision to eye his friend directly. "You chose her, not I, through no fault of hers, and I don't want her gossiped about," he said in no uncertain terms.

"What? Any more than she is already?" Hazard muttered.

Scholastica stepped into the schoolroom, carefully making her way around various boxes. The place smelled musty, and she left the door ajar to air it out. The small building was hardly more than a gardener's cottage and shed, set far behind Cubby's house, but he had graciously lent the premises to Matilda for her school, and all of her friends had been helping with the preparations.

Although Scholastica once might have complained about the task ahead of her, the unpacking of books that had been donated to the establishment, now she was grateful for the familiar chore. It was exceedingly dull work, and yet she welcomed it, for her thoughts were in such a turmoil as to need steady employment. Still, her attention kept drifting to the open door, where she could glimpse a fine summer's day.

However, it wasn't the ocean spray or long stretch of seaside or even the salt breeze that tugged at her thoughts so much as the question of what was going on out there in her absence. Particularly with a certain nobleman. Where was he now? What was he doing? How did he look? Questions that Scholastica would once have deemed nonsensical seemed to have taken over her thoughts. And although one part of her realized just how frivolous such ruminations were, quite another part of her, seemingly the larger part, embraced them as the only ones of any true worth.

She set a thick volume upon the desk and paused, cocking her head at an errant sound, then sighing with dismay as her pulse increased its pace in anticipation. In truth, she had no reason to believe that the man would call upon her again today. She had not seen him at all yesterday, and even during their drive the day before he had seemed a bit distant.

Indeed, she might never see him again, Scholastica noted with a pang. And yet, some heretofore untapped feminine intuition told her he would be back. If so, she knew the household would direct him here. Was she reckless to have come here alone? More reckless still to hope that he would join her? Scholastica had never been overly cautious, yet she told herself she was perfectly safe on Cubby's property in broad daylight. Until she remembered *the kiss*.

How could she forget it? Little else had occupied her mind since it had taken place, and certainly nothing else had filled her dreams. Scholastica shivered in remembered delight, her cheeks flushing, her heart pounding. Oh, she had been kissed before, but usually by fumbling young men who made a muddle of it, too inexperienced and too eager to do anything except dismay her.

Never had she dreamed that a simple kiss could melt her very body, and soul, as well. Of course, there was nothing simple about the Notorious Duke or his kisses. Complex, sensual, gentle, insistent, shockingly pleasurable, they had made her ache for more, to remain clasped in his arms forever. Scholastica shuddered, still a bit wary of the overwhelming sensations that such a man roused in her, a man well known for his way with women.

But the Notorious Duke had turned out to be altogether different than she had imagined, very different indeed than she had been led to believe. Surely a man of such ill repute ought to be a boor, or at least a bore with nothing but seduction on his mind. Instead, he was witty and knowledgeable and oh, so interesting! He wasn't perfect, far from it, Scholastica thought with a smile. She knew he was vain, but she had come to adore that vanity and to delight in teasing him about it. And, then, of course, there was his past. A man with his sort of reputation could hardly be ideal, but wouldn't perfection be dull anyway? Far better to be interesting!

Scholastica could practically recite what any other person in her father's house would say at any given moment. Those supposedly eccentric types had become all too easy to read. But she never really knew what Pagan was going to do or say or what went on behind those haunting, dark eyes of his. He was so confident, so sure of himself, *so sure of her,* that Scholastica was sorely tempted to succumb to his charms.

The thought was not so shocking as it might have been had she been any other genteel young woman of reasonably decent birth. Most of them were raised to be wives under a strict code designed to keep them pure until marriage. But unlike most young women of her station, Scholastica had been raised in a less restricting environment. The constant exchange of ideas in her household, the proposing of modern views and notions of equality between genders had led to a less rigid upbringing. She knew several women and men drawn together by intellect had gone on to become far more intimate. Some of these unions had led to marriage, some had not, and some had borne fruit in the way of children.

Scholastica included.

Although Cubby had claimed her as his own, giving her a name, he had not been married to her mother, an artist who had died not long after her birth, and Scholastica had been raised by a succession of committed women, some of them involved with her father, some simply taking refuge in his house with its atmosphere of intellect. Indeed, sometimes she even wondered if the tiny portrait she treasured was really her mother, or if one of the others who sometimes disappeared only to reappear with an infant, had given birth to her.

Although hers was not a typical childhood, Scholastica told herself that strong women who made a difference in the world, even luminaries such as Mary Wollstonecraft, paid little heed to society's strictures. Mary herself had a love child by one man before marrying another and dying in childbed.

Of course, Pagan was a little more hedonistic in his pursuit of pleasure. Indeed, what was shocking to Scholastica was that she, who had never been the least bit moved by any of the earnest young men who frequented her circle, was drawn to such a man. Which simply brought her thoughts 'round full circle to all the reasons why he, above all others, was preferable to her mind.

Scholastica was still standing there, lost in thought, a heavy book clutched in one hand, the rest unpacked beside her, when Matilda came in. "Woolgathering?" she snapped, taking the volume from Scholastica in a rather rough movement.

"What? Oh, yes, I suppose so," Scholastica admitted, and to her surprise, a blush rose in her cheeks.

It did not go undetected by her observant companion. Indeed, Matilda seemed infuriated by her reply as she moved to the box in front of Scholastica. "And sadly, the subject of your thoughts is quite apparent!" she noted.

"What do you mean?" Scholastica asked, baffled by her friend's ill mood.

Slamming down one heavy text with what seemed to be excessive force, Matilda glared at her. "Don't try to be coy with me, Scholastica. It doesn't become you, but then *he* doesn't, either."

"What are you saying?" Scholastica asked, truly bewildered.

Matilda fisted her hands at her waist and gave her the sort of fierce look a disappointing student might receive, not a friend of long standing. "I simply refuse to countenance what appears, by all accounts, to be a relationship of some sort between you and the Notorious Duke!"

She looked so furious that Scholastica thought she was acting, teasing perhaps, but there was no mistaking that scolding glint in her eye. Scholastica felt a little hurt, for though Matilda was outspoken, it wasn't like her to attack someone personally, especially one of her friends. She shrugged, in unconscious imitation of Pagan himself.

"The duke isn't as bad as people think," Scholastica said, reaching out for one of the books. "I imagine it amuses him to live up to his reputation," she added, almost casually, so not to reveal the depth of her feelings to Matilda's scorn.

But even that simple reply seemed to rouse Matilda further. She grabbed the volume out of Scholastica's hand, so as to claim her full attention. "He is a predator, Scholastica, a man who preys upon women!"

The force of Matilda's opinion had twisted her face into a fierce mask of fury that startled Scholastica. "Nonsense," she managed to reply. "He adores women, and they adore him. It is a case of mutual admiration," she said, taking up another text in a firm dismissal of the subject.

But Matilda would not let it go. "Is that so?" she asked. "I suppose his relentless pursuit of you was undertaken with your full consent and cooperation?"

Scholastica colored. It was true that Pagan's marked attention to her had been unremitting, despite all her initial efforts to discourage him. And yet she had come to like, even expect as her due, the attentions she had first spurned. Had he sensed some weakness in her that hinted of her eventual capitulation, or as Matilda was intimating, did he woo any female who caught his fancy in like fashion, without regard to her wishes? The thought made Scholastica pause, and Matilda quickly seized upon the doubt she had sown.

"I know that even the best among us have fallen victim to the honeyed lies of men, but I never imagined that you would be so foolish as to succumb to the dubious charms of one of *them!*" Matilda exclaimed.

The venomous words jolted Scholastica from her own uncertainties. "Matilda, I hardly think we can quarrel with all of mankind, nor would I want to. I have never claimed to despise every member of the male gender. Indeed, I thought we agreed that only through change of education and instruction could all people, boys and girls alike, be taught to respect each other."

"Children, perhaps, not grown adults!" Matilda said in a harsh, dismissive tone.

"But many of the gentlemen who frequent Cubby's gatherings see things differently, as do others outside of our limited circle, I'm sure. I don't hate men in general, nor do I think any of the females in Cubby's household do," she said, giving Matilda a pointed look. "I just hate the way women are denied educations and opportunities to be other than ornaments."

"Very well, I concede your point, that I cannot condemn all men, though the vast majority, by doing nothing, contribute to our plight," Matilda said, her lips pursed tightly. "But, Scholastica, that man, the Notorious Duke, is the embodiment of everything we stand against!"

"Nonsense," Scholastica murmured, unable to equate the handsome and seductive duke with the subordination of females. He seemed more like a boon to womankind…

"He is a powerful man, who by his title and position, supports and upholds male domination of our society. But what is worse, he personally degrades women by using them as no more than receptacles of his lust, to be

ruined and discarded!'' Matilda cried, working herself
into a fervor once more.

Scholastica blinked. Although she considered herself
as intelligent and capable as any man, she could not seem
to muster any outrage about Pagan, who seemed to provide women with one of the few joys to be had in life.
Or at least that's what she had heard. Unfortunately, she
could not really speak from experience...

''I hardly would refer to what seems, by all accounts,
to be a mutual, uh, experience as degrading,'' Scholastica said.

''You defend him?'' Matilda cried. *''You dare defend
him?''*

Her face twisted fiercely again in response to Scholastica's shocked silence, and she lunged forward. ''Defend *this,* then!'' she shouted. ''Your Pagan has got so
many brats upon his hapless victims that he opened his
own orphanage for them. They call it Pagan's Paternity.''

As Matilda stepped back, for the first time this day
she appeared pleased, apparently by the expression of
horror that crossed Scholastica's face. Then, with an evil
smile of contentment, she turned on her heel and strode
from the building, leaving Scholastica to ponder the de-
fense of a man who would father bastards without
thought or guilt or responsibility, for an orphanage was
certainly not her idea of responsibility.

She sank down, unseeing, onto a hard bench, surprised
by the ache in her chest. Really, she had known what he
was—if not just how depraved!—so why should she feel
the least bit dismayed at Matilda's announcement? Yet
she did. She felt hurt, not only by her friend turning upon
her, but by Pagan's perfidy. She had liked him, had
melted at his kiss, and now she wondered if he intended
to get her with child, too, only to lock it away! The

revulsion that thought induced made her struggle for breath, but her chest seemed to constrict, as if something hard had lodged there that no amount of sea breeze or saltwater dose could cure.

It was a new sensation, wholly unknown to her, this mixture of grief and disgust and pain, and for once in her life, Scholastica felt like indulging in that most weak of feminine behaviors: weeping. How maudlin! she scolded herself. And yet, awareness of her condition did nothing to alleviate it. Indeed, she might have gone so far as to cater to her own whim and weep, if not for a knock upon the open door.

Had Matilda returned? Scholastica gulped, feeling quite unable to face the woman and her righteous gloating, or, more likely, a fervid apology tendered with a request for forgiveness. Hastily composing herself, Scholastica stood and faced the opening. "Yes?" she said as calmly as she could muster. She was determined to brush off her friend and flee with as much dignity as she could gather to her.

But it was not Matilda's familiar form that appeared in the doorway. It was another, no less well-known for its brief acquaintance with her, yet even more distressing. At the sight of that dark hair, those wide shoulders and that handsome face, Scholastica shuddered.

"Good afternoon! I believe you hinted the other day that I might help you with your labors," Pagan said, his voice so smooth and rich and alluring that her own body was tempted to betray her. He tilted his head, his dark eyes seeming to search her own. "With the school?"

Before Matilda's arrival, Scholastica would have greeted him warmly, thinking it wonderful that a duke of the realm, with far more important things to do, would deign to help her sort books for the new establishment.

Now, however, she could only wonder if he had hoped to catch her here alone for his own nefarious purposes. To bend her back over the table? To get her with yet another by-blow?

"Scholastica?" Her name, spoken for the first time without the proper salutation, was painful to her, as was the look of concern, entirely false, no doubt, that crossed his gorgeous features. He took a step forward, as if to reach for her, and she fought the urge to flee, a coward in the face of his powerful allure.

Instead, Scholastica lifted her chin. "Your Grace, I bid you grant me leave to excuse myself now—and forever—from your presence," she said as firmly as possible.

Then, she made her exit, refusing, in a bow to her sudden weakness, to look at his face, whether for fear of what she would see there or for fear of what she would not, Scholastica wasn't sure.

Chapter Four

Scholastica returned to the house, eager to seek out the privacy of her room, only to be detained by the usual press of people. She realized, suddenly, just how much she hated Cubby's salons and the constant flow of visitors. Better to be with one person you cared about deeply than all these superficial acquaintances! And not one of her so-called friends questioned her about her well-being, although she knew that something must have shown upon her face, for hadn't Pagan seen it instantly? Despite his black behavior, he was far more perceptive than anyone else in her life, a discovery that shocked and disappointed her.

Even Cubby paid no heed to her agitation, but that was hardly surprising, for Cubby always was most concerned with himself. He seemed particularly jovial this afternoon, and Scholastica ducked out of his way, intending to flee upstairs, but his booming voice stopped her in her tracks.

"Ah, there you are, Scholastica, dear! There's been a change in plans for this evening," Cubby said, puffing out his considerable chest. "I've been invited to a little soiree by the Duke of Penhurst, who most *specifically* requested that you come along, too," he noted with a wink.

Scholastica struggled for breath to reply, but the lump in her chest seemed only to grow, making her throat tight. "I'm not feeling well, sir, and can hardly be assured of recovering sufficiently to be able to attend," she finally managed to respond.

"Nonsense!" Cubby answered with his usual lack of concern for anyone's welfare except his own. And this man claimed to be enlightened? Indeed, in his sudden desire for noble society, he seemed to have conveniently forgotten his views upon idle aristocrats.

"I wonder that you wish to keep company with such a man," Scholastica said.

"Pagan?" Cubby asked, as if surprised by her vehemence. "Oh, he's not a bad sort! One of the better fellows of his class, I daresay."

"Indeed?" Scholastica said, her voice thick with both pain and contempt. "I realize you are a modern thinker, but how can you condone a man who has so many bastards as to place them in an orphanage?"

To Scholastica's utter shock, Cubby laughed, quite loud and long, before pulling out a handkerchief with which to wipe his streaming eyes. "Lud, girl, you can't have fallen for that foolishness, have you? I would expect you to have a bit more sense, but even the best of us lose our wits in *some* situations, eh?" he asked with an indulgent smile.

Scholastica had no idea what he was talking about. She must have looked so lost that Cubby finally bestirred himself enough to pat her on the shoulder.

"You, my dear, have swallowed one of the ton's favorite bits of gossip, a total untruth, to be sure, but fine fodder for the wagging tongues," he said.

Scholastica's heart lurched within her breast, but she remained skeptical. Like a big, selfish boy, Cubby was not above manipulating the facts to suit himself. "You mean, there is no orphanage?" she asked, eyeing him closely.

"Oh, there's an orphanage, to be sure, and Pagan established and funds it. But I believe he is quite, uh, careful in his pursuit of the ladies. And no man, even one of the duke's notorious, ahem, talents, could father that many children so quickly. Unless, of course, you think of those foreign princes, those pashas with their innumerable wives," Cubby said, getting that look that told her he would happily expound upon a favorite speculation.

"Then why do they call it Pagan's Paternity?" Scholastica demanded, forcing him back to the topic at hand.

Cubby snorted. "Because the ton like to believe what they will. It's far easier for them to whisper nastily about by-blows than to consider that one of the realm's noblemen might actually be doing some good in the world. Lud, then they might be expected to put some of their wealth toward solving the ills of the country instead of spending it in mindless frivolity!" he said.

Scholastica felt stricken. "But his grace—" she began, only to have Cubby cut her off with a wave of his hand.

"I think it suits Pagan just as well to have that scandal added to his reputation. You know, some men don't care to be known for their Good Works," he said, shaking his head as though uncomprehending of such selflessness.

Scholastica blinked in confusion. "You mean to tell me that the Notorious Duke has established the orphanage as a Good Work?"

"Why, of course, my dear girl! In fact, I believe he has some other charitable establishments, not work-houses, mind you, but places where the poor can go. Not too popular with some of the politicians, who might have to admit that our country is not perfect, eh? I expect that's why he keeps it all quiet," Cubby mused.

Scholastica could find nothing more to say because the lump in her chest seemed to have dissolved in a burst of euphoria. Unfortunately, that elation was all too brief, replaced by abject misery as she remembered her recent behavior in the schoolhouse. She sank down on the near-est chair with a groan as her curt dismissal of the duke returned to haunt her. Although Scholastica still wasn't sure what Pagan had wanted of her and had been afraid to hope for more of his attention, now she was utterly certain to not receive it.

Thanks to her own reckless actions, whatever relation-ship she had with the Notorious Duke was over now, per her own fierce demand.

Pagan was not in a good mood. He hated hosting par-ties and was only doing so tonight to lure a certain lady into his lair, to prove once and for all that he had won the damn bet. Only he hadn't. She wasn't here and wasn't likely to appear, though he could not figure out for the life of him what, exactly, had gone wrong.

It had taken him a full day to recover his composure after their drive, but Pagan finally had convinced himself that the bizarre feelings he had suffered in the company of Miss Scholastica Hornsby were nothing more than a figment of a rather fevered imagination. All that sweating and groaning wasn't like him at all and could only be the product of excessive sexual frustration. Obviously, knowing that he wouldn't receive his usual reward at the end of his pursuit had driven him to the brink. How else to explain his overt reaction to one simple kiss?

Once this whole business was over, he would set about finding himself a suitable lover to satisfy needs he had let languish for too long. In the meantime, just because he couldn't fulfill his immediate desires, didn't mean he had to hand over his money to Hazard, who not only would take it gladly, but would spread the tale of Pagan's defeat all over Brighton—and London, as well.

Although Pagan's reputation could probably withstand the blow, his vanity decried it. And there was no reason for him to surrender the bet. Despite a momentary wariness on his part, he wasn't afraid of any woman, especially some female philosopher. Let her do her worst. She would find that he succumbed to no female's spell, now or ever!

Unfortunately, his vow could not be put to the test, for Scholastica was not here, nor did he expect her to arrive anytime soon. To Pagan's astonishment, she had given him the cut direct earlier this day, leaving him to gape after her in her wretched little school, laid low by a green girl! Certainly, some of the ton's ladies had feigned a protest when he pursued them, but none had ever pretended indifference, let alone refused him outright. Pagan was rather at a loss and did not care for the sensation. He shook his head, unable to understand her abrupt reversal. When he had left her at the house after their drive she had seemed ripe for the picking, and then…

Hazard! Pagan nearly growled the name out loud as he wondered if that thieving conniver had disclosed the details of the wager to Scholastica. If so, his friend could forget about ever receiving the money or anything else, for that matter, Pagan thought, his ire rising. Although well aware that at another time he might have applauded his friend for his ingenuity, now he could only shudder with rage.

When Pagan thought how the man had the audacity to come to his house and gloat, demanding his money this very evening! On top of that, Hazard had informed all those in attendance that this little soiree was a pre-birthday party. It was all Pagan could do not to snarl at each and every one of his guests. Now, at least, he could kill one of them!

With deadly determination, Pagan searched the reception rooms for his intended victim, only to be stopped repeatedly by several ladies who made it quite plain that they would love to help him celebrate in private. Unfortunately, the only thing he felt for them was irritation. Not one of them looked right or sounded right or even *smelled* right, he thought with disgust, and he couldn't even muster up the pretense of interest. Besides, he didn't have time for them when he had murder on his mind.

Pagan was just wondering whether Hazard, a cowardly wretch indeed, had left the premises, when, to his utter amazement, in walked Cubby Hornsby and several of his brood, including the only female to thoroughly confound him.

For a moment Pagan simply stared, dumbstruck by her appearance. Those other women had been too curvaceous, too bold, too perfumed, too *everything,* while Scholastica was perfection itself from the top of her shining dark hair to the tips of her slippered feet. Pagan felt his heart increase its pace, as though he had just gone several rounds with Gentleman Jackson and, like a man who had taken one too many blows from the famous boxer, he nearly swayed on his feet, so intense was his reaction to the mere sight of her. To dismay him further, the lady who had vowed never to set eyes upon him again was heading his way with a shyly determined look on her young face.

Pagan decided he was dreaming.

Indeed, as if through the haze of some fevered sleep, he heard Cubby's loud voice, chatting genially about some "little misunderstanding." And then Scholastica herself stood before him.

"May I speak with you for a moment, Your Grace? Privately?" she added.

He was *definitely* dreaming. Nevertheless, Pagan led her toward the library, motioned for her to precede him into the room and carefully closed the doors. She was dressed in a surprisingly simple willow-green gown, and he was enjoying a delightful view of her behind when she turned, and he was nearly struck dumb again. He realized now why those other women hadn't the slightest effect upon him. Innocence, along with a certain boldness, held an allure all its own, and he wondered with no little alarm whether he would ever be able to appreciate again the mature, experienced women he had once preferred.

As he watched her silently, Scholastica lifted her dark lashes and gazed at him with caramel-colored eyes that surely were enough, in themselves, to lay any man low. "I feel a bit like Elizabeth Bennet facing Mr. Darcy in *Pride and Prejudice,*" she said, her lovely lips curving upward even as she clasped her hands nervously before her. "I fear I have misjudged you, Your Grace."

Pagan tilted his head.

"No doubt, you will think me the most gullible of green girls," she said, drawing in a deep breath, "but someone told me about your orphanage, and I was quick to leap to the wrong conclusion." She squared her shoulders, completely covered in silk, and Pagan wondered what they would look like bared. No doubt, they were slender. And smooth. "I can only beg your forgiveness for believing such a thing of you," she said, her head downcast.

As he looked upon the top of her silky brown hair, Pagan finally digested her words. This tender young innocent was apologizing to a hardened rake for believing the worst of him? Either he was still dreaming or he had stepped onto the stage of some bad Covent Garden production.

"I can only feel ashamed for being so easily swayed to ill thoughts," she said as she took another deep breath. If a bit more worldly, she might have realized that the movement made her breasts rise in the most enticing fashion. Pagan didn't feel the need to enlighten her.

"And I am guilty, too, of lecturing you upon your duties to the world, when you already have undertaken Good Works, which I can only confess I knew nothing about. That is no excuse, I realize," she said, looking contrite.

Pausing in his admiration of her every feature, Pagan caught her last words and frowned. He was no philanthropist and certainly not praiseworthy. "It is not something I trumpet about," he muttered.

"Or else you would be besieged by those seeking charitable benefactors, I suspect," she said, glancing up at him with a rueful smile.

Pagan shrugged. "Perhaps my vanity demands I be known for other endeavors," he admitted.

"Still, you have done things, good things, and I, for one, am very impressed and grateful," she said.

Pagan stalked past her, uncomfortable at being cast in

the role of a hero, especially when Scholastica was far more inclined toward philosophy than he. "I've done little enough," he muttered.

"More than many others, and certainly much more than those at Cubby's gathering who would disparage you! You should have spoken up," she said, her voice rising in outrage.

Her passion was showing again, and Pagan smiled as he turned to face her once more. Crossing his arms over his chest, he leaned against the mantelpiece. "Anyone with a bit of sense can see that change is coming. But I don't need to waste my all-too-brief lifetime debating it, especially with the sort of philosophers that dangle on Cubby's coatstrings," he said.

"I admit that some of them only talk to hear themselves speak, but several are published. They are conveying their ideas to the masses, to try to improve the world," Scholastica said.

"Some writers do make a difference, but then someone like your beloved Mary Wollstonecraft undoes whatever good she might have accomplished by a lifestyle that can only call down the condemnation of those same masses," Pagan said. Sadly, her husband's biography, published after Mary's death, was a little too revealing for popular approval.

"But there are others," Scholastica protested.

"Yes. There are others all over the country, though I think the best minds converge upon London. If you really would like to exchange ideas with them, there are salons there for scientists, philosophers, artists and literary notables, which I can assure you are a bit more inspiring than your father's gatherings."

They might even be interesting, Pagan mused before he caught himself. The thought was so jarring as to jolt him from the dreamlike state in which he had been mired. *Salons, interesting?* Pagan shook his head. He was no dilettante to waste his time debating the latest thinking—and certainly not with some young chit in tow. He could feel a bead of sweat upon his brow again, and with sudden awareness, he realized he had already spent entirely too much time closeted here with an unmarried miss. Although no one had seen them enter, society had a way of ferreting out juicy gossip, and that was the last thing Pagan wanted.

He turned, abruptly wary. Scholastica's nearness, instead of giving him pleasure, now seemed vaguely threatening. There was something about her that he couldn't quite put his finger on, a sort of kinship that he couldn't recall ever feeling before, and it both fascinated and alarmed him. For no matter how intriguing she might be, Scholastica Hornsby could not be one of his lovers.

The pang he knew at that reminder struck him too hard. Indeed, he appeared to be feeling too much of everything lately, and he didn't like it. He had always kept a safe distance from everyone and everything, and against all odds, this young thing was getting too close to him. He could almost sense her burrowing under his skin, *bringing him to his knees.*

Pagan pushed away from the mantelpiece with an oath. *This was ridiculous.* Whatever her effect, whether real or imagined, he was spending far too much time brooding over a girl he would normally never even acknowledge. Obviously it was time to call a halt to this nonsensical bet and to collect his winnings. Hazard was out there. Pagan had only to show his friend just how kindly Miss Scholastica was feeling toward him, and then the whole business would be over.

He jerked at the thought, as if he had cut himself, and

glanced down at his hands only to find them trembling. It was an odd reaction, indeed, and he could only blame the strange nature of their relationship, not friends or lovers but something else entirely, for he had never minded parting from any of his women before. In fact, he was usually all too bored once the pursuit was over. Perhaps that was it. He had never consummated this liaison, so *he felt incomplete.* Or rather, *it* felt unfinished, he amended with a frown.

"We had better go," he muttered to his companion, who was saying something about London that he didn't heed. He felt harried, and hurried from the room as quickly as possible. But when he escorted Scholastica through the reception rooms, eager to be rid of her, Hazard was nowhere to be found. Indeed, when questioned, his friends said that Maitland had left quite precipitously, it seemed. Something about a wager?

Pagan swore under his breath.

He took her out driving again. Just to prove that he could. Just to prove that she had no power over him whatsoever, as, indeed, no woman ever had. And just to prove that he was the one in control, Pagan employed some of his favorite tricks, like casually running a finger along the nape of her neck. As he expected, she shivered helplessly in response. What he didn't expect was to find that his own hand was shaking. After that, he decided to forgo his usual techniques and cultivate an even more carefully distant air.

At first, he was annoyed when Hazard failed to appear as instructed, to surrender the wager, but after a while, he figured that the man hadn't the money to pay him. And if that difficulty necessitated a few more outings with Scholastica, well, Pagan was a grown man approaching thirty. He could handle one young woman. Perhaps they could even be friends, he thought, startling himself. Whenever one of his women had suggested that, he had wanted to retch, and yet, somehow Scholastica was far more interesting than his increasingly tedious acquaintances.

The more he thought about it, the more Pagan wondered why he was in such a hurry to win the bet. After all, he was enjoying himself thoroughly, for the first time in months, *maybe years,* and he didn't care to end it just yet. Besides, his vanity demanded that he demonstrate his own unflagging power over the female gender, Scholastica in particular. He had to prove that she was no different than any other, and yet, all he seemed to prove to himself was the opposite.

Lord help her, she missed him, Scholastica realized as she viewed the dining room. It was crowded with faces, but not one of them was *his,* and she knew a bone-deep disappointment. Suddenly the noise and the bustle and the strangers seemed overwhelming, and the way of life she had always known oddly uncomfortable. Nevertheless, she found a place even as her half brother, Godwin, dodged around her and grabbed up a couple rolls from a servant's platter, tossing one across the table to his brother while stuffing the other into his mouth as if he were starving.

Scholastica sighed. The eclectic atmosphere that Cubby so assiduously cultivated now seemed more the product of a spoiled boy too lazy to assert control over his household. Free thinking run amuck, Scholastica decided as she took her seat and inventoried the guests. There were two new fellows she didn't know grinning sappily at her, and, to her surprise, both Miss Rawlings and Matilda had joined them. She tendered a smile toward her old friend, only to be rewarded with a smart rebuff.

Looking down at her plate, Scholastica knew a sudden, sharp longing for Pagan that was so strong she nearly leaped from the table. Somehow one of the most notorious rakes in the country had come to represent stability to her, and she nearly laughed out loud at the paradox. How ironic, too, that not long ago she had thought he would flee the Hornsby table in horror, when now she was the one who wished herself elsewhere. But where? And how?

"Ah, Miss Crossthwaithe! We haven't seen you in a while. How goes things with the school?" Cubby's jovial voice rang out over the din of speech.

Matilda pursed her lips in a distinct sign of disapproval. "As well as can be expected, considering my lack of assistance," she replied, shooting a sharp glance at Scholastica.

Scholastica lifted her chin. The reproof was hardly fair since Matilda was the one who had broken off their friendship with her rude—and untruthful—tales about Pagan. And she had made no gesture for amends, either. Obviously she still harbored ill feelings both toward the duke and her old friend.

Although annoyed, Scholastica made no comment, for she did not intend to pursue personal disputes during supper. However, Matilda must have felt otherwise, for when Scholastica made no reply, she shot her another hard glance before turning once more to Cubby with a loud sound of disgust. "I have held my tongue long enough, Mr. Hornsby, and I find I can do so no longer, for the sake of my own integrity."

"What's that?" Cubby asked, looking vaguely befuddled. Scholastica tried to cut in, but Matilda, quite clearly in a froth, would not be silenced.

"I wish to know, sir, how you can countenance this…this *liaison* between your own daughter, your own flesh and blood, and a nobleman known only for his use and abuse of women? How can you allow her to associate with such a man?"

A deadly quiet settled over those seated near enough to hear Matilda's scathing rhetoric, even Scholastica's normally raucous half siblings, as all waited for Cubby's reply. Everyone knew he did not like to be taken to task for anything and those who would enjoy his good graces dared not openly dispute him. As for Scholastica herself, she was so dumbstruck by her supposed friend's outburst that she, too, held her breath.

"Well, I think Scholastica has a mind of her own, don't you?" Cubby asked, and the crowd released a collective sigh of relief.

But Matilda did not accept the reprieve that she had been granted, nor did she show any signs of her noted intelligence as she continued her attack. "Mind of her own? She is not thinking clearly, but is being ruled by pure emotion. Can't you see? She's in love with the man!"

"That is quite enough, Matilda!" Miss Rawlings said from her place beside the miscreant.

Before Cubby could reply, Scholastica recovered herself. "You need not speak of me as if I were not here," she said, looking directly at Matilda. "Indeed, you need never speak of me again." Rising from the table with as much dignity as she could muster, she left the room even as voices erupted in argument behind her.

Slipping into the library, blessedly quiet at this time of day, Scholastica moved on shaky limbs to the nearest chair and sank down gratefully. Her heart pounding, her mind spinning, she felt as if she'd been struck by a runaway carriage. But it was the truth that assailed her, a truth that she was only now beginning to accept: *she was in love with the Notorious Duke.*

While all the earnest young philosophers who frequented her father's gatherings had failed to capture her attention in the slightest, it had taken one of the ton's most infamous rakes to stir her interest, her blood, and her heart.

Scholastica sighed at her own errant judgment, for surely she could not have picked a gentleman less likely to return her regard. Everyone knew that Pagan's past was filled with women, if not children, and she was not so foolish as to believe that his current attentions toward her promised a long-lasting passion.

For Pagan, their acquaintance was just another interlude, but for her this was *love.* Recognizing that, how should she proceed? For a young woman who prided herself on sense, Scholastica feared herself unreasoning in this case, just as Matilda accused. For how could she stay her own reckless emotions? How could she dismiss such momentous sensations when she might never know them again?

Not being one to sit and watch life pass her by or to err on the side of caution, Scholastica knew she could not ignore her feelings, for they were something fine and beautiful. Thus, her decision was swift and sure. No matter what might come after, she must seize the day, grasp it in both hands and hang on for as long as she might. Flushed with the rightness of her choice, she stood, as if to run into her lover's arms, only to pause as another truth struck her.

She was not, exactly, Pagan's lover. Indeed, the country's most notorious rake had not been acting the slightest bit rakish lately. Matilda had warned her that the man only wanted one thing, to steal her innocence and ruin her good name. So far, however, the man had done no more than kiss her, much to Scholastica's disappointment.

Perhaps he was moving slowly in consideration for her inexperience, she mused. Or perhaps, in her inexperience, she had missed some signal from him! The thought alarmed her, for she realized that she had no idea how to conduct an affair of the heart. Indeed, for all her extensive education, she now found herself lacking in the one area that served as the entire curriculum for most young women: how to attract a man.

Scholastica groaned as she recognized just how very little she knew about the feminine arts. She couldn't sew a straight line, had never cultivated any musical ability, and never paid the slightest heed to the latest fashions. What was she to do? Fortunately, her momentary panic was soon overridden by her better sense. After all, she already *had* the man's attention. She just needed to nurture a closer *intimacy* between them. Unfortunately, she had no idea how to go about that, either.

Again her brief alarm was soon dispelled by reason, for whenever baffled by questions of science or philosophy or literature, where did she turn? To books, of course! And, fortuitously, here she was in the library, where Cubby kept a vast and eclectic amount of reading material on hand, encompassing all sorts of views. Surely something here would aid her.

Heartened, Scholastica began her search immediately, but soon discouraged once more. Although she found several French volumes that were most explicit in nature—some even with illustrations!—she had already glimpsed such things before. That was not the kind of knowledge she was particularly interested in, unless she planned upon leaping onto Pagan's lap. Somehow she couldn't quite picture that, though the thought of engaging in some of the activities detailed within the pages certainly set her pulse to racing.

Tossing the erotic volumes aside, Scholastica continued her investigation, and after a while, she managed to find a book containing a very good argument *against* feminine wiles, which she decided to use to her advantage. Smiling, she clutched the volume to her breast in satisfaction, certain she had only to adopt those behaviors with which the author took umbrage, and surely, she would soon have the Notorious Duke at her feet!

Or at the very least, in her arms.

Chapter Five

After an evening of reading, Scholastica felt more able to meet her task the following day, the first order of business being a new gown. Although fashion called for low-cut bodices, the better to expose a woman's assets, she had never felt the need to bare most of her breasts for the sake of a passing style or anything else. Now, however, it seemed best to use whatever she might to succeed in her quest. And since she had nothing that qualified in her own wardrobe, she was forced to ask Lady Byford. A recent visitor to Cubby's gatherings, the older woman appeared to have little interest in the salons beyond one of the other guests, a young poet half her age.

But Lady Byford had been more than eager to contribute a dress to the cause of love, which Scholastica suspected was her favorite pastime, and Scholastica was glad to accept the loan. A rich, deep burgundy, the gown's color was darker than her usual choice, the silk so thin as to seem indecent, and the fit extremely…snug. As for the bodice, Scholastica took one look at the pale, plump mounds of flesh that looked ready to spill out of their sheer confines, and she donned a shawl that she secured with a brooch. After all, she didn't care for the whole world to see her, only one particular gentleman.

Unfortunately, that gentleman had not come to call or left her with word of his whereabouts, but Lady Byford assured Scholastica that he would be at the Marine Pavilion tonight. Prinny was in town, and everyone who was anyone would be there. Of course, Scholastica had no invitation, but Lady Byford, who qualified as *someone* as far as the ton was concerned, had kindly offered to escort her.

Although this was her first visit to the Prince Regent's Brighton home, Scholastica knew its history as well as any other resident. The original farmhouse Prinny had purchased early on in his affair with the seaside town had been completely restructured in 1787 into the long Palladian villa that greeted Scholastica. Supposedly, it had once been tastefully appointed in the French style, but when building resumed in 1801, the Pavilion began to reflect the prince's passion for all things Chinese. Rumor had it that more remodeling was ahead, with John Nash to execute a more exotic design.

Having never been inside, Scholastica could only gape in amazement at the abundance of black lacquer and bright silk. But the wonders of the interior could not hold her interest for long. Despite Lady Byford's warnings to not appear eager, Scholastica glanced through the elegant crowd searching for one particular person, and when she saw him, he made the striking rooms appear rather outlandish compared to his stark black coat and startling white cravat, tied in some exquisite fashion.

Again, she marveled that a man she once would have dismissed as an idle, frivolous boor now seemed the most sensible man in the room. Was she the only one who could see that? Surely, she was not the sole member of society to discover the intelligence and wit and liberal spirit that lay behind the casual facade? Scholastica was not so vain as to believe so, and yet, she felt a certain possessiveness that came from her knowledge. It assailed her, along with a soul-deep yearning such as she had never known.

Unfortunately, the object of her desires did not appear altogether pleased to see her. Indeed, he acted oddly distant, as had been his way recently, and he kept craning his neck as though searching for someone else in the press of people. Scholastica felt a near-violent surge of jealousy that alarmed her until she caught him muttering something about "That damned Hazard. Where the devil is he?"

Not only did Pagan seem preoccupied with his friend's whereabouts, but it was proving exceedingly difficult for Scholastica to get him alone. How did all the legendary ladies of the ton manage such rendezvous? This dallying was difficult work, Scholastica decided, and she found herself longing for an ice for her dry mouth. She was tempted to send one of her admirers to fetch one for her, but Pagan, though less than attentive himself, glared at anyone else who came too close.

Indeed, that was how she finally coaxed a dance from him. Although subterfuge did not come naturally to her, Scholastica discovered that when she smiled at one of the other gentlemen who approached her, Pagan stepped in to whisk her onto the floor himself. It was wonderful, of course, to be in his arms, the fine fabric of his sleeve soft and warm beneath her fingers, the heat of his body so near to her own.

And the Notorious Duke was no stumbling clod of dubious gentility nor was he an orator unaccustomed to dance. Smooth, confident and elegant, Pagan moved with a masculine grace that nearly stole her wits. For a long while, Scholastica could do nothing but stare at him in what she hoped was not rapt adoration. Finally, however, she marshaled her errant thoughts to her mission, took a deep breath and fluttered her lashes in what she intended as a coy maneuver.

She was rewarded for her efforts almost immediately, for she could feel Pagan's intent gaze upon her, and Scholastica held her breath as he leaned close to whisper something in her ear. Unfortunately, his was not quite the response she was pursuing. "Have you something in your eye?" he asked.

"No," Scholastica answered sourly.

"I beg your pardon, but you keep blinking. Perhaps you need spectacles?" Pagan suggested.

"No," Scholastica maintained. "I assure you I can see perfectly well. Perhaps it is your own eyesight that is failing!" She could have bitten her tongue, for that little gibe, sure to prick his vanity about his age, would do nothing to advance her cause. And when they finished the waltz, all too swiftly, the intimate mood of the dance was gone.

Scholastica decided that women worked very hard for romantic success, and that there might be something to be said for teaching a few of the feminine wiles to the daughters of the world. After her last, disastrous effort, it took her a good quarter of an hour just to convince Pagan that she needed to speak to him privately on a most urgent matter. Instead of looking delighted at a chance to be alone with her, he assumed the expression of a long-suffering brother, making Scholastica question his intentions toward her.

When they were finally ensconced, as cozily as possible, in one of the Pavilion's elaborate rooms, Scholas-

tica perched upon the edge of a japanned sofa and tried
to look alluring. Pagan, however, appeared more intent
upon the trappings around him, and she frowned in disappointment. It seemed a veritable age had passed since
he had kissed her in Cubby's morning room. What had
she done then to rouse his interest except walk through
the door after delaying him unpardonably?

Obviously there was much more to this business between men and women than she had ever imagined.
Swallowing her dismay, Scholastica squared her shoulders, and decided to use one of her newly learned tricks.
Perhaps the age-old language of the fan might speak for
her? Unfortunately, it was not one of Scholastica's preferred tongues. Having mastered Latin and Greek and
French, as well as a smattering of German and Italian,
she had never even recognized the heretofore useless ac-
cessory as a form of communication. However, Lady Byford had enlightened her, as well as given her a rudi-
mentary grasp of the technique.

Unfurling one of the lady's fans, Scholastica began to
flutter it carefully, and she soon had reason to hope, for
she quickly captured Pagan's attention. Indeed he stared
at her in an extremely odd fashion until, finally, he strode
directly toward her. Success! Scholastica thought gid-
dily, only to gape in surprise as he snatched the acces-
sory from her hand.

"What the devil are you trying to do with that thing?"
he asked, snapping it shut and tossing it down upon the
sofa.

Perhaps, there had been some sort of miscommuni-
cation, Scholastica thought. Apparently he had read her
message as, "Seize my fan and throw it down." Scholastica frowned, momentarily nonplussed as Pagan paced

before her. If only she knew how to say, "Seize *me* and throw *me* down."

She was running out of ideas, and Pagan was growing impatient. "Are you going to keep me in suspense or enlighten me as to what is so important that you need speak privately with me?" he asked, his handsome face revealing some kind of strain.

Unable to face the question in his dark eyes, Scholastica shook her head in unaccustomed failure and stared down at her lap. The presence of her shawl, fortunately, made her realize that she had forgotten her daring neckline. And now that they were alone, and all her other feminine tricks unsuccessful, it was time to bring out the big cannons, so to speak.

Surreptitiously, Scholastica released the clasp that held her shawl and let it slip downward, but to her immense disappointment, Pagan wasn't even watching her. Again, she tried an alluring glance, taking a deep breath and widening her eyes as Lady Byford had instructed, but she had the feeling she looked more like a tick about to pop.

"Are you all right?" Pagan asked, his dark brows lowering. "Is it something you ate?"

Having had quite enough of futile feminine wiles, Scholastica rose to her feet in outrage. "No! It's you, you charlatan! You fraud! Notorious Duke, my foot! You, Your Grace, are a counterfeit!" Snatching up the discarded fan, she struck him with it on one of those wide shoulders—shoulders reserved apparently for every other female's arms except her own.

"What the devil are you shouting about?" Pagan said, ignoring her blows.

"If you are Society's idea of a rake, then it's a wonder the entire ton is not dozing on its feet for want of any excitement!'' Scholastica replied. ''I can only assume that just as the rumors about your orphanage were unfounded, your reputation on a whole has little basis.''

''What *are* you talking about?'' Pagan asked, his handsome face wearing an expression of annoyance.

''You are supposed to be a rake and yet, you have not made the slightest move to seduce me,'' Scholastica said, crossing her arms in front of her.

Far from appearing chagrined, Pagan looked aghast. ''You think I would have my way with you here, in the Pavilion, practically in public?''

''Why not? Isn't that where lovers tryst?''

''We are not lovers!'' he answered heatedly.

''You needn't remind me of that fact! You have made it quite clear this evening while I have been making a fool of myself with these ridiculous feminine trappings! Alluring looks! Fluttering eyelashes!'' Scholastica threw both the fan and the shawl down in a fury. ''Tonight I have gone against everything I believe in, and for what? A most mortifying experience. But it has been most enlightening, having confirmed my belief that women are degraded by the use of such mannerisms. These arcane mating rituals must be discarded once and for all, if men and women are ever to achieve some kind of parity!''

Scholastica paused in her impassioned speech long enough to glare up at Pagan, but her gaze was immediately arrested, for he was staring at her bodice, or rather, where her bodice usually was. Tonight, it was the bare expanse of her breasts, nearly popping from the burgundy silk that had captured his attention, and most thoroughly, too. As his gaze lifted to her own, Scholastica drew in a breath, for something glinted in his eyes, something dark and feral and seductive.

''You did all that for me?'' he asked, his voice so low

and rich that Scholastica could have lapped it up with her tongue.

She nodded slowly, suddenly wondering just why she had worked so hard to rouse the slumbering beast, for Pagan resembled nothing so much now as some kind of dangerous animal, dark and menacing and sensual. He stepped toward her, and Scholastica was tempted to back away, but his eyes held her prone.

"I'm afraid that's a case of overkill, darling. All you have to do is breathe and I want you," he drawled. He stood in front of her now, only inches from where Scholastica watched him with enormous eyes. "No. All you have to do is be," he said. And he reached for her.

This time he didn't coax her with a gentle wooing, but pulled her close, wrapping his arms tightly around her, as he lowered his head, his gaze never leaving hers until his lashes dipped and his mouth closed over hers. Hot. Wet. Delicious. And *plundering*. Scholastica could barely draw a breath so forceful was the assault on her senses. But she had never been a cautionary maid, and so she clung to him, returning his ardor as best she could.

His hands roved down her back, pressing her to him, and she felt the blatant hardness of him against her belly. She whimpered when his mouth left hers, but he only moved to her throat, spreading kisses down to the swell of her breasts. The shock of lips upon that expanse of skin made her gasp and she moaned as he slid one finger inside the edge of her bodice to stroke one taut nipple.

"Pagan!" she whispered. The sensations were too new, too overwhelming, and she swayed against him.

"What? Isn't this what you wanted?" he asked. His dark gaze met hers over the swell of her breasts, and Scholastica tried to gather her wits. Was he warning her, or trying to frighten her away? She blinked at him, unsure. Was this all another one of his poses? But, if so, why was his breath coming just as quickly as hers? Why was his face flushed, his body hard?

The rattling of the door made him release her, and Scholastica nearly fell to the floor without his steadying arms. Obviously he had locked them in the room, but the sudden awareness of her surroundings made her wonder if she had not been just a bit too precipitous in her boldness. Perhaps Pagan was right not to want to tryst here in the Marine Pavilion, subject to any and all interruptions.

"This has got to stop. *Now,*" Pagan said, as if echoing her thoughts. He drew in a ragged breath and moved away, and Scholastica could see the distance he put between them, far more than mere inches would indicate. "You are too intelligent for this, too committed to your ideals," he said.

Scholastica straightened her shoulders. "I've never had anything against love," she said. "It was your reputation that made me hesitate."

Scholastica saw surprise flicker in his eyes, along with something else, dark and undefined, before his expression was shuttered once more. "Well, I guess I'm not that much of a free thinker," he muttered.

When she only stared at him blankly, he swore soft and low. "You want to know why I sought you out? Why I took you driving? Because I bet someone that I could."

Scholastica blinked at him in bewilderment. "What?"

"Hazard made me a wager that I could not manage to charm a woman of his choosing. He saw you handing out pamphlets and picked you," Pagan said, his voice harsh, his dark eyes glinting.

Scholastica drew herself up and lifted her chin. "Well,

then, let us find him and finish this business once and for all, shall we?''

She had the pleasure of seeing startlement cross his face before Pagan shook his head. ''He's not here,'' he said. He frowned. ''And you shouldn't be, either.''

In imitation of his own casual pose, Scholastica shrugged. ''I'm afraid that your opinion holds little weight with me, Your Grace,'' she said. She managed to move past him and open the door without losing her composure, though his pronouncement had certainly affected her.

How mortifying it was to discover she was no better than those witless females she had long held in contempt! She had held herself up as superior, but now proven herself just as susceptible to a smooth tongue and a handsome face. Worse yet, those other women might have fared better than herself, for wasn't she so detached from her own femininity that she could not even tempt a man of the Notorious Duke's infamous appetites?

She had been soundly rejected, and yet, some hidden instinct of her gender made her believe that Pagan was not so indifferent as he seemed. Was she being foolish, clinging to a hope unfounded? She heard him call after her, but ignored him, seeking out Lady Byford among the crowd.

''Ah, Scholastica!'' The lady greeted her with a smile of delight. She leaned close, to whisper behind her own eloquent fan. ''How did you fare?''

''Most dreadfully,'' Scholastica admitted. ''I fear he has sent me packing.''

''Oh, dear!'' Lady Byford clasped her in a loose embrace, and Scholastica felt smothered by breasts and strong perfume. When released from the well-meaning woman, she took a deep breath.

"Well, you are young and lovely, and Penhurst is excessively particular, especially these days. He is notoriously selfish, as well, and cares not a fig even for his lovers, so perhaps it is all for the best. You must not waste any time fretting over him, but move on to someone else more likely to return your regard," the lady said, scanning the crowd as if searching for a likely replacement already.

Scholastica opened her mouth to protest only to shut it again as Lady Byford, looking over her shoulder, lifted her brows over eyes wide with surprise. "Your Grace," she said, dipping her head in acknowledgment.

Scholastica turned to see Pagan hovering behind her, looking rather menacing. "You are the one who brought her here?" he asked Lady Byford in a decidedly accusatory tone.

When the older woman nodded in rather amused fashion, his expression grew even more fierce. "Well, this is no place for her, as you well know, so I'd advise you to see her home immediately."

"I'm afraid that your grace has no say over my behavior or my whereabouts!" Scholastica said, turning away from him only to come face-to-face with someone far more powerful—and ultimately more dangerous.

"I say there, Pagan, who is this pretty lady who looks so vexed with you?" the Prince Regent asked while Scholastica gaped, wide-eyed.

"Your Highness! How well you look this evening," Pagan said, interposing himself between Scholastica and his monarch. He had assumed his casual air once more, but Scholastica saw the tightness of his jaw as he took her elbow in a proprietary fashion. "Your Highness, may I present Miss Scholastica Hornsby? And you know Lady Byford, of course."

Prodded by Lady Byford, Scholastica managed to curtsy as the Prince Regent nodded his formidable head. "My dear, it is a pleasure," he said, smiling affably, but Scholastica knew that beneath that genial exterior beat the heart of a rake just as notorious as the duke and far less appealing to her personally.

"What a fortuitous meeting this is, Your Highness," Pagan said, assuming his most charming persona. "I had hoped to introduce you to Miss Hornsby this evening. Indeed, that is why we came," he said, patting Scholastica's arm in an avuncular fashion.

"Oh, really?" the Prince said, eyeing Scholastica far too avidly for her own comfort.

"Yes, Miss Hornsby is quite the proponent of education for women, and I told her that you might be interested in her views," Pagan said, even as Scholastica blinked in astonishment.

Prinny's grin fled, replaced by a pained look. "Indeed?"

"Yes, Miss Hornsby has contributed to the establishment of a school right here in Brighton and has many modern theories on the rights of women, most especially in terms of their education," Pagan said.

The Prince Regent looked horrified, then suspicious. "A schoolteacher? No, really, Pagan," he said, giving the duke a sly look.

"Yes, Your Highness," Pagan said. "I know it is hard to believe in one so young, but I have such faith in her concepts that I intend to fund the creation of another school in London," he noted smoothly.

Scholastica heard Lady Byford's low sound of surprise, caught the expression of shock on the Prince Regent's face, and was certain her startlement mirrored their own. Pagan was establishing a school? Because of her? Hadn't Lady Byford just claimed that he never bestirred himself for any woman? Suddenly it was as though their encounter in the other room had never occurred, his damning words never spoken, and a warm feeling swelled inside her. What it all meant, she didn't know, but the Notorious Duke had her heart, now and forever, in his keeping.

Ignoring the stunned reaction of his audience, Pagan blithely continued. "I'm sure you would find our plans for the curriculum most enlightening and forward-thinking, in the manner of Your Highness's own famed education," he said.

"But I am a man!" the Prince Regent protested with an appalled expression.

"Yes, of course, but females can think, as well, Your Highness," Scholastica pointed out. "Indeed we—"

Prinny cut her off with an expression of alarm. "Yes, I'm sure you do. Well, good luck to you, miss!" he said, intimating just the opposite as he practically fled her presence. Scholastica could just hear him muttering to himself. "Pagan Penhurst setting up a school for women? It is hardly to be borne, hardly to be borne."

Scholastica felt like laughing, so profound was her joy and so amusing the Prince Regent's flight, but she bit her cheeks as Pagan whispered something to Lady Byford. The older woman immediately began leading Scholastica away, toward the doors, apparently having been convinced that the Marine Pavilion was no place for Scholastica, after all. Scholastica had to agree, for she counted herself lucky to have escaped the Prince Regent's attentions.

Lady Byford, under the guise of fanning herself, was smiling wickedly. "Clever man! I'm not certain whether he did you ill or not, but Penhurst definitely made you appear unappealing to his highness, which I'm sure was his intention.'' Her eyes narrowed as she called for her carriage.

''I'm surprised, though, that he would bestir himself, indeed, risk the wrath of his sovereign, on your account. It is not like him. Not like him at all. I find it very interesting. You know, there have been some rumors bandied about that Hazard Maitland has been making highly unusual wagers involving the duke.'' She paused to touch the tip of her fan to her lips.

''I wonder...'' she began, but Scholastica pointed out that their carriage had arrived. She definitely did not care to discuss Hazard's bet with Pagan. She just wanted to hold on to that bright, amazing moment when he had pledged himself to a school for women.

And as she stepped away from the magical world of the Prince Regent's pavilion, the climax of her own dreamlike summer, Scholastica knew that even should she never see Pagan again, she would keep that moment precious in her memory forever.

For perhaps the first time in his life, Pagan wasn't certain of himself. His initial, most basic instinct was to retreat to London or his family seat and be done with Brighton and its residents. But to do that, he would have to pay off Hazard, a notion that still rankled. Yet how could he claim the wager now, even though he had won it, after revealing its existence to Scholastica?

Pagan loosed a harsh breath at the memory of that encounter. He had certainly never expected to see her at one of the Prince Regent's soirees. What the devil had possessed Lady Byford to take her? But he knew the answer already: Scholastica, who was too daring and determined for her own good.

And she had been determined to seduce him. The woman he wanted more than his next breath had offered herself up to him, and he had denied her. Pagan would have laughed at the thought of the notorious rake refusing the advances of a beautiful, young woman if it hadn't been so painful, so very nearly disastrous. He shook his head at his own folly. He'd thought to scare her away, to show her not to tempt a man, but he should have known better than to try to teach Scholastica anything. She had met the force of his passion with her own, diverting him from his intention until he was so aroused as to be nearly insensible.

If someone hadn't tried the door, God knows what would have happened, Pagan thought with a groan. When he considered how he might have taken her maidenhead on the floor of one of the Pavilion's rooms, he cringed, well and truly horrified by his own behavior. Yet, even now, as appalled as he was by the thought, another, deeper, darker side of him urged him to take what she offered, just as he would from any other woman.

But Scholastica wasn't any other woman.

And that knowledge held him to his decision. No matter how tempting, how appealing, he would not and could not ruin her. It would be an insult to her, a defiling of her young spirit, a statement to the world that he valued her no more than any mistress he might set up in London.

And she was far more than that. She deserved better than to be some man's courtesan, fated to be looked down upon by Society when she was above it, just as she was above him. Pagan frowned at the acknowledgment. An orphanage and a couple of other establishments, though well-intended, hardly made for a lifetime's achievement, while his true avocation, the pursuit of women, now seemed embarrassingly childish, a pastime hardly worthy of a grown man approaching the ripe old age of thirty. The thought made him swear under his breath. He certainly didn't want to end up like the Prince Regent, an aging roué from whom no female was safe!

Pagan stiffened as he was reminded, once again, of Scholastica's narrow escape from Prinny's clutches. He could only hope that he had disengaged the Prince Regent's interest in her not only for last night, but *always*. Pagan shook his head, seized by a sudden desire to lock Scholastica away in a tower somewhere, far from the temptation of *any* man. Perhaps he should talk to her father about keeping a closer eye on her, he wondered, only to dismiss that notion as a waste of time. Cubby was too much of a so-called free thinker, as well as too wrapped up in himself to consider his daughter's well-being, should the headstrong female allow him.

Pagan fought against a surge of anger toward the man even as he told himself that Scholastica's future was *not* his concern. And yet, he knew he was guilty of bringing her to the notice of the kind of people he had once called friends, but who now seemed ill favored and unscrupulous. And now it was too late, for he could not give her any sort of protection, without it being deemed the wrong sort.

At least he had saved her from Prinny last night. Unfortunately, thanks to that little episode, he was committed to funding a school for girls! Pagan frowned ruefully. Of course, it wasn't as though he didn't believe in the project. Far from it. He saw no reason why only a select few of the ton's wealthiest, most influential widows were allowed to have opinions. Scholastica had proven to him many times over that her wit was the equal of his. Indeed, it seemed to work upon him like a tonic, sharpening his own.

For her sake alone, he could not abandon the project that was so dear to her heart. However, Pagan knew, with a sense of dread, that it wouldn't take long for the rumor of his latest scheme to spread, and that knowledge was enough to make him want to seek one of his outlying properties—preferably the one in Scotland.

Wait until the news reached London! No one would believe he actually intended to set up a school for decent females, for the simple reason that his reputation assured every misconception. Pagan groaned as he pictured the jests and innuendos: the Notorious Duke's School for the Demimonde, for the care and training of high-class prostitutes. It would make Pagan's Paternity look tame! Unless he distanced himself totally from the blessed school, no parents in their right minds would send a daughter there, making his effort to aid Scholastica's cause an abject failure.

Yet, how could he convince any woman to endorse it? He had no female relatives to speak of, and, unfortunately, most of the ladies he knew were not likely to lend any more credibility to the project than his own name provided. Indeed, the only woman he knew with a spotless reputation and unassailable integrity was Scholastica herself, a young girl whose attachment to anything to do with him would only provoke comment. Unless…

Pagan reeled at the sudden notion that struck him, then stood stock-still, suspended by the enormity of what he was considering. It was both outlandish and frightening, and his mind screamed out a protest. But, seized by something other than reason, he headed toward the door—before he could talk himself out of it.

Chapter Six

Scholastica left behind the noise and bustle of the house by escaping to the schoolroom, which she found much changed since her last visit. The women who supported the endeavor, mostly Matilda's friends, had managed to scavenge some desks, and Scholastica busied herself by cleaning and arranging them toward a central space at the front of the building.

The peace and quiet, along with the fresh air coming through the open windows and door, was therapeutic. Surely, as Dr. Russell had claimed, there was no place better than Brighton to recuperate, though Scholastica did not think he had her particular ailment in mind. Still, if the sea water could cure various diseases of the glands, rheumatism, consumption, and even madness, why not a broken heart?

She was glad now that she had agreed to accompany Miss Rawlings bathing this afternoon, for immersion in the ocean might aid in her recovery. She only hoped that Matilda would not be joining them, Scholastica thought with a frown, for no doubt her former friend would gloat over her ill usage at the hands of the Notorious Duke. But had Pagan really used her so ill? He had done naught but make her fall in love with him through no fault of his own. After all, how could he be blamed for possessing looks and charm that devastated most of the female populace, including herself?

He should not have accepted the wager, of course, but Scholastica could see all too well how his vanity would impel him to agree. And if he had not? Did she really wish she had never met him? Scholastica smiled, sadly. Never! For he had filled her life with something beyond price and regret. It was simply too bad that she could not treasure the memory of the best moments, without undergoing the pain and longing that filled her now.

Scholastica sighed, only to start as a knock came upon the door. Recollecting well her last visitor here, she held her breath as she turned, hardly daring to hope even as she saw him. Dark hair, wide shoulders encased in forest-green superfine, and handsome features well worth any amount of heartache appeared in the doorway. "Pagan!" she whispered in surprise.

He nodded and stepped forward slowly, as though uncertain of his reception, and Scholastica wondered if he, too, remembered his last visit here. Recovering her composure, she stepped forward to take his hands in her own, determined to be gracious, for he deserved no less after what he had done for the cause.

"Thank you so much for your promise of a school," she said. "And for declaring your support before the Prince Regent himself. Word of it can only aid our endeavors!"

Pagan shook his head, as if uncomfortable with her gratitude. "I'm no hero. I only did it to convince Prinny that, despite your obvious appeal, you were too much the feminine philosopher for his taste," he said with a wry expression.

Scholastica smiled, for somehow she didn't quite believe this explanation. Surely he could have managed to do that without offering to fund a school. But she knew he was reticent about his Good Works, and so she did not argue. "So you say," she murmured, loving him all the more for this unexpected modesty mixed in with so much arrogance.

"How old are you?" he asked abruptly, and Scholastica glanced up at him, again surprised.

"Nineteen," she answered.

He appeared decidedly relieved, for some reason. "You look much younger."

She laughed. "Thank you. I think."

"Tomorrow's my birthday. I'm going to be thirty, you know," he muttered, as if the admission tasted poorly in his mouth.

"I know," Scholastica said, trying not to smile.

"Well? Aren't you going to accuse me of being in my dotage?" he asked. His dark brows drew together, though he spoke as smoothly as ever.

Scholastica laughed again. "I hardly think you are ready to keel over just yet," she said.

The answer didn't seem to please him too well, and although she hesitated to feed his enormous ego any further, she lifted her hand to his cheek. "You are altogether perfect as you are, and well you know it," she added.

Scholastica was rewarded with a sensual grin of acknowledgment, as his familiar confident manner returned, but his next words could only dismay her. "About that school I offered to fund?" he asked, lifting his brows.

Scholastica studied him closely, suddenly anxious. Would he now rescind his promise, with the claim it had been tendered only for show? "It's too late to back out," she warned, clasping her fingers together.

"I'm not backing out, but I do have a condition," he drawled, recapturing her hands with his own.

Scholastica's cheeks flushed as she imagined the kind of bargain a man like Pagan would make. Although she thought he had refused her attempts at seduction, perhaps they were simply at odds last night, or he had suffered a change of sentiment today. Excitement sent her senses humming at the notion, for whatever he offered, she knew she would agree. "And just what are you proposing?" she asked.

"Just that," he answered. When she gazed up at him blankly, he smiled. "My condition is that the establishment be named the Lady Penhurst School for Female Education. Lady *Scholastica* Penhurst."

Scholastica blinked at him, certain she had not heard him aright, but his dark eyes glinted and his lips curved upward in a sensual smile that held no mockery. She swallowed hard. He wanted her to *marry* him? Stunned beyond belief, she stared up at him for a long moment, then tried to draw in a breath and compose herself. Failing miserably, she burst into tears.

"Yours is not exactly the reaction I envisioned." Scholastica heard Pagan's murmur as he drew her into his arms. She rested her head against the expanse of his chest, warm and unyielding, but could not stop crying. Another man might have balked in outrage, but Pagan simply held her close and whispered against her hair.

"Would you care to explain?" he asked. "I admit that I've made a lot of propositions to ladies in my life, but this is the first time I've ever asked one of them to marry me. And something tells me yours are not tears of happiness. What is it? Am I too old?" His tone roughened at the last question, and Scholastica gurgled, torn between tears and laughter.

"Oh, Pagan, you are so easy to tease!"

"You are *teasing* me?" he asked, his voice laced with incredulity.

"No! I mean about your age. You are not old, and my taunts were only an attempt to puncture your excessive vanity. You are perfectly wonderful, and you have nothing to do with my...my refusal," Scholastica managed to return before succumbing to fresh despair.

"Since I'm the one you are refusing, I beg to differ," Pagan said dryly. Then she felt his lips against her forehead. "If you don't cease, I shall be forced to kiss you. And I don't think that is wise, considering that the issue of our engagement remains unsettled."

Even through her grief, Scholastica could feel the heat between them, and she caught her breath at the thought of it. Temptation, like a live thing, threatened to overwhelm her misgivings with the promise that she could indulge in a lifetime of seduction, if she would but agree to his outrageous proposal. Only her own personal principles prevented her surrender as his mouth moved over her hair.

"Tell me, my little philosopher," Pagan urged. "Is it my past? My reputation? I assure you that I intend to honor our vows, perhaps far better than another man with less knowledge of the world."

The whispered promise only made Scholastica feel worse. She sniffed. "I told you, it has nothing to do with you. The truth is that I don't have the money or power or proper...antecedents to be your wife, and you know it," she stated. There, she had said it. Now could they be done with this nonsense?

Unfortunately, as usual, Pagan had an answer for everything. "Since I already have plenty of money, I don't see how that, or some vague notion of lineage, could possibly matter. You are not a racehorse, after all. As for your antecedents, you are a gentlewoman, are you not?" He lifted her chin and looked at her with a fierce intent that made her throat tighten.

"I can't marry you, not with my, uh, hazy heritage," Scholastica said, unable to hold that dark gaze. "I'm not even sure who my mother was, let alone if she was married to Cubby at the time."

Scholastica waited for him to exhibit some sign of shock and distaste, for despite her sheltered and eccentric upbringing, she knew that such things mattered in the world, especially in the exacting world of the ton.

"And you think that is relevant?" Pagan asked as he stroked her cheek, wiping away a tear with his thumb. "My darling girl, I could wed a fishwife, and no one in the land would dare question me," he said with his usual supreme arrogance.

"They would probably be too shocked to speak," Scholastica murmured.

"Shocked by what, the fishwife, or the fact that I'm marrying?" he asked, grinning wickedly.

Scholastica shook her head even as she moved from his embrace, for he was far too tempting. She could hardly trust her judgment when he held her close and whispered of possibilities.

"Indeed, it would probably start a new trend, and all the young bucks would be seeking wives upon the wharves," Pagan said. "Prinny might have to take a third wife just to be fashionable."

His reference to the Prince Regent's clandestine marriage to Maria Fitzherbert, as well as the Princess Caroline, obviously was designed to show her that not even the future king behaved as he should, but Scholastica remained unconvinced.

"I just don't know," she murmured, feeling trapped by his relentless pursuit of his objective. She needed time to consider such a momentous offer.

"This is my modern-thinking woman? Why not make a stand for the rights of women by marrying whomever you please?" Pagan challenged. "And this for what anyone else believes," he added, snapping his fingers.

"I...just don't know, Pagan," Scholastica repeated, unsure whether the part her that prompted acceptance was being reasonable—or selfish.

Pagan frowned, obviously losing patience with her reluctance. "Last night you were certain enough when you offered yourself up to me in one of the Prince Regent's rooms. Or have you forgotten your determination to seduce me?" he drawled, his tone holding a certain edge to it that dismayed her even more.

When Scholastica didn't answer, Pagan's dark brows lowered. He paused to study her long and hard, and she flushed, uneasy under his intense scrutiny. "Scholastica, please don't tell me that you would agree to become my lover and not my wife," he said in a harsh voice that evidenced his disapproval.

"Well, I..." Scholastica hesitated, unwilling to speak when he appeared so disinclined to hear her answer.

"Scholastica!"

"I fail to see how you can complain about it, but, yes, I would," she answered, lifting her chin.

Unfortunately, the black expression that crossed Pagan's face left no doubt of his reaction to her bold claim. Indeed, Scholastica had never seen him so angry, never witnessed such a loss of composure in the preternaturally relaxed nobleman. He swore under his breath, his jaw

tight, and stalked to the door. Obviously the arrogant
duke was not used to having his wishes thwarted! For a
moment Scholastica stared at him wide-eyed, wondering
if he would leave without a word, but he paused on the
threshold and turned.

"Well, I won't," he said before making his exit.

For a while, Scholastica fumed, annoyed by Pagan's
high-handed behavior as well as his perverse attitude.
After all, she had agreed to a liaison with a notorious
rake, only to have him storm off in high dudgeon, in-
sulted! The situation was so laughable as to finally wring
a smile out of her. Was Pagan worried about his reputation? His honor? Did he think she would ruin him?
Overwhelmed by the emotions of the past few days,
Scholastica finally began giggling, a rather manic response to her troubles that might have continued but for
the arrival of Miss Rawlings, fetching her for bathing.

As much as she had looked forward to it earlier, Scholastica was hardly in the mood now for a dip in the sea,
but she hated to disappoint the older woman. And she
supposed that the activity might help her sort out her
thoughts, jumbled to near hysteria by Pagan Penhurst's
unlooked-for proposal.

And who could have looked for it? As far as Scholastica knew, the Notorious Duke had never so much as
hinted at marriage to anyone in his life. Of course, the
knowledge that she alone, of all his women, had moved
him to propose, was most flattering. Indeed, the more
she thought about it, the more wonderful it seemed.

Unfortunately, he had caught her off guard, and all
she could do was protest her own inappropriateness. Yet
now, her unaccustomed tears over, her reservations dismissed by Pagan, Scholastica was more inclined to feel

a swell of warmth at his offer, instead of a lump of misery. And, of course, it wasn't as though she had much choice in the matter, given the duke's ultimatum. Who would have thought that the man would stand firm on his previously precarious morals?

Although his decree, in itself, did not sit well with her, Scholastica had to admire his principles, which were so different than anyone suspected. She smiled, loving him all the more for them. And given the choice to marry him or to never see him again, Scholastica's own beliefs were wavering. After all, she had registered her misgivings. Pagan knew the truth, and if he was willing, however misguided he might be, to accept her hazy history, who was she to argue?

"I say, the dipper on the end there seems most anxious for our business," Miss Rawlings said, and Scholastica was forced to wrest her attention back to the present as they neared the seaside. "Perhaps she is in need of money to support a family," Miss Rawlings added, always ready to help a female in distress.

She hurried Scholastica along until they reached the bathing machine, little more than a wooden box on wheels, where the dipper, a strong-looking woman with a Gypsy-like cast to her features, welcomed them happily. Scholastica moved up the small set of stairs that led to the tiny room, but the dipper shook her head when Miss Rawlings tried to follow.

"We wish to go together," Miss Rawlings protested.

"One at time. You go there," the dipper answered, pointing to the next machine, much further along the beach. "Half price for both," she added.

Miss Rawlings sighed. "Very well. I shall join you after the immersion, then," she said to Scholastica. Scholastica was rather inclined to take the other machine and spare Miss Rawlings the walk, but the dipper urged her into the wooden unit rather fiercely. Indeed, Scholastica had barely entered when the woman shut the small door, plunging her into darkness, and the machine lurched forward, the horse backing it into the water before she even had a chance to change into her shift and cap.

Scholastica reached out to steady herself against the rough-planked side wall and drew in a swift breath only to gasp in disbelief. Surely, her senses were deceiving her, for instead of musty, wet wood, she smelled something oddly familiar and wholly alluring. It was the scent of horses and leather and soap and man that belonged only to one person.

"Pagan?" she whispered disbelievingly into the blackness.

"Your cleverness astounds me, as always, darling, though I must admit I was hoping to stay hidden until you had removed some of your clothing, at least," Pagan said, his low drawl unmistakable.

"Pagan Penhurst, what are you doing here?" Scholastica asked, torn between annoyance at his underhanded behavior and excitement at his unrelenting pursuit.

"I find that I am ruthless, after all, and unaccustomed to being thwarted in my desires," he said, his voice so deep and smooth and seductive that she swayed upon her feet. "I must admit that you are the only woman ever to confound me, and I hope you continue to do so for the rest of my life. But, being unaware of your current mind-set, I thought it advantageous to arrange for a meeting without giving you a chance to refuse it," he explained as the machine rolled to a stop.

While Scholastica pressed herself against the wall, disoriented by the near complete darkness, he stepped past her to open the door. Blinking in the sunlight, Scholastica saw the vast expanse of the ocean stretching out before them, the other bathers far away and her dipper nowhere in sight. If she wanted to leave, she would have to flounder in deep water, fully clothed, back toward shore. She glanced up at Pagan, half outraged and half amused, only to find him grinning at her wickedly.

"Since there really isn't any escape from our trysting place, I thought it the perfect spot for me to exercise my powers of persuasion," he said, his tone rife with promise.

Scholastica's outrage melted away, heat surging through her in reaction to his implicit pledge. He had gone to an awful lot of trouble to arrange to see her alone, and the knowledge both pleased and excited her. Scholastica cleared her throat. "What, exactly, did you have in mind?" she asked, her own voice wavering.

Pagan took a step toward her. "You claim to be considering me, but I don't believe you are doing so with your usual astuteness," he said. "Do you honestly believe I would rather have society's approval than you as my wife? How can you imagine so, when I've been courting its disapprobation for years? And what of my line, Scholastica? Do you think I don't deserve heirs? Do you find me too much a rogue to raise up children, to cherish a family?"

Scholastica felt a pang and shook her head.

"Good. Because I've talked to Cubby, and he said that you are definitely his daughter, that he was married to your mother, however briefly, and that the Duke of Carlyle will most assuredly come to our wedding," Pagan added as Scholastica gaped in surprise.

"Now, I'm hoping that bit of news causes you to realign your skewed priorities because I don't think I can stand two rejections in my lifetime. One was quite harrowing enough, I assure you,'' Pagan said, his eyes glinting as he advanced another step. ''I can only suggest that since you apparently feel it is your life mission to prick my inflated pride, then by all means do so, but under the guise of wedlock, if you please.''

He paused, his expression becoming more serious. ''And, in case I didn't mention it before, I...love you,'' he whispered, the force of his emotion plainly evident in his eyes. He drew in a deep breath. ''Now, do you need more convincing?''

Shaking her head, Scholastica launched herself into his arms. However, she had not taken the rickety bathing machine into consideration before her impulsive leap. The force of her weight made Pagan step back, the wood creaked, and suddenly they both landed in the water.

Scholastica came up, laughing and sputtering, too giddy with happiness to protest the dousing, while Pagan shook the water from his dark hair with a frown. ''This wasn't exactly the sort of persuasion I had in mind,'' he muttered. But when Scholastica drew his head down for a kiss, he seemed to suffer a change of heart quite rapidly.

The water was cold, but he was hot, and soon Scholastica was, too. Breathless and fevered from several long, deep kisses, she moaned a protest when his mouth left hers. ''Just a moment,'' he said, reaching for the bathing machine, and to Scholastica's astonishment, some sort of gauzy drape descended around them.

''What is this?'' she said, fingering the material.

''A curtain patterned after those used at other seaside resorts,'' Pagan replied. ''Thin enough to let in the light, but heavy enough to thwart the telescopes glued to prying eyes. I find that I don't care for an audience," he muttered as he drew her back into his arms.

To Scholastica the experience was like a dream, for not only was she in Pagan's embrace, but she was immersed in water up to her waist, while the pale fabric drifted around them like some kind of phantasm, casting light and shadow over the moving sea. The breeze was gentle, the air tinged with salt and the scent of Pagan as he plied her with his lips and his tongue and his hands.

Somehow, he managed to tug down her wet gown, freeing her breasts, and Scholastica gasped as he caressed her with dripping hands, the wetness sliding over her, chilling and heating her at the same time. And when he lowered his head and licked at the moisture, she arched back at the feel of his tongue stroking her sensitive skin, moaning frantically as he took her nipple into his mouth.

It was too much, and yet, not enough, and she tried to pull at his damp shirt, eager to touch his body, as well. He wore no coat or waistcoat, and she finally tugged the clinging fabric over his head, tossing it into the bathing machine. Then he pulled her close and the feel of his chest against her own was so glorious that she held him fast.

The sea made her buoyant, and Pagan lifted her easily, wrapping her legs around his hips so that Scholastica felt the press of his hardness against the juncture of her thighs. As the water lapped about them, they rocked together in a rhythm as ancient as the tides, ever closer, ever tighter. Pagan's breath was harsh and fast against her throat, and Scholastica thought she felt his fingers tremble as they touched her hair.

"I want to love you now, but I can't," he said in a hoarse voice.

"What?" Scholastica could barely speak, so dazed was she by the feelings he engendered, not only of heat and desire, but of love and longing and a rightness so strong and clear, it banished any remnant of doubt from her heart.

"I don't have any envelopes with me," Pagan whispered, as if the effort of speech cost him.

"What?" Scholastica asked again.

Pagan lifted his head to meet her gaze. "*French* envelopes. I never intended my persuasion to go this far, but somehow you manage to overset all my plans effortlessly. What is this power you have over me?" he asked, his expression stark.

"The power of love," Scholastica answered with a smile. Then she pressed her mouth to his, nipping at his lips provocatively.

Pagan groaned. "Where did you learn to kiss like that?" he demanded harshly.

"You taught me," Scholastica answered as she sprinkled kisses across his face and down his throat.

When she tugged at his ear with her teeth, he loosed a sigh. "This has got to stop. Now," he muttered, even as he lowered his head to allow her to continue her explorations.

"Why? Surely the ocean is an improvement over the Marine Pavilion," Scholastica said, smiling against his neck. In truth, she didn't care where they were, as long as they were together. And it seemed she had waited so long for the Notorious Duke to seduce her. How could she wait another moment?

"Hardly!" Pagan answered with a harsh exhalation. As if her words had recalled his will, he stopped her ministrations by reaching out to cup her face in his hands. Despite his harsh breathing, his eyes glinted fiercely as he held her fast. "Sometimes I think you've saved me, darling, and sometimes I think you've destroyed me."

At Scholastica's blank look, he shook his head. "I find it wholly unnerving to admit after years of nurturing my notorious reputation, that I am, at heart, a prig," Pagan said with a wry smile. "I don't want any child of ours growing up in the sort of ramshackle household you did. I want us to be married. I want you to be certain who is the father of your child, and I want us to raise our child together, so he or she is not prey to the doubts that have disturbed you."

Scholastica blinked, moved beyond words by his consideration and perception. And, in spirit, she agreed with him, but right now, clinging to his wet form, she had to admit that other things were uppermost in her mind. "Then let us be married posthaste, for I would not delay a moment longer," she urged.

Pagan stared at her, muttered some oath under his breath, and then, as if she had unleashed the beast in him as she had once before, he kissed her hard and fierce. But Scholastica again met his passion with her own, even when she felt the unfamiliar thrust of his body against hers beneath the water and the growing sensations that gripped her until she cried out, pleading with him, and he pulled her hard against him, grinding his body to hers while they both shuddered with pleasure.

Afterward, he stroked her back and pressed kisses to her hair, but Scholastica thought she heard him mutter something about his will being stronger than hers, "Just barely," and she smiled into his shoulder. There would be no babies from today's encounter, but someday, and soon...

"About our children," Scholastica said. "You had

better hope, for your peace of mind, that we don't have any daughters.'' Feeling him jerk at the thought of protecting his own from the sort of rogue he had been, she laughed softly, enjoying, as always, the chance to tease the Notorious Duke.

"Well, there is one thing that will serve to their advantage," he drawled.

Scholastica lifted her head to gaze at him with adoration. There would be so many things, not the least of which would be two loving parents in a household of luxury and privacy, as well as ideas. "What is that?" she asked.

Pagan grinned. "They'll be assured of only the best education."

He was having a birthday celebration. Pagan laughed out loud, still unable to believe it when not long ago he had dreaded the day, determined to ignore its passing. But both the birthday and celebration were welcome today, for it gave him an opportunity to announce his engagement. And he had to admit that he had thoroughly enjoyed watching the jaws of all the guests drop, especially those of the Prince Regent, in reaction to the news.

That moment alone would be worth shackling himself to one woman, Pagan decided. *As if all the other reasons weren't enough,* he thought, glancing toward the only female ever to confound him and delight him and close the distance he put between himself and the world. He shook his head, still amazed, which probably would be a lifelong condition. Pagan grinned. He hoped so.

"Congratulations!" A hearty slap on the back drew Pagan from his delightful musings, and he turned to find Hazard smiling in a most satisfied fashion. Although his friend had managed to hide his surprise better than the rest of the guests, Pagan had looked forward to their meeting. At last, there could be no doubt about who had won the wager. So why did Hazard look so pleased with himself?

"And may I wish you a happy birthday, as well!" Hazard said. "One presumes that despite coming into your dotage, you will manage to find something to occupy your time," he added with a wink and a glance toward Scholastica.

Pagan said nothing, but crossed his arms over his chest and waited expectantly for his friend's capitulation. His lips curved upward in a smug expression, for after all Hazard's hazing, he was going to savor every minute of it.

But Hazard did not appear the least bit contrite. In the ensuing silence, he lifted his brows speculatively, as if he had no idea why Pagan was eyeing him. Then he grinned. "Ah, you're waiting for my gift, perhaps?" He shook his head and clucked his tongue. "Foolish man! I've already given you your birthday present!" he announced, and to Pagan's astonishment, he grasped Scholastica by the shoulders and turned her, presenting her, with a flourish.

Pagan stared, dumbfounded, while his bride-to-be greeted his friend happily. "Ah, Hazard! I do believe I owe you my thanks, concerning a certain wager you are rumored to have made with my husband-to-be?" she ventured.

Hazard threw back his head and laughed. "You are most welcome, my dear," he said, bowing graciously. Then he sent Pagan a rebuking glance. "At least someone recognizes the value of my efforts."

"Are you saying that you planned *this?*" Pagan asked,

waving a hand to encompass Scholastica, the celebration and all that was now his future.

Hazard flashed his white teeth with immodest glee. "Well, I did my best, although I must admit that several times I feared that you were too dense to seize your prize."

Pagan frowned at him, annoyed. "I am not so stupid as to fail to recognize and embrace my fate when it stares me in the face," he said, conveniently ignoring all the times he had broken out in a sweat, fearful of Scholastica's power over him. However, Hazard was not to be fooled. When he smirked knowingly, Pagan sighed. "Well, I don't have to be hit over the head too many times, anyway," he admitted.

Scholastica laughed, reaching out to touch his arm, and the warmth of her presence was enough to make Pagan forget all those old doubts in an instant. Besides, if she brought him to his knees, he could say the same of her, he thought, grinning wickedly.

"By the way, I believe I owe you some money," Hazard said, drawing Pagan once more away from his pleasant musings.

"No. Let us leave it be," Pagan said, for he had won something far more valuable than mere coin. And, although he was not prepared to concede it as yet, he might very well owe Hazard for his good fortune, a lifelong debt, indeed.

"I wouldn't dream of it!" Hazard said as he tendered the agreed-upon amount.

Surprised at his insistence, Pagan noted that his friend was smiling rather complacently for someone relinquishing payment. "Are you sure you can afford this?" Pagan asked, suspicious.

"Very sure, my dear man. In fact, thanks to you, I am now quite flush," Hazard said.

When Pagan lifted a dark brow in question, Hazard shrugged. "You see, after I made this bet with you, I wagered every acquaintance of yours something else entirely," he explained.

"Which was?" Pagan prompted.

With a glance toward Scholastica, Hazard grinned. "I bet them all that you at last had met your match."

* * * * *

DEBORAH HALE

Since selling her first book to Harlequin Historicals in 1998, Deborah Hale has enjoyed hopscotching through history, from medieval England to nineteenth-century Atlantic Canada, from Regency ballrooms to a Montana ranch. With every book, this award-winning author invites her readers to "escape to an enchanted past."

Deborah Hale lives in historic, romantic Nova Scotia with her medical physicist husband and their four imaginative children. She loves to hear from readers at P.O. Box 829, Lower Sackville, Nova Scotia B4E 2R0, Canada or through her Web site, www.deborahhale.com.

Please address questions and book requests to:
Harlequin Reader Service
U.S.: 3010 Walden Ave., P.O. Box 1325, Buffalo, NY 14269
Canadian: P.O. Box 609, Fort Erie, Ont. L2A 5X3

CUPID GOES TO GRETNA
Deborah Hale

For my sister Cyndi Corscadden,
whose charm is matched only by her
brains and beauty

Chapter One

Bath, England 1815

"Mr. Armitage, will you please elope to Gretna with me?" asked Miss Ivy Greenwood in a breathless rush.

He must be dreaming. He had *better* be dreaming!

Oliver Armitage glanced up from his latest experiment and shook his head hard to dispel the vivid hallucination of Miss Greenwood standing in the open door of his study. This was what came of working thirty-six hours without a wink of sleep. Perhaps he should take better care of himself, as his aunt Felicity constantly urged.

This was not the first time Oliver had been vexed by dreams of the beautiful and vivacious Miss Greenwood. Nor the first time thoughts of her had interrupted his work. It was becoming a right bloody bother!

"Oh please, Mr. Armitage, don't say no until you've heard me out." Unaffected by the shaking of his head, or the stinging slap Oliver now delivered to his right cheek, the relentless mirage of Ivy Greenwood stepped into his study and closed the door behind her.

A fragrance wafted from her, sweetly at odds with the faint reek of chemicals in the room. Some floral distillation—*Dianthus carophyllus,* perhaps. Commonly known as clove pink, the flower's oil was often used in compounding soaps.

Oliver had heard of overtired minds imagining sights and sounds. But never smells.

She must be *real!*

"Miss Greenwood, what are you doing here?" He leaped from his desk chair, trying to adjust his spectacles with one hand, while raking the other through his disheveled hair in a vain attempt to make himself presentable.

It didn't work, or so Oliver judged by the look of pitied exasperation in Ivy Greenwood's eyes. Remarkable eyes they were, too, the precise melding of blue and green produced by the combustion of copper. Looking into them produced a curiously combustible sensation in Oliver Armitage.

"What am I doing here?" echoed Miss Greenwood. "I told you straightaway, or did you not hear me? I need you to elope with me to Gretna Green. The happiness of your aunt and my dear brother depend upon it. Will you help me?"

His fatigue-addled mind struggled to fathom what she was talking about. At the same time a number of alarming sensations diffused through his chest, provoked by the mere thought of wedding this baffling, bewitching creature.

"I must confess myself at a loss, Miss Greenwood."

Intellect being his·sole source of pride, Oliver shrank from admitting his confusion. From the moment he'd met her, Ivy Greenwood had confused him on too many levels for his liking. "While I would like to oblige you, I have no intention of marrying you or anyone else, no matter how greatly Aunt Felicity may desire it."

"But she doesn't desire it—that's the whole point." Ivy Greenwood swept a glance around the makeshift laboratory he'd contrived in the guest room of his aunt's town house. Perhaps she thought he could use a wife to impose a little order on the scientific clutter.

"I assure you, I have no intention of compromising your bachelor state, sir. Let me explain myself better. My brother and sister understand me so well I've fallen into the lamentable habit of jumping into the middle of a discussion and expecting other people to follow me."

A trill of laughter at her own expense shook Miss Greenwood, making the lustrous curls that peeped out from under her bonnet dance. Their color put Oliver in mind of a freshly burnished copper-gold alloy.

"Pray have a seat while you explain." As he scooped a pile of books and papers off the nearest armchair, Oliver wondered why the news that Miss Greenwood had no designs on his bachelorhood did not prompt the anticipated rush of relief.

"Thank you, Mr. Armitage." She gave the embroidered chair seat a rather dubious look before perching herself on it. "Now, let's see…begin at the beginning. I don't want to go too far back, or it will take me ages to tell, and we haven't much time."

"Perhaps if you clarify the points on which I'm confused." Oliver lowered himself back onto his desk chair, belatedly wondering if his cravat might be hopelessly stained with the residue of mineral salts. "You wish us to elope, but not get married. That's a bit of a contradiction, you must admit. And what do Aunt Felicity and your brother have to do with the eloping business?"

"That's it!" A smile of blinding intensity lit Ivy Greenwood's delicate features. For an intoxicating instant she regarded him with a look of dazzling admiration, as though he had just unlocked the secret of the universe for her. "I expect you know that your aunt has been my brother's mistress for the past two months."

The shock of hearing her refer so casually to such intimate, scandalous matters made Oliver's lips open and shut rapidly without engaging his other vocal organs.

Miss Greenwood ignored his mimicry of a beached fish. "I've never seen my brother happier than he's been lately. Watching them together, I'm convinced your aunt is quite as smitten with Thorn as he is with her."

Oliver managed a nod. Though not as perceptive of people's emotions as Miss Greenwood appeared to be, he had sensed a change in his aunt Felicity. It had almost seemed to him as if the twelve year difference in their ages had narrowed further still, making him the senior of the two. On that account Oliver had warmed to Hawthorn Greenwood as he had to few other men—including his own uncle Percy, Lady Lyte's first husband.

"If you and I can see how well suited they are, how can Thorn and your aunt be so blind to it?" demanded Miss Greenwood.

"You're losing me again." Oliver strove to concentrate his weary wits on what Ivy Greenwood was saying, instead of how her eyes sparkled or the way she cocked her head to one side when she spoke, like a winsome little bird. "What makes you think they *are* blind to it?"

"Be-cause," explained the young lady with the exaggerated patience of a schoolmistress tutoring a particularly backward scholar, "she gave poor Thorn his marching orders yesterday."

"Oh dear."

"Oh dear, indeed." Ivy Greenwood's voice sharpened. "Without a word of warning or explanation that I could tell. Thorn's wandering around in shock, as though he'd been hit by a runaway mail coach. If I didn't like your aunt so well, I'd be furious with her for treating him so badly."

As he tried to digest this information, Oliver found himself wishing someone cared enough to be as indignant on his behalf as Miss Greenwood was for her brother. "How does Gretna Green figure into all this?"

Since the introduction of Lord Hardwick's *Marriage Act,* some sixty years before, couples desiring to wed against their families' wishes had often fled to Scotland, where matrimonial law was scandalously lax.

"It's very simple, really." Miss Greenwood treated Oliver to a most disarming smile. "I'm sure all Thorn and your aunt need is a little time and privacy to sort out whatever's gone wrong between them. But I know my brother. If he thinks Lady Lyte wants nothing more to do with him, he'd never impose himself upon her, which may be exactly what she's hoping he *will* do."

Oliver rubbed his brow, behind which he could feel a vicious headache brewing. He doubted whatever else Ivy Greenwood had to say would prove soothing.

As she watched the young scientist massage his fore-

head, a mystifying urge overtook Ivy. Never one to resist
an impulse, she sprang from her chair, and knelt beside
his. Reaching up, she pushed an unruly lock of chestnut
hair from his brow.

"Are you ill, Mr. Armitage?"

The hazel gaze he turned upon Ivy unsettled her. It
was plain to see the man did not take proper care of
himself. And for the first time in her life, she yearned to
look after someone.

Her precipitous arrival and nonstop chatter couldn't
have done the poor fellow any good. "I probably
oughtn't to have barged in on you like this. But when
the idea came to me, I *knew* it might be the only chance
for Thorn, and I had to act upon it without delay. Does
that sound quite ridiculous to you?"

"O-on the contrary, Miss Greenwood." Though he
appeared alarmed by her nearness, Oliver Armitage did
not move away. "It's the first thing you've said that I
understand completely. Sometimes when I've been
brooding over a particular experiment, I'll get a sudden
flash of insight into what's happening or how I could do
it differently. Then I cannot rest or sleep or eat until I've
tested my theory."

A smile seemed to take his angular features as much
by surprise as it took Ivy. If he spruced himself up and
made an effort to look less sober and serious all the time,
Oliver Armitage might have a bevy of belles pursuing
him for more than his fortune.

His voice softened, and for a dizzying instant his gaze
played over her face like a caress. "What flash of in-
spiration has brought you to me, Miss Greenwood?"

For possibly the first time in her life, Ivy found herself

at a loss for words. All at once the notion of running off to Gretna Green with Oliver Armitage didn't seem quite so comical. True, he wasn't the kind of dashing rake she fancied, but there was something curiously compelling about the young scientist she'd never appreciated until this very moment.

"When you first came in, you asked if I'd elope with you," he prompted her. "I still fail to see what that has to do with your brother and my aunt Felicity."

This admission freed Ivy's tongue from its unaccountable paralysis. "For a man who's wont to be so clever, you don't understand very much about people, do you?"

His smile faded and a shadow darkened his eyes. "I fear you're correct. The human heart is one conundrum beyond my ability to resolve. Perhaps from so little practice."

For no reason that she could work out, Ivy felt herself ashamed. She almost blurted an apology for disturbing him and quit Lady Lyte's town house then and there. But she remembered the stricken look on Thorn's face when he had finished reading the letter from Oliver's aunt.

Dear Thorn had been mother and father to her since long before their father had died. Ivy would do anything to see him as happy again as he'd been during the past two months.

"What do you suppose your aunt would do if she discovered you'd set off for Scotland to marry some unsuitable young woman?" she asked Mr. Armitage.

He shrugged. "Try to stop me, I hope."

"*Ex*-actly!" Perhaps her plan had a chance of succeeding, after all. If only she could win his cooperation.

"Thorn would do the same if I eloped. I know he would. And what better opportunity for the pair of them to talk out their problems than on the long carriage ride to Scotland?"

Understanding flickered deep in his eyes and one corner of his wide mouth inched upward again. "You're proposing we stage a sham elopement in order to make your brother and Aunt Felicity follow us to Gretna?"

Ivy gave a vigorous nod. "Isn't it a stroke of genius? By the time they arrive, I expect they'll be ripe to step in front of a clergyman and take their own vows."

Her enthusiasm for whole project rekindled. "I have a natural talent for matchmaking, if I do say so. I managed to bring my sister Rosemary together with her destined husband. It was no easy task, either, what with her foolish pride and his unaccountable modesty. They're blissfully happy now, thanks to me, and I won't rest until I've done the same service for Thorn and your aunt."

"I applaud your goal, Miss Greenwood, but—"

"Do call me Ivy, or Miss Ivy, if you must. Back in Lathbury, Rosemary was *Miss Greenwood* to everyone. Whenever I hear that name I want to check if she's standing behind me."

"Very well, Miss Ivy. About this scheme of yours—"

"Brilliant, isn't it?" Ivy almost hugged herself.

Another agreeable consequence of making this match between Thorn and Lady Lyte would be to bring Oliver Armitage into the Greenwood family. Once she got to know him better on this little jaunt to Gretna, she'd have an idea what sort of wife he needed. He struck her as just the sort of unassuming fellow who could use the help of an astute matchmaker.

For some reason, however, the notion of finding Mr. Armitage a wife left a sour aftertaste.

Ivy had no time to consider why that might be. "If we're to succeed we must act quickly, before Thorn and Lady Lyte have gotten used to being apart. Can you jot a note to your aunt and pack a portmanteau straight-away?"

"Surely you must be—"

Another thought occurred to her. "Do you have a carriage of your own, or shall we need to hire a coach?"

"I've never felt the need of my own vehicle since Aunt Felicity has always lent me the use of hers."

"A rented coach it is, then. Thorn had to let all of ours go—they're such an expense to maintain." Ivy squashed down a pang of regret. One could never count on hired transport to be as comfortable or reliable as a family's private equipage.

Still, it was a small sacrifice to make for the sake of her brother's future happiness. "We must leave Thorn and your aunt the means to give chase as soon as they discover we've gone. We'll need money, too, I suppose. For coaches and inns and such. Do you have any? My dear brother-in-law gave me twenty whole pounds to kit myself out for the Season. I hardly spent any of it and this is a much more worthwhile enterprise, don't you think?"

Before she could say anything more, he raised his hand and pressed his fingers over her lips with firm but gentle pressure.

"Miss Greenwood...Miss Ivy, please hear me out. Your goal is a laudable one, but you can't be serious about this addlepated scheme. Your brother and my aunt are both past thirty—old enough to know their own minds, surely. We would do better not to meddle in a situation we may not fully understand. If either of them seek our counsel, then we can offer our advice.''

How dare he patronize her as if she was a silly child who could not comprehend the consequences of her actions? Ivy struggled to maintain her indignation when some foolish part of her enjoyed the sensation of his hand on her lips.

Just because Oliver Armitage had read all these thick dusty tomes piled around the room, didn't mean he knew everything. He'd confessed himself mystified by the workings of the human heart, and on that account she felt sorry for him. She'd rather understand about important things like love than have all the book learning in the world.

If Mr. Armitage believed he'd had the final say in all this, then the young scientist had made a serious miscalculation.

Chapter Two

Oliver woke with a start, praying he'd find himself in his own bed or fallen asleep hunched over his desk.

Instead he discovered himself slumped on a hard seat upholstered with dry, cracking leather, inside a bouncing, swaying, rattling coach. A coach he vaguely recalled hiring in Bath during what he'd hoped was a nightmare. How had he let Ivy Greenwood talk him into such rash folly?

Almost against his will, Oliver's gaze strayed to the opposite seat. The moment his eyes encountered the slumbering form of Miss Greenwood, he found his answer in her beauty.

It was not an answer to his liking.

He purported to be a man of science, didn't he? A man of science should collect facts, weigh them, then make a rational decision based upon solid information. Dimples, red-gold ringlets and eyes like shimmering aquamarines had no place in such deliberations. Neither did that immeasurable, intangible, thoroughly suspect quality known as *charm*.

Ivy Greenwood had not charmed him! Oliver's intellect protested. She'd merely taken advantage of his ex-

hausted state, nattering on about love and happiness and
family obligations until he'd have promised her anything
to secure a moment's peace. Now that he'd got a few
hours' sleep to shore up his willpower, he'd order this
blasted vehicle turned around and driven straight back to
Bath before anyone missed them.

Wouldn't he?

As he let his gaze linger over Miss Ivy, Oliver wasn't
so sure. In sleep her features had taken on a soft, ingen-
uous caste that accorded well with her temperament.
Like a child, she was full to the brim of high spirits and
sunny optimism without a thought to spare for the harsh
practicalities of life or the troublesome consequences of
her impulsive actions.

Oliver couldn't help comparing her to the other ladies
he'd met in Bath—comely and controlled, with a glitter
of avarice in their eyes that no amount of fan fluttering
could hide. After their suffocating attention, Ivy Greenwood had breezed into his life like a zephyr of clover-
scented country air. No wonder such a singular creature
had captured his interest.

Captured and held it hostage. That would never do,
because Miss Greenwood was not a child. The bewitching curves beneath her light muslin gown were those of
a woman, as were her ripe, inviting lips.

Oliver Armitage needed to concentrate all his mental
powers upon his research, without feminine distractions.
In short, he needed to purge Ivy Greenwood from his
system.

If there was an enterprise calculated to make him
heartily sick of her, Oliver could think of none better
than a tedious carriage ride of over three hundred miles.

Having satisfied himself with a sound, logical reason
for continuing their journey, he settled back in his seat

with a contented sigh and studied Ivy Greenwood as though she was some exotic botanical specimen.

When a pedantic little voice in the back of his mind carped at his pathetic excuse for lingering in her company, Oliver told it to keep its opinions to itself.

"Miss Ivy, wake up, will you?"

Ivy's fuzzy, half-asleep mind sensed she had been ignoring similar appeals for some time. This one sounded more insistent and more vexed than the ones before.

Surrendering to a wide yawn, she coaxed her eyes half open.

"I hope your bed curtains never catch fire while you're asleep," said a pleasant masculine voice with just a hint of asperity. "You sleep as soundly as any hibernating animal."

Ivy stretched, then rubbed her eyes. "I'm sorry, Thorn. What time is it?"

"It's nearly sunset," replied the voice. "And I'm not your brother. Luckily for you, he hasn't caught up with us…yet."

Her eyes flew open. "Mr. Armitage!"

She glanced around the dim interior of the coach. "What…? How…?" Her heart galloped faster than the faint beat of horses' hooves upon the highway as she struggled to marshal her memory.

What had she done?

"We've left Avon behind." Oliver Armitage spoke in a calm, patient tone, but the crinkled line of his mouth suggested wry amusement at her expense. "We aren't far over the border, but it's past time we put in somewhere to dine and sleep. Newport's as good a place as any. Since it's on the provincial route north, we should have little trouble hiring fresh transport in the morning."

Dine? Sleep! The recollection of what she'd done slapped Ivy wide-awake. The consequences of her folly threatened to overwhelm her.

"I know a good inn where we can take supper." Mr. Armitage sounded far more enthusiastic about the whole venture than when she'd first approached him. "We'd probably better not spend the night there, though."

Sleep—with him? No wonder he looked so gratified all of a sudden. When she'd first hit on this plan, Oliver Armitage had seemed the perfect accomplice. Quiet, steady, bookish—just the sort of fellow with whom her virtue would be safe. Not a dashing young rogue who would tempt her and be tempted in turn.

Perhaps all men were rogues at heart. That enormous miscalculation dropped onto an already teetering pile, which threatened to fall on Ivy and bury her.

"How could you let me go through with this?" she wailed. "Did you never stop to think what will happen if Thorn and your aunt *don't* come after us? This will all be for naught, that's what. And Thorn will probably call you out, or worse, insist you marry me to salvage my reputation."

The notion of being tied for the rest of her life to an unromantic intellectual filled Ivy with dismay. "Why didn't you talk some sense into me? I've always been prone to speak and act before I think. But you're a man of science—you ought to have known better!"

"I did my damnedest to dissuade you, silly child!" In the gathering darkness, emerald sparks seemed to flash in Oliver's hazel eyes. His features took on a razor-sharp definition that was both frightening and stimulating to behold.

His voice echoed the raw crack of the coachman's whip. "I might just as soon have tried to talk a river out of flooding its banks, or warn a hurricane that it could unleash destruction. Did it ever occur to you that you should've staged this mock elopement with a man you *would* be willing to wed if worse came to worst?''

His outburst rocked Ivy back in her seat, speechless and strangely roused.

In the astonished silence that followed, she heard him mutter some words that he might not have meant to give voice. "I know I'm the last fellow in Bath a vivacious beauty would want for a husband. You needn't rub it in.''

A nettle-sharp blush stung in Ivy's cheeks. Vivacious beauty—was that how he thought of her? Silly child had been nearer the mark. What a perfect little wretch she'd been!

"Nonsense. I'm not half good enough for you.''

Oliver Armitage had far more to lose in all this than she had. What if Lady Lyte didn't make up her quarrel with Thorn? What if Oliver's aunt cut off his inheritance as punishment for taking part in this ridiculous escapade? Ivy knew she'd never forgive herself.

Leaning forward, she reached across the narrow space between their seats and grasped Oliver's hand. "I'm most awfully sorry for dragging you into this. And sorrier still for expecting you to talk sense into me when I should be taking responsibility for my own actions. How can I ever make it up to you?''

Oliver stifled a grin. He didn't dare tell Ivy what manner of compensation he found himself wanting from her.

Charm might be immeasurable and intangible, but he could not deny its existence. Nor the fact that Ivy possessed this mysterious power in ample quantity. How else could she have tempered his fury into indulgent amusement with a few disarming words of remorse and an impulsive squeeze of his hand?

One day science might unravel the riddle and translate

it into a dry equation that made perfect sense, but Oliver found himself hoping such a desecration would never come to pass in his lifetime.

At least Ivy Greenwood was forthright about not wanting any lasting attachment with him. Better that than playing the coquette and mouthing sentimental nonsense, all the while keeping a calculating eye trained on his bank balance.

"There, there." He patted her hand and released it...while he still could. "The situation isn't as dire as all that. And it wasn't as though you held a cocked pistol to my head, forcing me to come with you. However ill-considered on both our parts, we're in this up to our necks now. If we mean to salvage anything worthwhile, we shall have to work together. Agreed?"

"Agreed." She heaved a sigh of relief. "You sound as though you have some plan of action in mind."

Off to the west, across the Severn and over the Welsh hills beyond, the May sun had set at last. Even though he could not make out Ivy's expression, Oliver sensed her interest bent upon him. Was there some force of personality akin to magnetism? he wondered.

"Plan...yes. I propose we stop at the King's Arms in Newport and dine there. If my aunt does follow us, that's the first place she's apt to stop and inquire. We often break our journey there when we travel between Bath and her house in the country."

Ivy clapped her hands. "And you want to lay a clear trail for them to follow—how clever!"

The candid ring of admiration in her voice went straight to Oliver's head like a bolt of brandy on an empty stomach. He hadn't realized how intoxicating it might feel to be valued for himself rather than on account of the fortune he stood to inherit.

"That's not all." He resisted the urge to preen for her,

but failed miserably. "While we dine, we must talk as if we plan to press on for Gloucester tonight. Perhaps make a point of asking the innkeeper where we can get fresh horses to continue our journey."

"But…we…won't?"

Oliver shook his head. "We need to be certain Aunt Felicity and your brother are following us…together. Otherwise, we might as well pack it in, head back to Bath and hope we can concoct a plausible story to avert scandal."

Why didn't the prospect of extricating himself from this whole mess hold more appeal for him?

"I see what you mean." Ivy's rising inflection told Oliver that she still didn't follow him completely.

"We'll spend the night across the way at the Green Dragon and keep watch," he explained. "Depending on whether Thorn and Aunt Felicity turn up looking for us, we'll decide how to proceed from there."

"A sound course, indeed." Her endorsement took on a somewhat doubtful tone. "When you say *spend the night,* what manner of sleeping arrangements did you have in mind?"

Thank heaven she hadn't waited to pose that question over supper. If he'd been partaking of beer or wine, Oliver feared he might have choked or expelled the libation out his nostrils! As it was, he could blush and sputter under the benevolent cover of darkness.

"For…for a num-ber of reasons, I think it best we share a room. If I can secure one with a window onto the street, that is. I doubt either of us will be much inclined to sleep after dozing in this coach all afternoon. Would you be agreeable to taking turns at watch? Say three hours at a spell. The one off watch may make use of the b-bed."

Ivy chuckled. "Is that what people mean when they say a lady and gentleman have shared a bed?"

"Miss Greenwood!" Oliver managed to squeak before his neck linen almost strangled him. He was already bedeviled by too many such thoughts without her taking pains to torment him.

"Oh, please don't let's be formal," she cajoled him. Despite his best effort to resist, Oliver could feel it working. "We're running away to Gretna, remember? And if our brilliant plan works as it's sure to, we'll soon be some sort of relations by marriage and then…"

"Then?" He wasn't sure he liked the sound of that.

A flickering glow from the lighted windows of shops and houses told Oliver they must be driving into Newport. After conversing in darkness for some time, he could see Ivy's face clearly again. The sudden vision made him catch his breath.

How many young bucks in Bath would give up a year's allowance to trade places with him? None of them would be fool enough to share a bed with her only turnabout.

A qualm of doubt wriggled deep in the pit of his belly. Would a close-quarter journey to the ends of the earth be sufficient to sicken him of Ivy Greenwood's sparkling company?

"Then?" He managed to ask again from a mouth gone dry.

"Then—" her eyes twinkled brighter than the evening star "—I have brilliant plans for *you*, my dear Mr. Armitage."

Chapter Three

"My dear Mr. Armitage, that was as brilliant a performance as I've ever seen on the stage." Two hours after their coach had rattled into Newport, Ivy concentrated to keep her words from sloshing around like wine in the bottom of a cup. "Every soul at the King's Arms from the hostlers to the waiter will be tripping over themselves to assure Thorn and Felicity that we've driven off to Gloucester, tonight."

Her feet seemed much farther away than usual. It put Ivy in mind of her childhood back at Barnhill, staggering around on a pair of stilts Thorn had built for her. Had she drunk too much, perhaps? The notion made Ivy chuckle to herself.

Unfortunately, she didn't seem capable of laughing and walking at the same time. At least not with any amount of grace.

"Steady on, old girl." Oliver took her arm when she stumbled. "Perhaps I'd better take the first watch, so you can sleep this off."

She sagged against him with a grateful sigh. For such a clever boots, he really wasn't a bad old stick, particularly once he got outside a glass of wine and started to talk about his research. Much of it Ivy hadn't understood, but that only whetted her curiosity to find out more. As she primed him with question after question, he fairly radiated his passion for discovery.

Animated and aglow, his features took on an appealing cast that caught Ivy by surprise. He would never be handsome in the manner that had previously caught her fancy—dark, devilish and dangerous. But there was a certain distinction about his well-shaped, expressive features and his alert, penetrating eyes that somehow dimmed the luster of those swarthy rakehells.

"The first watch?" It took her a moment's concentrated thinking to figure out what he meant. "Oh, *that* first watch. Of course. I shall have the bed well warmed for you when it comes your turn to sleep. You know, Oliver, you'd be my perfect accomplice in all this, even if you weren't Felicity's nephew."

They entered the Green Dragon Inn, where Oliver had secured them lodgings before taking her to dinner across the way. When Oliver had told the innkeeper they were newlyweds on their honeymoon tour, she had almost burst out laughing. Now the notion didn't seem quite so funny.

"Perfect in what sense?" murmured Oliver, steering her up the narrow twisting stairs.

Ivy was grateful for his warmth, strength and steadiness.

"Perfect in playing the tactician to my strategist." She lolled against the wall as he opened the door to their room. "I dream up this lofty plan, as full of holes as a ruddy sieve, then you weave in all the practical bits to make it hold water."

"We do make rather a good team, don't we? I haven't

the imagination to dream up such an idea in the first place.''

Oliver lit a candle that cast dancing shadows around the room. The chamber was so tiny it could barely hold the modest furnishings of a narrow bed, a washstand and a single chair.

Throwing off her bonnet and light shawl, Ivy reeled the few steps it took to carry her from the threshold to the bed, then collapsed onto it.

''You don't have much of a head for drink, do you?'' Oliver pulled off her slippers and covered her with an extra blanket that lay folded at the foot of the bed.

As he drew it up over her shoulders, his hands lingered there for an extra second in something near a caress. Ivy wondered if he might press his lips to her brow in a good-night kiss. When he pulled back at the last moment, then dragged the chair to the window, and extinguished the candle, Ivy couldn't decide whether she felt relieved…or sorry.

''Thorn always used to tuck me in at night, when I was a little girl.'' Ivy's drowsy murmur drifted out of the darkness behind Oliver.

He wished she'd go to sleep. Then perhaps he could focus his thoughts on some scientific conundrum, like the relationship between electricity and magnetism, and forget she was there.

He'd felt something very like static electricity crackle between them this evening while they'd dined at the King's Arms. Her eager curiosity about his research had rubbed against his enthusiasm, igniting a positive charge in their conversation that energized him. Now the knowledge that she lay so close by, soft, warm and languid, tugged on him with a force as powerful as ever a magnet had exerted on an iron nail.

"A strange duty for a brother," he mused, not certain if she was even still conscious to hear him. "Why should Thorn tuck you into bed, rather than your mother or father?"

"I don't remember my mother." Did Ivy's sleepy words sound wistful, or was he reading his own feelings into them? "I'd barely been weaned when she died. Father always seemed to be off in London on some manner of business. We had servants, of course, but Thorn and Rosemary pretty much took charge of me. I sometimes think they gave up any kind of proper childhood for themselves to afford me one. That's why I do so want to help Thorn now, if I can.

"Such good times we had..." In a soft, dreamy voice, Ivy wove a bright tapestry of words and wrapped it around Oliver, until he felt almost as if he'd taken part in her golden, carefree summers at Barnhill. Even the name of the Greenwood's estate in Buckinghamshire conjured up the scent of new-mown hay and the distant lowing of cattle on a sun-drenched afternoon.

"What about you, Oliver?" she asked at last. "Where's your home? What family have you apart from your aunt?"

"None."

That sounded too bleak, too heavily weighted with self-pity, which was foolish since he never let himself dwell upon it. "My father was an army officer in India. That's where I was born. I can still speak the odd word of Hindi I learned from my amah. My parents sent me to school in England as soon as I was old enough to make the journey. That climate is hard on English children."

In the shadow-wrapped street below, Oliver could picture his younger self howling and thrashing as strangers manhandled him aboard that ship bound for an impossibly distant land. His amah keening on the quay while his mother waved a handkerchief, her face almost as pale as that square of bleached cotton.

"You parents aren't still in India, are they?" asked Ivy.

Oliver shook his head. "My father was killed in the Third Mysore War."

"I'm sorry."

"I wasn't. I scarcely remembered him. I was happy, because it meant my mother would come back to England."

After so long a pause, he thought she must surely have fallen asleep, Ivy asked, "Did she?"

For the first time in almost twenty years he made himself say the words. "She drowned in a shipwreck on the voyage home."

Silently he begged Ivy not to offer sympathy. With the wine in his belly and his emotions stirred to a pitch he ordinarily took care to avoid, he might just break down and blubber a schoolboy's tears. The kind he used to hoard and only release a miserly few at a time. Very late at night, like this. In dark, cramped, malodorous little rooms like this one.

He'd been twice a fool to let Ivy Greenwood beguile him into this madcap escapade! If only her brother and his aunt would stay put in Bath like sensible folk, he could trot her back tomorrow and wash his hands of the whole enterprise.

Almost as though she could sense his thoughts, Ivy spoke. "Did you go to live with your aunt then?"

"Heavens, no!" Oliver pulled off his spectacles and dashed the back of his hand across his eyes. It came away only a little damp. "Felicity wasn't even my aunt, then. Now and again Uncle Percy would spare a thought for me—he was my mother's younger brother. Then he'd fetch me up to his house in Staffordshire for a bit of a holiday. Never could count on his remembering or scraping together the cash to finance it. Once he married Felicity he had plenty of blunt from her fortune. She was the one who arranged for me to come at Christmas and every summer.''

By then all those unshed tears had settled in his heart and frozen, and he'd become a junior version of the man he was now—polite but insular, his nose buried in a book most of the time.

With less than a dozen years difference in their ages, Felicity had never tried to mollycoddle him or anything. She had given him the first taste of real family life he'd ever known, though. He'd developed a closer bond with her than with anyone else. It had grieved Oliver, in an abstract fashion, to watch the marriage sour when she could not provide his uncle with an heir.

More to herself than to him, he heard Ivy whisper, "I know my brother could make her happy, if only she'd let him."

"Ivy, Ivy, Ivy." A mordant, mocking chuckle burst out of Oliver as he rose from his chair and stretched. "If only it were that simple."

Was he talking about Thorn and Felicity? Oliver wondered as he settled his spectacles back on his nose and scanned the deserted street once again. Or himself? Surely it couldn't be as simple as letting a woman make him happy.

He could only imagine one who might be equal to the task. And he doubted she would be inclined to undertake it.

* * *

He snored! As the first feeble light of dawn stole through the inn's mullioned window, Ivy clapped a hand over her mouth to stifle a giggle. It seemed impossible that a paragon of intellect and decorum like Oliver Armitage should do something as *human* as belch or break wind…or snore.

She rather liked the sound of it, though—a hushed, husky buzz that assured her he was sleeping peacefully. The poor fellow deserved a little peace after the upheaval she'd visited upon his tranquil life in the last eighteen hours. With one or two forgivable lapses, he'd been a jolly good sport about the whole madcap enterprise.

For a moment she spared her attention from the deserted street below to watch her traveling companion as he slept. Oliver rested on his side, his face turned toward her.

With his spectacles off and his features relaxed in sleep, Oliver Armitage looked years younger than his early twenties. Ivy could picture him in a schoolboy's high starched collar, his nose pressed to a window watching for a carriage that might fetch him away for the holidays. And when it failed to appear, hiding his face behind a book so no one might see the disappointment and longing in his eyes.

The thought of it gave her heart a queer twinge. Battling the urge to throw her arms around him and offer comfort that would be at least a dozen years too late in coming, Ivy forced her gaze back out the window.

Still no sign of activity at the King's Arms. Might all her matchmaking come to naught, except to land her and Oliver into a boiling cauldron of scandal broth?

Behind her, Oliver mumbled something in his sleep and rolled over. The sounds somehow lured her eyes to him again. This time he lay under the blanket in a boneless sprawl, his arms thrown wide. He'd peeled off his neck linen sometime in the night and the top few buttons of his shirt had come undone. The rumpled garment gapped open to expose a wedge of surprisingly muscular chest, lightly matted with fine dark hair.

If an inspection of his face had made her see the affection-starved little boy behind his unsociable facade, this glimpse of his bare chest reminded Ivy in most forceful terms that Oliver Armitage was a man grown.

She swallowed a lump that suddenly materialized in her throat. Had the stuffy little room gotten warmer all of a sudden? Perhaps the innkeeper had a lit a fire downstairs.

The impulse to pitch herself onto the bed with Oliver reared once more, stronger than ever.

"Don't be such a goose, Ivy," she whispered to herself. "When you set yourself to find him a proper wife, a girl anything like *you* would be the last to make your list of prospects."

Though she seldom heeded the voice of reason, this time Ivy found she couldn't ignore it. Why would she want to, indeed? The past day's excitement must be making her fanciful.

Her attention was so engaged upon Oliver that at first she paid no heed to the muted noises in the street below. When at last she spared a glance back out the window, a fine barouche sat parked in front of the King's Arms. Could it be…?

Elation vaulted her out of her chair and across the tiny distance to the bed.

Forgetting all her sister's warnings about waking sleepers gently, she grasped Oliver by the shoulders and shook him. "Wake up! I think they're here. Come tell me if that is your aunt's carriage!"

"What...? Who...?" He sat bolt upright, almost knocking his forehead against hers.

"There's a carriage pulled up across the street." Ivy clutched his arm and dragged him toward the window. "I can't imagine why anyone else would be abroad at such an hour. Is it your aunt's?"

Oliver's hand flailed out toward the washstand, snatched his spectacles and fumbled them onto his nose. He and Ivy pressed close together so they could both see out the tiny window.

"I do believe..." began Oliver.

Before he could say more, the familiar figure of a tall man opened the door of the barouche box and offered his hand to a familiar lady who emerged from within.

"It's *them!*" Ivy squealed. "Together!"

Relief surged through her like a powerful Atlantic gale, sweeping everything before it—sense, propriety, caution. She threw her arms around Oliver's neck, kissing him with a force that surprised even her.

Chapter Four

For the first time since he'd set foot on English soil, over fifteen years ago, Oliver Armitage heeded the dictates of his heart rather than those of his head. When Ivy launched herself at him, her whole slender body fairly vibrating with joy and excitement, he did not resist the kiss she lavished upon him.

The press of her soft, warm lips overwhelmed his senses with a force that elated and alarmed him in equal measure. Not quite equal, perhaps. Elation came on at a swifter velocity, propelling his arms to close around Ivy, his mouth to respond in a manner he'd never learned, but which somehow felt *right*.

His head tilted a fraction, to engage her more deeply. His lips parted, enticing hers to do likewise. One hand plunged into the silky floss of her hair while the other held her fast about the waist.

With the speed and energy of a violent chemical reaction, desire swept through him. His pulse raced and his nostrils flared, as though driven to consume as much air as possible to stoke the blaze within him. His head spun with a delicious dizziness, perhaps because all the blood in his body had rushed straight to his loins.

"I'm sorry, Oliver." As abruptly as she had hurled herself at him, Ivy pushed away. "I let my excitement get the better of me."

She wasn't alone.

Her words doused Oliver as thoroughly as a pitcherful of ice water over the head, allowing his laggard caution to catch and overtake him. Any power capable of shattering the barrier of reserve he'd labored for years to erect around himself was far too dangerous for him to meddle with.

Wrenching his hands away from Ivy, he put as much distance between them as the room's cramped quarters permitted. "I apologize for responding as I did. I must have been half-asleep still and fancying myself in a dream."

A rosy blush blossomed on Ivy Greenwood's fair face, but an impish grin arched her lips upward at the corners, calling forth a pair of devastating dimples.

"You must have very…stimulating dreams, Mr. Armitage. I suspect you may be a man of hidden depths."

How dare she provoke such an irresistible current of sensation within him, then turn around and laugh at him for surrendering to it?

"You find me amusing, Miss Greenwood?" He raked his discarded stock off the floor and twined it around his neck almost as tight as a tourniquet. Perhaps that would keep the blood up in his head, where it belonged.

"Of course I find you amusing, and lots of other nice things besides." Refusing to be cowed by his icy tone or his sullen glare, she disarmed him with her candor as she hunted up her slippers, shawl and bonnet. "I couldn't abide a man who didn't amuse me sometimes."

How could he stay angry when she appeared to mean it as a sincere compliment? And what "other nice things'' did she find him besides amusing? While logic insisted he didn't and shouldn't care, his foolish curiosity fired all the same.

Determined to resist, Oliver turned the conversation to the one subject certain to distract her. ''I must admit your plan to reunite Aunt Felicity with your brother appears to be succeeding. Last night, I would have rated the probability of their showing up together as very slight.''

She responded to his words with the kind of luminous smile most women reserved for compliments on their appearance. Although it was pointless to compare any other woman's smile with that of Ivy Greenwood's, Oliver mused, for she eclipsed them all with ease.

''You may know about probability and other such subjects, sir.'' Her eyes sparkled with the most engaging mischief. ''Perhaps now you'll admit I have certain insights into the mystery of the heart.''

''Granted.'' He wished he dared ask her to explain the baffling emotions that tugged him in several directions at once. Given that she was the one who'd provoked those emotions in the first place, perhaps it would be wiser to avoid the subject.

''Well?'' Ivy nodded toward the window. ''You said we'd decide how to proceed once we discovered if they were following us. They are hot on our trail—together. After yesterday, I expect you want to march me across the street to Thorn and be done with it.''

Part of him did, without a doubt. The considered, rational element that had ruled his life for many years. Another part, almost foreign to his nature, resisted the idea of abandoning this imprudent adventure. Resisted the idea of parting from Ivy Greenwood a moment sooner than events made necessary.

Besides, there was Aunt Felicity to consider. He did

want to see her happy and on some distant level he sensed that Thorn Greenwood might well be equal to the task. For all her kindness to him, Oliver knew she was a strong-minded woman, not apt to be persuaded by ordinary means.

Ivy pulled a rueful face. "I'll admit I hadn't taken into account all the bother involved in a trip to Gretna. I don't mind it for myself, but you will find it both uncomfortable and tedious, I expect. It was good of you to come this far with me after my brutal arm-twisting. If we continue, I want it to be *your* choice."

Hazarding a look into her eyes, Oliver saw reflected back an image of himself that he scarcely recognized. Once again he felt the subtle undercurrent of electricity and the magnetic pull between two polar opposites of emotion and intellect.

"I suppose we might as well be hung for a sheep as a lamb." Though he tossed the words off in a most casual tone, Oliver knew what a serious step he'd just taken.

He had made a commitment to this mad venture. He had made a commitment to this woman who represented a puzzle as challenging as any avenue of scientific inquiry. It was high time he dispensed with any illusion that this trip to Gretna would purge Ivy Greenwood from his system.

Unless he was very careful, he suspected her constant company might prove addictive.

"Life is going to seem rather flat after this little adventure, don't you think?"

As a fresh coach whisked them north to Tewkesbury, Ivy rummaged in the hamper of food she'd hurriedly purchased from the shops in Gloucester. Lifting out a golden-brown game pie, she passed it to Oliver on a napkin.

"*My* life, perhaps," he replied, giving the pie an appreciative sniff. "I expect you make the dullest day something of an adventure for yourself and everyone around you."

Another man might have delivered that pretty compliment with a verbal flourish, but Oliver spoke with an earnest, self-conscious air that went straight to Ivy's heart.

Her mouth crammed with ham sandwich, she could manage no better reply than a lopsided, cheek-bulging smile. True, she did her best to enliven life for herself and those around her. Nothing in ages had provided stimulation to equal her journey with Oliver Armitage.

Surely it was the thrill of the chase, and of matchmaking between Thorn and Felicity. Nothing gave Ivy quite the same sense of heady elation as playing Cupid on behalf of a man and a woman who were perfectly suited for one another but didn't recognize it.

Swallowing the well-chewed food in her mouth, she washed it down with a sip of ale. "Do you suppose there's any chance of them overtaking us?"

With the day waning, they'd stopped in Gloucester just long enough to hire another coach, buy this food, and bribe an innkeeper to say they'd spent the previous night in his establishment, if anyone inquired.

"It's possible," Oliver said. "That barouche of my aunt's is a fine rig. With frequent change of horses, Thorn and Felicity are bound to make good time. We must assume they won't be satisfied with lagging a day's ride behind us, either."

"But we aren't really a day's ride ahead." Why did her insides quiver like jelly at the notion of being caught and dragged back to Bath? Thorn would be vexed with her, of course, but he never managed to stay angry for long.

"I pray they don't find out how close we are." Oliver took a drink of his own ale. "Now that I'm satisfied they're well on our trail, I believe we should try to put more distance between us. If we drive through the night, morning should find us the better part of the way to Birmingham. It won't be a comfortable night's sleep, I fear…"

"I'd be willing to suffer worse than a sleepless night on my brother's account," vowed Ivy.

At least that would spare them any bother about sleeping arrangements at an inn. When Oliver had informed the landlord of the Green Dragon they were newlyweds on their honeymoon tour, she must have blushed almost purple. The heat of that blush had spread from her face all the way down her bosom and her belly, to her bottom. And that had been before she'd experienced the reckless intensity of Oliver's kiss.

They ate the rest of their rolling picnic in companionable silence, now and then exchanging a look, but more often staring out the coach windows at the Vale of Gloucester's rich farmland.

"By midday tomorrow we should arrive at Trentwell," remarked Oliver as Ivy stowed the remains of their supper in the hamper. "That's Aunt Felicity's country house. We'll be able to stop there long enough for a decent meal and a wash up. I also can collect some papers I left behind."

"Do you continue your research even during summers in the country?" asked Ivy.

Oliver nodded. "That's my real work. During the winters in Bath I play about with scientific inquiry in a variety of areas, but in the summers I concentrate on applied science. I've written a book on crop rotation and I'm working on a formula for a new pottery glaze.''

Though she did not find this practical research quite as engrossing as some of the scientific matters they had discussed the previous evening over dinner, Ivy still gave Oliver her undivided attention and prompted him with questions she hoped he would not consider too dimwitted. She found herself admiring the dedication he brought to his research. Oliver Armitage was not motivated by ambition for gold or glory, she sensed, but rather the noble ideals of mastering an intellectual challenge and finding ways to improve the livelihood of his neighbors.

Outside the coach, daylight slowly ebbed and a brisk wind blew up the Severn. Ivy pulled her shawl closer and closer around her.

Oliver paused in his explanation of porcelain manufacture. ''Your teeth are chattering!''

Ivy clamped them together. ''It's getting a bit ch-chilly, but I'll be f-fine, honestly.''

''Nonsense.'' From out of the darkness his hand latched onto her arm and tugged her over onto the seat beside him. ''They don't call this garment a greatcoat for nothing. It can easily accommodate the pair of us since we're neither very portly.''

Ivy parted her lips to protest, but all that emerged was a sigh as the warmth of Oliver's coat enveloped her. How could she protest this necessary intimacy, when she'd already plunged them into potential scandal by spiriting the poor man off to Gretna?

''T-thank you, Oliver.'' She snuggled against his toasty torso, savoring the warmth of his arm around her shivering shoulders. ''You've been far kinder to me t-than I merit. I promise, though, I will make it up to you. Once Thorn and Felicity are happily settled, I'll do everything in my power to set you up with the perfect wife.''

Their nearness and the subtle scent of him dispelled her chill in way no quantity of blankets or bed-warming pans could have managed.

"What makes you think I need a wife?" She sensed a teasing note in his voice, so close to her ear. "Or want one, for that matter?"

For some reason his second question left her vaguely unsettled. Perhaps that ham sandwich hadn't agreed with her digestion.

"You may not want a wife—" the tart reply burst out of her "—but, depend upon it, you require one. To see to practical matters so you can concentrate on your work. And to keep you from starving yourself or going without sleep. Besides, don't you ever feel the need…of a woman in your bed?"

The muscles of his arm stiffened, accompanied by a sharp intake of air. "Do you have any idea what you're asking?"

"I certainly do," she said. "Perhaps more than you, Mr. Nose-in-a-Book. My sister told me all about it once she got married. She didn't want me going to my wedding night a poor green goose like she was. I'll admit I was a bit shocked by the information at first, but now that I've gotten used to the idea I believe it might be quite pleasant."

"Hmm…yes…well…" The temperature inside Oliver's coat rose several degrees.

"Aren't you the least bit curious?" Ivy persisted.

Some wicked streak in her relished the opportunity to make Oliver Armitage squirm. It would serve him right for saying he didn't want a wife—as though women were, and would forever remain, superfluous to his monkish existence.

Why that should perturb her quite so much, Ivy could not work out. Perhaps she understood less about matters of the heart than she had boasted to Oliver.

Chapter Five

Wasn't he the least bit curious?

On the contrary, Oliver Armitage had never burned so with curiosity about a subject. He'd heard enough to guess what must transpire when a man and a woman joined their bodies. He'd gathered there was physical pleasure involved, but he'd never been able to reconcile himself to the sordid means by which most of his male acquaintances had satisfied their ''thirst for knowledge.''

Dashed if he would admit his ignorance to this brazen chit for her further amusement! Particularly when she roused his interest in the whole matter as no other female ever had.

Pointedly ignoring her question, he posed one of his own. ''How would you describe this *perfect wife* you mean to find me? And what makes you think such a paragon would want a tiresome fellow like me, other than to get her clutches on my aunt's fortune in due time?''

''I didn't say she'd be perfect in the absolute sense, just perfect for you. And what makes you think she'd only want you for your fortune? You have plenty of first-rate qualities that any wise woman would prize above material considerations.''

Ivy angled herself and titled her face toward him. He could feel the whisper of her breath on his cheek. Oliver continued to stare straight ahead into the darkness. He didn't trust himself to turn his lips in her direction.

''You are in the minority of your sex for thinking so, I fear. Or perhaps having been the target of more than one fortune huntress has jaundiced my opinion of women.''

Ivy pressed her head to his chest. If she meant it as a gesture of comfort, Oliver was surprised to discover it worked.

''I'm sorry if they hurt you. I can tell you from experience, though, being in straitened circumstances changes the way a lady must look at possible suitors. Many families pressure their daughters to make the most advantageous marriage, but that does not mean they would marry an odious man for his money. Only that they might have to give up a nice one if he had no prospects, as Papa made Rosemary do when my brother-in-law first began courting her.''

Swathed in discreet darkness, Oliver permitted himself the hint of a smile. Earlier that day, during their headlong rush from Newport to Gloucester, Ivy had related all the particulars of her sister's second chance at love. By the sound of it, she had reason to be proud of her match-making skills. Would Rosemary Greenwood and Merritt Temple have found their way back to one another, Oliver wondered, without a blatant push at opportune moments from Rosemary's meddling little sister?

''The ideal Mrs. Armitage won't care a fig for your

aunt's money,'' announced Ivy with reckless confidence. ''She'll have to be a bit of a bluestocking, that goes without saying, but not *all* prunes and prisms. Pretty but not bandboxy. A pinch of bossiness wouldn't hurt, to make certain you take regular meals and go to bed at a reasonable hour...''

''What else?'' Oliver asked.

''I just thought it mightn't go amiss if she has the sort of attributes men fancy in women, so you'd be glad to tuck into bed early.''

''You, my dear Ivy, are incorrigible.'' Even as he joined in her laughter at her own expense, Oliver reflected on Ivy's description of his ideal wife.

He doubted the bluestocking part was necessary. Ivy herself had demonstrated that a woman could have a keen mind and a lively curiosity without being aggressively studious. Oliver had a few other attributes he'd add to her list, as well. A loyal heart, a ready wit and an impish sense of fun to draw him out of himself.

It didn't take a genius logician to recognize that only one young lady of his acquaintance answered to that description. Might he be approaching this whole trip to Gretna from the wrong angle? Oliver asked himself. Rather than using the time to work his attraction for Ivy Greenwood out of his system, perhaps he should set himself to winning her.

Was it possible he could turn this mock elopement into the genuine article by convincing a certain charming little matchmaker that he might be a worthwhile match for her?

For the first time in her career playing Cupid, Ivy regarded a chance to matchmake with decidedly mixed feelings. Describing the young lady she planned to locate for Oliver, she found herself resenting the future Mrs. Armitage.

Don't be a ninny! she scolded herself. *It's only because she's an abstract set of qualities, not a flesh-and-blood girl.*

Yes, that must be it, she decided. When she met a real young lady who answered to that description, no doubt "Miss X" would have a flaw or two to humanize her. Then Ivy would learn to like her without reserve and take genuine pleasure in watching her succumb to Oliver's courting...perhaps.

A deep yawn stretched Ivy's mouth so wide it ached. She hadn't slept well on that musty-smelling mattress at the Green Dragon. Oliver's firm chest made a much more satisfactory pillow. Her head lolled against him and her eyes slid shut.

"What about your ideal husband?" he prompted her. "Any plans to make a match for yourself?"

The words reached her right ear in the normal fashion, but the left one, pressed against his topcoat, heard a deeper echo transmitted through his flesh, accompanied by the brisk rhythm of his heartbeat.

"One of these days, perhaps. I haven't met him yet, but I'll recognize him the moment I do. I've been dreaming of him for years, you see."

"Indeed?" Oliver heaved the word on a faint sigh, or did Ivy only fancy it from the muzzy twilight of half sleep? "Tell me all about him so I can keep a sharp eye out. Why, you may turn me into as incorrigible a matchmaker on your behalf as you are on mine."

Giddy with fatigue, the notion made her chuckle. "I fear you would be a dismal failure in that regard, my friend. You'd want a nice neat equation with all the figures tallied. Matters of the heart often go by contraries. Take my brother and your aunt for instance. You must admit, Lady Lyte is a rather unconventional creature."

"I would be the last to deny it." Oliver shifted in the seat, leaning back somewhat into the corner, making it even more comfortable for Ivy to rest against him. "I believe Aunt Felicity invited Thorn to become her lover, rather than the usual way 'round."

"It amazes me that he accepted." Fond thoughts of her brother flittered through Ivy's mind. "Though I adore him, I'll be the first to admit Thorn is as conventional and responsible a solid old citizen as you would meet in a fortnight. Yet, some special connection developed between him and Felicity, in spite of their differences. How would the cold logic of science account for that?"

She heard and felt the laughter roll through Oliver. Both the sound and the sensation proved highly infectious.

"I would account for it by hypothesizing that opposites attract. It is a well-documented principle of magnetism. There may be more science at work in matters of the heart than you might suppose, Miss Cupid."

Opposites attract? That made a kind of sense. Weren't men and women opposites in many respects already?

"I will concede you that point, and I'll tell you all about the man of my dreams, though I doubt you'll find his like among any of your acquaintance."

"And why is that?"

"Because he's rather wicked, Oliver. Does that shock you? A wicked, dashing rakehell with a dark past. My love will reform him, of course."

"Or his wickedness will corrupt you." Oliver's quip stung her with a barb of censure.

"Nonsense!" Ivy proceeded to spin a dramatic account of her imaginary suitor, though somehow her fantasy lacked its accustomed fire.

Gradually it sputtered out altogether as she subsided against Oliver, whose nearness made her feel warm in a way she'd never imagined.

Though Ivy's presence in his arms heated Oliver's blood to an almost unbearable degree, her words chilled his heart. The assurance that she would never pursue him for his money was equally cold comfort. She'd made it clear that he was not, nor could he ever be, the kind of man she wanted for a husband.

To think so would be deluding himself, and a good scientist must never allow wishful thinking to color his evaluation of the evidence. The way he'd once persuaded himself that his mother had not perished in the Indian Ocean, but miraculously washed ashore to appear one day at his school and reclaim him.

Was Ivy Greenwood deluding herself with her romantic fancies? Oliver asked himself through that long night as he held her in his warming, protective embrace.

He didn't for a moment believe the adage about a good wife steadying the kind of wild young man Ivy had her heart set on. The rakehell might be content until the novelty wore off, then he'd revert to his true form and break Ivy's heart with his philandering. The way Uncle Percy had done with Felicity.

Why did he care, anyway? Oliver's pride and logic scoffed. If the little fool wanted a scoundrel rather than a reliable but unexciting man of learning, no one had appointed him her keeper. He should have heeded his own sense of caution and never let Ivy Greenwood charm her way past all the barricades he'd erected around his affections.

While their coach sped through the sleeping Worcestershire countryside, Oliver struggled to shore up his defenses and to subdue a mutiny by his body and his heart.

Chapter Six

"So *this* is Trentwell." Ivy pressed her nose to the coach window as it trundled down a wide lane canopied with lofty arching elms. "It looks so much more grand than old Barnhill."

Oliver responded with an offhand, dismissive-sounding grunt. His vacant gaze did not stray from some fixed point off in the distance.

He must be deep in contemplation of some arcane chemical formula or complicated scientific theory, Ivy decided, for he'd been even quieter and more abstracted than usual all morning. She could hardly believe he was the same man she'd snuggled close to last night, exchanging confidences and easy banter. Today he exuded all the warmth and ease of a granite statue.

Might his behavior indicate more than intellectual preoccupation? Had she said or done something to make him angry with her, perhaps? Did he resent her well-meant aim of finding him a wife?

For the first time, Ivy pitied the future Mrs. Armitage. If she possessed a sensitive, affectionate nature, the poor young lady might well be grieved by the sort of chilly indifference Oliver had exhibited today.

Not that it mattered to Ivy in the least.

Oliver Armitage was simply her cohort in this scheme to reunite Thorn with Lady Lyte. If she'd begun to fancy any more tender feelings toward him, it could only be due to the enforced intimacy of their long coach ride. Ivy hoped the lengthy carriage ride would have an even stronger effect of that nature on her brother and his mistress.

As for she and Oliver, the pair of them could obviously use some time apart, even a few hours. If her chatter grated on his sensibilities as his glacial silence grated on hers, Oliver would doubtless agree.

The coach slowed as it reached the end of the drive, which looped around a dainty marble fountain. Their approach had clearly been noted by Lady Lyte's remaining servants, for a middle-aged footman waited in front of the house to greet them.

"Master Oliver, this is a pleasant surprise, sir." The man beamed when he recognized his employer's nephew. "What brings you away from Bath so soon?"

"The most agreeable of reasons, Dunstan." The forced heartiness of Oliver's tone made Ivy wince. "I am bound for Scotland to be married."

He climbed out of the coach with a gait as stiff as his manner had been all morning. "We shan't be staying long. Just a few hours to eat a decent meal, change clothes and stretch our limbs a bit. Be on our way again before nightfall. Don't want to delay the happy day, you know."

"Indeed, sir." The footman appeared to be struggling to digest this surprising information. "Well, congratulations to you and your lady, sir, and every happiness to you. Will you be coming back this way to pass your honeymoon, Mr. Armitage?"

The question brought a furious blush to Ivy's cheeks, prompted by thoughts of she and Oliver engaged in some of the honeymoon activities Rosemary had described to her. It appeared to fluster Oliver, too, for he made no direct reply to the question, but pretended to fix all his attention on helping Ivy out of the coach. Afterward, he sputtered a brief introduction to the footman, disengaging his hand from hers at the earliest opportunity.

"Would you be so good as to unload our bags, Dunstan, then direct Miss Greenwood to a room where she can wash and change clothes before tea." As he issued his orders, Oliver's gaze flitted to Ivy and away again, as if he felt obliged to look at her when he didn't much want to. "I'll go speak to the stable master myself about tending our hired rig and horses."

"Very good, sir." The footman accepted Ivy's portmanteau, which the coachman handed down to him. "This way if you please, miss."

After a parting glance in Oliver's direction, which he did not return, Ivy followed the servant through a magnificent entryway, up a massive staircase, and down an echoing corridor hung with paintings. The still, immaculate elegance of the place subdued her usual sunny spirits, already clouded by Oliver's distant behavior.

Back in Bath the numbing extent of Lady Lyte's wealth had not been so apparent. No wonder her nephew and heir had a bevy of debutantes throwing themselves at his head!

If Ivy had entertained any foolish romantic notions about Oliver Armitage, which she most emphatically did not, this evidence of his brilliant expectations would have been more apt to dampen her enthusiasm than to promote it.

A door suddenly opened in front of the footman and

We'd like to send you **2 FREE** books and a surprise gift to introduce you to Harlequin Historicals®. Accept our special offer today and

Indulge in a Harlequin Moment!

HOW TO QUALIFY:

1. With a coin, carefully scratch off the silver area on the card at right to see what we have for you—**2 FREE BOOKS** and a **FREE GIFT**—**ALL YOURS! ALL FREE!**

2. Send back the card and you'll receive two brand-new Harlequin Historicals® books. These books have a cover price of $4.99 each in the U.S. and $5.99 each in Canada, but they are yours to keep absolutely free!

3. There's no catch. You're under no obligation to buy anything. We charge nothing—ZERO—for your first shipment and you don't have to make any minimum number of purchases—not even one!

4. The fact is, thousands of readers enjoy receiving books by mail from the Harlequin Reader Service®. They enjoy the convenience of home delivery… they like getting the best new novels at discount prices, BEFORE they're available in stores…and they love their *Heart to Heart* subscriber newsletter featuring author news, horoscopes, recipes, book reviews and much more!

5. We hope that after receiving your free books you'll want to remain a subscriber. But the choice is yours—to continue or cancel, any time at all. So why not take us up on our invitation with no risk of any kind. You'll be glad you did!

SPECIAL FREE GIFT!

We can't tell you what it is…but we're sure you'll like it! A FREE gift just for giving the Harlequin Reader Service® a try!

Visit us online at
www.eHarlequin.com

The **2 FREE BOOKS** we send you will be selected from **HARLEQUIN HISTORICALS®**, the series that brings you rich and vivid historical romances that capture the imagination with their passion and adventure.

Books received may vary.

BUSINESS REPLY MAIL
FIRST-CLASS MAIL   PERMIT NO. 717-003   BUFFALO, NY

POSTAGE WILL BE PAID BY ADDRESSEE

HARLEQUIN READER SERVICE
3010 WALDEN AVE
PO BOX 1867
BUFFALO NY 14240-9952

NO POSTAGE
NECESSARY
IF MAILED
IN THE
UNITED STATES

If offer card is missing write to: Harlequin Reader Service, 3010 Walden Ave., P.O. Box 1867, Buffalo NY 14240-1867 a smooth, masculine voice inquired, "What's all this, then—company? Oh, good. I've been starved for amusement."

A young man lounged against the door frame, regarding her with a dark, admiring gaze. For a moment Ivy wondered if her fatigue-fogged brain had conjured him down from one of the old portraits on the walls. Sporting a black moustache and goatee, the fellow looked more like a cavalier of King Charles's day than a gentleman of the Prince of Wales's Regency.

Disheveled raven hair fell around his shoulders. The rumbled state of his shirt, breeches and waistcoat suggested they'd been slept in.

No sense holding that against him, Ivy decided. Her muslin gown must look a fright on that account, as well. She flashed him a comradely smile—one ragamuffin to another, out of place in these pristine surroundings.

The footman nodded toward Ivy. "This is Miss Greenwood, Master Rupert. She and Master Oliver are breaking their journey here on their way to Gretna Green."

"Is that so, by George?" The young man called Rupert let his dark eyes linger on Ivy's face with an obvious mixture of admiration and interest. "Who'd have thought old 'Books' would snare such a beauty?"

Ivy couldn't decide whether she was flattered on her own behalf or affronted on Oliver's. Who was this fellow, anyhow? He obviously made himself at home here, and the footman had addressed him as though he was a member of the family. But Oliver claimed he had no family apart from Lady Lyte.

Perhaps the question blazed on her face, for the young man's smile twisted into a mocking grin.

"Rupert Norbury at your service, miss." Performing an extravagant bow over her hand, he pressed his lips to it. "Or perhaps rather than using my mother's name, I should take to calling myself Rupert FitzPercy. I'm the eldest of his late lordship's merry-begotten brood. Lady Lyte suffers my presence at Trentwell, particularly when she is not in residence herself. It makes a convenient spot to hide out when my creditors grow tiresomely insistent."

"A pleasure to meet you, sir." It was, too, Ivy realized. A great pleasure to converse with a man who looked her in the eye when he spoke. A man who appeared to regard her as more than an inconvenient article of baggage. A man who answered in every particular to her dashing, wicked ideal.

"I regret we won't be much company for you." She should make some reference to her fictitious engagement, Ivy's conscience prompted her. "We're only stopping for a few hours. Oliver had some books and papers he wanted to collect since we were passing this way."

"A great pity you can't stay longer." Rupert Norbury heaved a deep sigh. "Though I hardly blame 'Books' for wanting to whisk you in front of a parson before some importunate fellow steals you out from under his nose."

Why did such an impudent bit of flattery not make her blush as red and hot as radishes, Ivy wondered, when any offhand remark or chance touch from Oliver Armitage seemed to make her cheeks blister?

Before she could contrive a satisfactory answer, she noticed the footman standing there with her portmanteau, trying for all the world not to appear impatient.

"I must go make myself presentable to be seen in a house as grand as Trentwell." She pulled a rueful face. "Books—I mean, Oliver and I will be taking tea before we go. I hope you'll be able to join us."

"A regiment of dragoons couldn't keep me away."

Rupert Norbury bowed again. "Dunstan, after you've shown Miss Greenwood to wherever you're taking her, have someone bring me hot water. I could do with a bit of sprucing up before I dine with my cousin and his intended."

The fresh, beguiling trill of Ivy's laughter drew Oliver toward the more intimate of Trentwell's two dining rooms. At the threshold, he froze, his limbs and voice paralyzed by the sight of Ivy pouring tea for his *cousin* Rupert. The fellow looked as though he'd been engineered precisely to Ivy's specifications, with an extra dash of wickedness thrown in for good measure.

"What are you doing here?" The words issued from his mouth at last as he willed his feet to carry him into the room.

Ivy was seated at the head of the table with a fine porcelain tea service arrayed before her. Rupert sprawled in the seat to her right, leaning as close to her as possible without falling out of his chair.

At Oliver's peremptory interrogation, Rupert glanced up, fixing him with a lazy, mocking stare. "Really, Books, old fellow, you must make an effort to address your betrothed with a bit more courtesy. Miss Greenwood is taking tea with us, of course. Wasn't that part of the reason you stopped here on your way to Gretna?"

"I didn't mean *her*." Making a determined effort to ignore the jeer, Oliver dropped heavily into the seat at Ivy's left. "I was talking about *you*. Last I heard, you were in Ireland."

"I was." Rupert turned his full attention back to Ivy, his gaze roving over her bare arms and slender neck in the most impertinent manner. "It didn't suit me, so back I came, like the prodigal...son. Nobody's offered to kill a fatted calf for me, but at least I have a roof over my head.''

Perhaps more importantly, access to Aunt Felicity's wine cellar. The unspoken words curdled on the tip of Oliver's tongue, but he swallowed them. He'd learned long ago the folly of rising to Rupert's baiting. Today, for some reason, Uncle Percy's natural son proved more difficult than usual to ignore.

"Sugar, my dear?" Ivy asked. "Cream? Lemon?"

For a moment Oliver didn't realize she was speaking to him.

"Ask him again, louder," Rupert urged in a tone of exasperated amusement laced with pity. "He's probably lost in some lofty thought, and—"

"Just lemon!" Oliver rapped out his reply.

With the silver tongs, Ivy deposited a sliver of pale yellow fruit into the steaming amber brew. Did she slide a covert glance sideways at Rupert as she handed the cup to Oliver? And did the line of her lips arc a degree or two at the corner in response to his outburst?

Let her laugh at him—let them both laugh! The last laugh would be his, since Oliver refused to care how Rupert preened for Ivy's attention or how she simpered for his.

Rupert plucked a dainty sandwich from the tray and popped it into his mouth. "Are you certain I can't prevail upon the pair of you to hang about a little longer? I'm starved for society, particularly the charming variety offered by the future Mrs. Armitage."

He regarded Ivy with an appreciative look so sticky sweet, Oliver expected it to draw flies.

Deep in Oliver's chest, his heart seemed to skip a beat at the sound of his surname applied to Ivy. In his temples, his pulse thundered as he watched Ivy and Rupert exchange a flirtatious glance.

"We must be off straightaway."

Oliver tried to speak dispassionately, as if relating a bald fact of the matter. Instead the words spat out of him. He sounded like a schoolboy, vexed at losing a few marbles, declaring his intention to quit the game.

He tried again. "I believe Aunt Felicity may be following us in an effort to prevent our wedding, so we must make all possible haste."

"Surely you could extend your visit another hour or two." Rupert addressed himself to Ivy. "Trentwell has some of the most beautiful grounds in this part of the country. They are at their best now. Really, Books, it's quite unfeeling of you to bring Miss Greenwood here, then whisk her away before she's had a chance to see them."

"Oh, please, Oliver!" Both Ivy's hands clutched his before he had time to pull away. "Can we not take a stroll to stretch our legs before we set off again?"

This time her touch did not provoke a passing jolt of static, but the sustained galvanism of a voltaic pile battery. If he spent the next hour with her, ambling along the wooded paths perfumed with spring flowers, what sort of foolish nonsense might he end up spouting?

"Very well." He detached his hand from hers on the pretext of reaching for another sandwich. "Perhaps we ought to take a little exercise while we have the chance. I believe I shall row around the pond."

For an instant, Ivy looked as though she would ask to join him. Against all reason, Oliver found himself hoping she would.

Before she could frame that request or any other, Rupert dove into the conversation again. "If Books is going to be occupied at his oars, I should be honored to escort you on a tour of the grounds, Miss Greenwood.''

Ivy hesitated, ''Oliver?''

What did she want him to do—forbid her going off with Rupert when she was obviously so anxious to?

Beg her to come out in the boat with him? Not likely.

Oliver made himself shrug, though his shoulders resisted the simple motion. ''Please yourself. It's of no consequence to me. Just don't stray out of earshot so I can call you when it's time to leave.''

Something in her blue-green eyes told him he'd given the wrong answer. But when he glimpsed Rupert's gloating grin, Oliver could not bring himself to retract his words.

Chapter Seven

What she did was of no consequence to him. *She* was of no consequence to him.

Very well, then, decided Ivy as she flounced out of the dining room on Rupert Norbury's arm. She would not allow Oliver's opinion to be of any consequence to her, either.

Easily said.

Somehow the fresh, sharp greens of spring foliage and the bright fragrant blossoms paled before her eyes, while small clouds collected to obscure the sun. Even Mr. Norbury's sparkling patter did little to lift the subtle weight oppressing her heart.

"Tell me, my dear." He led her down a hedge-bordered path. "How on earth did you manage to woo a dry old stick like Books into such a grand adventure as eloping to Gretna Green? I'm dumbstruck that he was willing to risk Lady Lyte's displeasure, not to mention tear himself away from his tedious research for so long."

Even though she was vexed with Oliver, Ivy couldn't help resenting the fellow's mocking tone. "You're rather talkative for a man who claims to be dumbstruck, Mr. Norbury."

He threw back his head and laughed as though monumentally pleased with himself and with her. "Well played, Miss Greenwood! I concede the hand to you. I should have known my cousin wouldn't saddle himself with a stupid wife, no matter how decorative."

If Rupert Norbury meant his comments for flattery, they fell somewhat short of their target.

Through a gap in one of the hedges, Ivy spied the pond. Oliver had just pushed away from the bank in a narrow boat. He began rowing with smooth efficient strokes.

If only he'd given her a crumb of encouragement, she might be sitting in that boat now, too, lulled by the soft, rhythmic dip of the oars and the tranquillity of companionable silence.

Instead, she must suffer Rupert Norbury's animated prattle about card games won and lost, ridiculous lengths to which he'd gone in evading his creditors, and bits of scandalous personal gossip concerning the unprincipled set of people he considered his friends.

"...then Miss Deagle pushed Mrs. Forrest backward into the fountain, which fortunately wasn't deep. But when the poor creature rose from the water, of course, the drenched gown was plastered to her like a second skin, leaving...I declare, Miss Greenwood, I don't believe you've heard a word I've said."

A badly spoiled five-year-old could not have sounded more petulant.

Ivy hadn't been paying much mind to his conversation—if one could call it that when Rupert Norbury did practically all the talking. She'd been more occupied with trying to avoid his hip brushing against hers so often. The sensation put her in mind of the time she'd trod on a eel while wading in the brook near Barnhill. It sent a shiver through her, but not of the pleasant kind she experienced when Oliver touched her.

"I'm sorry. What were you saying?"

Oliver's cousin rolled his eyes skyward. "Perhaps you're a better match for Books than I first thought, Miss Greenwood, with your wandering mind."

Was this how *her* discourse affected Oliver? Ivy wondered, casting a glance down the sloping lawn toward the pond. Did it strike him as so shallow and self-absorbed that he had no choice but to slam the door of his attention in her face, then turn his mind to worthier subjects?

"I apologize for my preoccupation, sir." She let go of Mr. Norbury's arm and put a distance of several steps between them. "A bride may be forgiven, I hope, for letting her thoughts often stray to her future husband."

His pique forgotten, Rupert Norbury laughed until tears rolled from his eyes and he had to gasp for breath.

"I fail to see what you find so amusing." To Ivy's ears, his laughter held more scorn than merriment. She fumbled for an excuse to put more distance between herself and this odious man. "I believe I shall return to the house. The way the sky is darkening, I fear we may soon have rain."

As she skirted around him to go back the way they'd come, Mr. Norbury's hand whipped out and caught her by the wrist. "Pray, don't deprive me of your company so soon, Miss Greenwood. You haven't seen the fruit tree arbor yet."

She tried to shake off his hand, but Rupert Norbury hung on with a strength of grip that surprised her. He had fleshier hands than his cousin, Ivy realized, their skin softer than most women's. Had they ever done more strenuous work than rolling dice, tipping a wine cup, or peeling off a woman's clothing?

That last thought made Ivy's gorge twitch.

"Kindly let go of me, Mr. Norbury. My tour of the arbor can wait upon a future visit."

If Thorn married Lady Lyte, Ivy wasn't sure she'd want to visit Trentwell again, particularly if her ladyship's illegitimate stepson might be in residence.

"But the blossoms are at their peak, now." He pulled her toward him. "Who knows if you might catch them in such perfection again. 'Gather rosebuds, while you may.'"

"Mr. Norbury—please!"

The midnight glitter in his dark eyes made the flesh on the back of her neck tighten. What childish folly had ever led her to believe there could be anything romantic or exciting about wickedness?

"You may drop this pose of missish devotion to Books, my dear. If you're preoccupied with anything, it might be the notion of one day being mistress of Trentwell."

"I am *not* after Oliver's fortune." For some reason it felt more urgent to challenge that assumption than to protest Rupert Norbury's importunate grip on her.

"You mistake me, my dear. I don't hold it against you. Why, I've tried to spirit more than one young heiress off to Gretna in my day."

An uncharitable judgment of those young ladies' taste and intelligence crossed Ivy's mind, followed by a swift, stinging indictment of her own. She'd been lured by Rupert Norbury's striking looks and glib allure. If she hadn't been acquainted with another sort of man—one who, despite his flaws, had genuine worth and ability—

she might not have seen past Norbury's appealing facade so quickly.

"Having a husband who's so blind to your needs and charms can have its advantages, my dear." He pulled her Ivy into his embrace. "Books isn't likely to notice if you seek satisfaction elsewhere."

"Stop calling him that and let go of me!" Ivy struggled to break his grip.

Turning her face from his approaching lips, Ivy almost retched at the loathsome sensation when he kissed her ear instead. She brought her foot down hard on his toes, but her flimsy slippers were no match for Mr. Norbury's riding boots.

"No need to play coy, now." The blackguard chuckled and tightened his grip further. "My dear cousin's too far off to hear us, not that he'd pay much mind if he did. You and I are quite alike, Ivy. With me, you won't need to make any tiresome pretenses."

She wasn't anything like him...was she? The hideous notion slapped Ivy into a moment's limp, stunned silence.

"Ah, that's better." Mr. Norbury accosted her bare neck with his lips. Between kisses that made Ivy's flesh crawl, he murmured, "I wouldn't hurt you or force you, of course. And we haven't the time to indulge ourselves just now. I only want to give you a little foretaste of what awaits in the future."

Perhaps she should allow him to kiss her and paw her a little, thought Ivy. Endure it as a fit punishment for her stupidity. Oliver wouldn't care one way or another.

Somehow she couldn't let herself give Rupert Norbury the satisfaction of believing she preferred him to a man like Oliver.

Feeling his grip slacken, she wrenched one hand free

and scored his face with her nails. He bellowed a shocking oath and called her an even more shocking name.

Perhaps thinking she meant to scream, the rogue
clamped a hand over her mouth with bruising force. Feral fury surged through Ivy. She bit down on one of his
fingers, glorying in the howl of pain it provoked.

When he let her go, Ivy released his finger from her
teeth and made a bolt for freedom. She'd scrambled only
two steps when something checked her headlong rush.
The bounder must have grabbed a handful of her skirt,
Ivy realized as she pitched to the ground, the screech of
tearing muslin filling her ears.

Oliver endeavored to channel his anger and agitation
into the force of his oars against the water. Perhaps the
rhythmic, repetitive movement would soothe his over-
wrought emotions and distract his attention from the pe-
riodic glimpse of Rupert and Ivy through the hedges.

Why did the sight of them together poke his heart with
sharp sticks? Surely it came as no surprise that Ivy would
prefer his engaging, worldly, rascal of a cousin to him?
Even if she hadn't professed herself disposed to a dashing, wicked young man, Rupert would have lured her.

If he had a crumb of sense left, Oliver knew he ought
to thank his cousin for this harsh but necessary lesson
about the folly of allowing emotion to ride roughshod
over intellect. Scientific quandaries might baffle and
frustrate him by times, but matters of the heart baffled
and frustrated him *all* the time. Unlike the austere, elegant realm of scientific theory and pure mathematics, the
kingdom of Cupid could be messy, ugly and even painful.

What were Ivy and Rupert up to now? For the three
hundred and fifteenth time, Oliver assured himself their

actions were of no consequence to him. Not even if they had stopped walking. Not even if they were standing so close together he could hardly tell if they were two people or one. Not even if they might be kissing.

Without noticing that he'd changed direction, Oliver found himself rowing toward them instead of away. Perhaps he had better interrupt their little tryst, after all.

The decision had nothing to do with his thwarted feelings for Ivy. He was responsible for her, though. In her naiveté, she might hanker for a rake like Rupert, but she deserved far better. If she could not exercise a little common sense in the matter, Oliver would elect himself her voice of reason.

He had almost reached the far bank of the pond when Oliver heard his cousin roar a curse. In his haste to scramble ashore, he tipped the boat and tumbled into the pond. The cold water did not succeed in cooling his temper. He wallowed ashore and surged up the slope in time to hear Rupert cry out again.

When he reached the path an instant later, Oliver found his cousin poised over Ivy, who had fallen to the ground, or perhaps been pushed. Her skirt and undergarment had both been torn from hem almost to waist and a breathtaking expanse of shapely leg protruded through the long slit.

Oliver's pulse throbbed in his forehead…and lower. For the first time in his adult life, he could not grasp the reliable rope of logic. Instead it slid through his fingers as if greased, leaving him swamped in the stormy seas of passion.

"Damn you…Norbury!" His breath heaved in and out in such gusts, he could scarcely gasp the words out. "Get your…lecherous hands…*off* her…this instant!"

Rupert turned on Oliver with a sneer. "Stay out of this, Books."

Three red lines in parallel blazed on the wastrel's cheek. Taken together with his earlier loud cries, they suggested Ivy had not submitted tamely to his liberties.

Oliver's mind whirled in such a tempest of savage urges, he sensed himself all but incapable of rational thought. Instinct, potent and undeniable, demanded he protect the woman and punish any man who challenged him for her.

Forgetting that he had long eschewed violence as the conduct of fools, Oliver grabbed his uncle's misbegotten son by the neck linen and wrenched him to his feet. Norbury flailed out, fetching Oliver a glancing blow to the stomach.

Though he doubled over for an instant, Oliver did not release Norbury's stock. If anything, he gripped it tighter, holding his cousin's handsome, scornful face steady for the tightly clenched fist he slammed into Norbury's jaw.

The blow Oliver struck hurt his knuckles as much as the blow he'd taken pained his abdomen. When Norbury reeled back into the hedge, Oliver released his cousin's neckcloth, so he would not be dragged along. Some manner of bloodlust, completely foreign to his nature, sang in Oliver's veins, urging him to beat his rival senseless. With enormous difficulty he resisted it, turning to Ivy instead.

"Are you injured?" As he lifted her from the ground, Oliver yearned to wrap her in his arms and hold her for as long as she would let him, kissing away any residue of fear or pain.

A wave of queasiness seethed through his stomach. Perhaps it was only a consequence of the clout he'd taken from Norbury. More likely it was guilt that he'd left Ivy alone with his unprincipled cousin, because he'd been too much afraid of his own feelings for her.

Setting Ivy on her feet, he stepped back, crossing his arms in front of his chest to keep them from reaching for her again. And as a token shield for his heart.

For the first time since he'd met her, Ivy Greenwood looked thoroughly chastened.

"Injured?" She forced a gallant smile, which soon wavered, then vanished. "Only my pride...and my gown."

She shot a withering glance at Norbury as he struggled to extract himself from the shrubbery. "I'd just put on fresh clothes, too."

Oliver glanced down at his own sodden garments. "As did I. We'll have to change again as quickly as we can and get back on the road before Thorn and Aunt Felicity overtake us."

A look of dismay twisted Ivy's winsome features. She raised a quivering hand and pointed at something over Oliver's shoulder. "I fear we may be too late."

Why he even bothered to turn and look, Oliver could not fathom. He knew what would see.

Pulled by two teams of hired horses, his aunt's barouche rolled up the stately drive toward Trentwell.

Chapter Eight

Oliver turned back to Ivy. With the white linen of his shirt plastered to his chest and his arms crossed in front of him, he had never looked more attractive to her. Nor had he ever looked more forbidding.

"What should we do now?" he asked.

"What *is* there to do?" Ivy's shoulders slumped. The wellspring that fed her bubbling fountain of optimism had suddenly run dry and it was all her own fault. "They've caught us. We must give ourselves up, I suppose, and hope Felicity and my brother have had enough time to mend their quarrel."

She'd made such a dreadful botch of everything, dragging Oliver halfway to Scotland on a fool's errand. They might have been safely on the road to Stoke-on-Trent this very minute if she hadn't been engaged in her silly flirtation with Rupert Norbury.

As Norbury staggered to his feet, rubbing his jaw, and looking terribly sorry for himself, Ivy knew she would never regard a handsome rakehell the same way again. Though part of her wanted to wilt in a puddle of petulant tears, she resolved to start acting like a grown-up. She owed Oliver that much, no matter how belated.

"I'll tell your aunt I originated the whole scheme and you only came along under protest, to prevent me from coming to harm." She wouldn't have to stretch the truth on that point.

Oliver stood quite still, as if weighing her words. Then he held out his hand to her. "There may be another way. I have a plan, if you're willing."

"A plan?" A slender jet of hope shot in a high arc from Ivy's fountain. It splintered a stray beam of May sunshine into a hundred tiny rainbows. "Then let us pursue it, by all means."

She placed her hand in Oliver's. As his long deft fingers closed over hers, a feeling of warm tranquillity stole over Ivy such as she sensed whenever she returned to Barnhill after a long sojourn away.

"See here, Rupert," Oliver ordered his cousin. "Will you help us, or shall I tell Aunt Felicity and Ivy's brother what devilment you were getting up to with her?"

"Very well." Rupert Norbury pulled a sulky face. "What do you want me to do?"

More than Oliver's threat compelled him, Ivy felt certain. Perhaps the scoundrel hoped to nudge Oliver out of favor with Lady Lyte.

"Tell Aunt Felicity and Mr. Greenwood that we've gone for a stroll around the grounds and won't be back until supper," said Oliver. "Then load our luggage into a gig and fetch it to the village. You'll find us waiting at The Fox and Crow. Mind you are not spotted and followed, though."

Norbury made a show of dusting the tiny hedge leaves off his coat. "Don't go telling me my business, Bo—er, Armitage. I've had more practice sneaking around than you'll ever have."

A fine thing to boast of! Ivy and Oliver exchanged a look, their brows arched.

"This way." Oliver tugged her down the hedged path toward a stand of trees. "I hope this will give us a few hours' jump on them, if we can trust Rupert to carry out his part."

Ivy gave an exaggerated shudder. "He's awful, isn't he?"

"You seemed to find him most diverting at tea time." Oliver let go of her hand as they entered the woods. "I thought he answered to the description of your ideal man in every particular. Perhaps you didn't find him wicked enough. He's not really. Just vain and selfish and irresponsible."

"You must think he and I make a perfectly matched pair." Though Ivy tried to toss the words off as a jest, shame soured her tone. There wasn't anything funny about Oliver Armitage despising her.

"I think nothing of the sort." Oliver held back a sapling that barred the overgrown woodland path so Ivy could squeeze by. "I blame myself for allowing you to go off with him. I should not have done it, except…that is…I should have known better. I'm…sorry."

She couldn't stand to see Oliver hold himself accountable for her imprudence. She would relieve his conscience of that burden, even if it meant exposing the sum total of her foolishness. Lobbing the words over her shoulder or addressing them to his back would not do, either. Ivy turned to face him, reluctant but determined to make a clean breast of the matter.

"You needn't reproach yourself, Oliver." What business had she making matches by manipulating other people's feelings when she'd been so blind to her own? "I went with your cousin for an even more ridiculous reason than because I thought I fancied him."

Oliver raked his long fingers through his wet hair and adjusted his spectacles, which had been knocked askew. He gazed at her with the sort of bemused questioning countenance he'd turned on her when she first barged into his study and demanded he run away with her to Gretna. All the feelings he'd quickened in her since then deluged Ivy's heart in a bittersweet, bewildering tangle.

Curiosity, exasperation, respect, tenderness, pique, fascination, desire—and none of it with a hope of being returned, apart from the exasperation, perhaps.

Oliver couldn't think less of her than he did already, so she might as well blurt out the humiliating truth. "You hadn't been paying me much mind, so I wanted to see if I could make you jealous. How's that for nonsense?"

Oliver made no reply at first. He just stared at her as Ivy felt her once boundless self-confidence shrivel into a small but weighty lump in the pit of her stomach.

In the leafy canopy above them, birds warbled as if their tiny bodies would explode with joy unless they released it in song. The aroma of may blossoms perfumed the still woodland air. The forest wore a spring mantle of lush, expectant green.

But in Ivy's heart a cold November drizzle settled over bare branches and brown, dead bracken. She longed to vent her feelings in a good cleansing cry, but that could wait until she was alone. She would not burden Oliver more than she had already.

"I...don't understand." Oliver gave his head a vigorous shake. He'd heard Ivy's words and he knew their individual meanings. Taken together, however, they refused to make sense for him.

Or perhaps the muted sparkle of Ivy's springtime eyes had driven all rational thought from his head.

"You were *trying* to make me jealous?" She'd succeeded beyond any measure she could have intended. It had taken every ounce of restraint, cultivated over many years, to keep him from pummeling Rupert's comely face to a jelly. "Why?"

Ivy pursed her lips in a rueful grin, but her eyes betrayed a hint of moisture. "If you cannot deduce that simple conclusion from the evidence, Mr. Armitage, I fear for your future as a scientist."

If she'd been speaking of any other man, indeed, he might have summed the equation with ease. "Y-you *care* something for me?"

"So it seems." A stray shaft of sunlight pierced the leafy canopy above, further gilding Ivy's riot of red-gold curls and her rapidly blinking lashes. "It took me long enough to sort out. I don't believe I've properly sorted it out yet. Doesn't speak well for my boast of understanding about love, does it?"

Ivy had admitted she cared about him. She'd even used the word *love,* however indirectly. That much Oliver could take in, though he still had difficulty believing it. What he couldn't fathom was why it made her look so woeful.

"Don't fret." She started to turn away. "I promise not to throw myself at your head for the rest of our journey. I'm well aware that I don't answer to the description of your ideal match."

The tiny catch in her voice acted like a key, unlocking Oliver from his confusion. Her feelings for him dismayed Ivy for the same reason he'd been alarmed by his mounting attraction to her—because she believed he could not return them.

Part of him wanted to sit down and puzzle it out. Weigh the facts. Make a well-considered decision. One that wouldn't overturn his whole life the way his precipitous leap from the boat had capsized it.

As he wavered, Ivy took a few steps along the path and disappeared behind the thick trunk of a towering oak tree. All at once the sunlight seemed to lose its luster and the vibrant colors of the leaves grew dull.

"Wait!" Oliver rushed after her, almost tripping in his haste and not caring if he did.

Ivy glanced back, prompted perhaps by the sound of his hurried footsteps. A delicious expanse of her bare leg protruded through the tear in her skirt. Her hair had captured a few stray leaves—an emerald chaplet fit for a queen of the woodland nymphs.

His longing for her must have blazed on his face. Whatever she saw lit an answering smile in Ivy—one so bright and warm it eclipsed the spring sunshine.

Somehow he knew this was not the time for questions or discussion, or words of any kind. Instead he scooped Ivy up and whirled her around, setting his head in a dizzy spin to match his heart.

As his arms closed around her and his lips sought hers, a whisper of doubt chilled him as surely as a stray breeze over his wet clothes. Would Ivy welcome such an ardent demonstration of his feelings so soon after Rupert had forced his odious attentions upon her?

Before Oliver had time to recant his rash action, Ivy's arms closed around his neck. Her lips greeted his in an eager kiss that distilled all the green, fragrant promise of spring.

She was his springtime, Oliver realized—unpredictable, vivacious, romantic, invigorating. The gentle rain of her sympathy and the clement sunshine of her temperament had chased cold, barren winter from his heart and nourished the fragile seed of his fancy for her.

When they paused to catch their breaths, Ivy pressed her brow to his until all he could see were those turquoise pools he longed to immerse himself in at the start of every day.

Her slender body vibrated with laughter. "If you are bewitched, Oliver Armitage, I must warn you, I shan't make the least effort to locate an antidote."

"Oh, I am bewitched, Lady Cupid." A week ago he'd have sneered at any fool who mouthed such fanciful drivel. Now he pitied anyone whose life was uncolored by a little romance. "You cast a spell on me the minute you barged into my study and demanded I run away with you to Gretna Green. I have fought against it with every weapon of logic at my disposal, but you have vanquished them all."

"Well, I have learned a little wisdom to temper my romantic fancies." She rubbed her pert little nose against his straight jutting one and lavished him with a look of bewitching impudence. "Only a very little, mind. Enough to recognize that you are as dashing and masterful as any rogue, but a good deal more interesting and congenial once the shallow gilding of glamor has warn off."

"In that case—" Oliver set Ivy on her feet again and dropped to his knees before her "—my very dear Miss Greenwood, would you do me the honor of becoming my wife once we reach Gretna?"

No one in Oliver's recollection had ever looked at him with such transparent affection. He wondered if, like the songbirds, his chest might burst from the happiness swelling inside him.

"Indeed, I will," whispered Ivy. Her lower lip trembled for an instant, then twisted into an impish grin. "Provided you don't come to your senses before then."

Oliver pulled her toward him, nestling his cheek against the soft bounty of her bosom. "If you perceive any danger of that happening, I hope I may count on you to kiss me senseless again."

"That I shall." She chuckled, nuzzling her cheek against his damp hair. "Now, much as I hate to be the one to bring up practical matters, we had better hie ourselves to this Fox and Crow establishment where you told Rupert to bring our luggage."

With a grudging nod Oliver regained his feet. Much as he would have liked to linger in the woods with his pretty nymph, they would now have a perilously slender lead on Thorn Greenwood and Aunt Felicity. For the remainder of their journey, he and Ivy would be fleeing headlong to Gretna Green in earnest.

Chapter Nine

"Carlisle, at last." Ivy sighed as their coach rattled past the crumbling ruin of Hadrian's Wall. "One more change of horses should see us to Scotland."

"Not far now." Oliver roused from his restless doze and let his right hand stray from Ivy's shoulder down her arm. "Soon we'll be husband and wife."

As his hand veered inward to graze over the subtle rounding of her bosom, a sound issued from his bride-to-be, like the purr of a contented kitten. When she nuzzled her cheek against his chest and rubbed her hand over the too-sensitive flesh of his thigh, Oliver gained a very personal understanding of the heat produced by friction. If he didn't kiss Ivy immediately, he feared his whole body would burst into open flame.

The way she snuggled against him made it impossible to engage her lips without a series of contortions to which his spine would be quite unequal. Instead, he seized her and spun her around, landing her deliciously rounded backside onto his lap. Her head tilted over his arm in the perfect posture for kissing.

As their lips met and mingled and a blast of delicious

heat surged through his body, Oliver wondered if there could be a better way to begin every day for the rest of his life.

Had she ever imagined Oliver lacking in passion? Ivy marveled at her own ignorance. Perhaps the angels did watch over well-meaning souls whose good intentions outstripped their good sense, she decided as she clung to him. Certainly she'd been blessed beyond anything she deserved.

"The minute we're safely married, I shall haul you away to some inn for a hot meal." She ran her fingertips over his lean, unshaven cheek. "I may not possess many practical skills of a good wife, but I have mastered cookery. So I serve you fair warning—you've missed your last meal, sir. From now on, I will make it my mission to keep you well nourished."

He raised her hand to his lips and swiped them across her knuckles. "You're talking like a wife, already. If you keep it up, I shall find myself calling you Mrs. Armitage."

Oliver might have meant to tease her, but Ivy heard the barely suppressed longing in his voice. He wanted the kind of looking after she yearned to lavish on him.

"Just think." Ivy yawned and stretched. "By tonight we'll be married, we'll have eaten our first hot meal in days and we'll get to sleep in a proper bed rather than sitting up in some drafty, rattling old coach."

A hint of emerald devilment glittered in Oliver's luxurious hazel eyes as he caressed her bosom through the light fabric of her bodice. "I hope you aren't counting on getting too much sleep on our wedding night. I'm anxious to discover all the intriguing information your sister imparted to you.''

A sound broke from Ivy's lips—a whimper of desire roused but unsatisfied. ''For a sober man of science, you've demonstrated lamentably passionate tendencies in the past day or two.''

She pulled his face toward hers for another kiss. A kiss she'd come to know and enjoy and crave ever since their precipitous flight from Trentwell. Lost in that deep, passionate kiss, neither she nor Oliver took much notice as their coach slowed and stopped.

Then the door of the vehicle wrenched open and a familiar gruff voice thundered, ''I suggest you take your hands off my sister, Mr. Armitage.''

''Thorn!'' For the first time in her life, Ivy wanted to bludgeon her beloved brother, or take some other equally violent action against him. ''What are you doing here?''

''Spoken as if you had no idea,'' Thorn growled. Seizing Ivy by the arm, he hauled her out of the coach and onto the cobblestones in front of a prosperous-looking inn. ''Have you made it your sworn aim in life to turn me gray-headed before I'm forty?''

Ivy had never seen her brother so angry. His deep brown eyes, usually so calm and steadfast, now flashed with dark fury. That look made her want to crumple before his displeasure like a naughty six-year-old caught at dangerous mischief.

Then she felt Oliver's hands close over her shoulders. The warm resonance of his voice enveloped her.

''Don't be angry with your sister, Mr. Greenwood. The responsibility is mine.''

Thorn cast Oliver a scathing glance. ''I have plenty

of outrage to go around, Armitage. You'll come in for your share, never fear. I'm hardly surprised to discover my sister up to such high jinks, but I had credited you with better sense."

Twisting her arm out of her brother's grip, Ivy traded him glare for vexed glare. "I will not permit you to speak to my fiancé in that tone, Thorn. Kindly apologize at once."

"He is *not* your fiancé and I will speak to him in any tone..." Suddenly aware of the curious stares his tirade had drawn, Thorn swallowed his last words.

"Is Lady Lyte with you?" asked Ivy. Perhaps if Thorn understood what had set them on the road to Gretna, he might not be so angry with them.

"She is." His tone considerably subdued, Thorn nodded toward the inn. "Let us go inside and see what she has to say to the pair of you."

Thorn sounded so ominous. A chocking lump of shame rose in Ivy's throat. She clung to Oliver's hand as they entered the inn and mounted the stairs behind her brother, meek as mice. When Thorn opened a door and ushered them through, Ivy guessed how a condemned criminal must feel on her way to the gallows.

As they stepped into a small sitting room, Felicity Lyte rose from her chair by the hearth. She looked different than when Ivy had last seen her. Her face had lost flesh—hardly surprising if she and Thorn had been living on a diet of cold pies and sandwiches as Ivy and Oliver had.

There was more to it than that, though, unless Ivy was very much mistaken. Lady Lyte gave the impression of a woman who had drunk deeply from the cup of happiness, yet feared to drain it in case she might discover poison in the dregs.

Thorn shut the door, then moved to stand behind Felicity. Beneath his determined scowl of brotherly censure, Ivy glimpsed a befuddled grin, barely held in check.

"It worked!" she cried, hurling herself upon her startled brother and his equally bewildered mistress. "I knew it would. I just knew it."

She kissed Felicity on the cheek, then threw her arms around Thorn. "I told Oliver if the pair of you were cooped up together in a carriage all the way to Scotland you'd soon realize how much you cared for one another. And you did, didn't you?"

Felicity drew back from her impetuous embrace, staring at Ivy as if she was a lapdog who'd just messed on the floor. "Do you mean to say you *planned* all this? Did you not have any intention of marrying my nephew?"

"Not at first." Something about Felicity's voice and stiff posture bothered Ivy, but she was too elated by the success of her matchmaking to pay it any mind. "It started as a ruse to bring the pair of you together, but one thing led to another...and..."

Felicity fixed Thorn with a horrified accusing stare. "You were in on this, as well, weren't you? Did you put them up to it? I can't believe I was gullible enough to let you twist me 'round your finger this way."

Pushing past his sister, Thorn tried to reason with Felicity. "I knew no more of it than you did, I swear. Surely you can't believe I'd stoop to such a thing."

"Keep your distance." Shrinking back from him, Lady Lyte looked ready to vomit. "Don't touch me."

If the woman he loved had hurled vitriol in his face, the acid could not have eaten into Thorn's flesh as viciously as her caustic suspicion seared his spirit. Even as Ivy's temper flared on her brother's behalf, she could feel the distress that radiated from Felicity.

Lady Lyte turned her eyes from Thorn and Ivy as if she could not bear to look at them. Her anguished gaze fell on Oliver.

She held out her hand to him. "I don't hold you to blame for any of this, my dear boy. We have been abominably used, both of us. Just take me home now, please."

Oliver stood there, trying to make sense of what had happened so quickly. Like Ivy, he'd sensed a renewed attachment between Thorn and his aunt, beneath their displeasure over the elopement. For reasons that baffled him, Felicity's feelings for her lover had undergone an instantaneous shift in polarity. What had formerly attracted now repelled with a vengeance.

"Don't be angry with Ivy," he begged his aunt. "She only wanted to make the pair of you happy. And her brother knew nothing about it, of that I can assure you."

He could tell Felicity was not listening. Could he find the words to convince her when all he knew of love he'd learned in the space of a few short days?

"In any case, I cannot take you home just now. Ivy and I mean to wed. Before nightfall, if I can persuade her brother to give us his blessing. I know this has all fallen out like a comedy of errors, but that won't signify if we can give it a happy ending. Won't you and Thorn come with us to Gretna and make it a double wedding?"

The glow of perfect admiration on Ivy's face elated him even as the hurt and rage in his aunt's eyes cast him down.

"You stupid boy, can't you see she's just like all the others—after you for *my* money?"

His aunt's accusation boxed Oliver in the stomach, driving the wind out of him. Could it be true? Experience contended that it must.

But this was no orderly scientific experiment, where repeated results supported or refuted a theory. Love retained an element of sweet, capricious magic. His own Lady Cupid had taught him that lesson.

"All evidence to the contrary, I believe Ivy loves me, Aunt Felicity. And I know I love her." He turned to Thorn Greenwood. "Will you please permit your sister to marry me, sir? I promise to do everything in my power to make her happy."

Ivy took her brother's hand. "Oh, please, Thorn, please say yes! Don't do to me what father did to Rosemary by forbidding her to wed Merritt."

Clearly Thorn Greenwood had trouble denying his sister anything she'd set her heart on. "Well...if the two of you made it all this way without killing one another..."

"I don't believe this," cried Felicity. "Don't tell me you mean to indulge this silly whim of theirs, after everything we went through to stop them? If you ever had the least genuine feeling for me, Hawthorn Greenwood, you'll forbid this match and fetch your sister back to Barnhill, where she belongs."

Though his countenance remained impassive, something in Thorn's eyes betrayed the bitter tug-of-war taking place within him. "If you have the least feeling for me, Felicity, you wouldn't ask me to sacrifice my sister's happiness."

He looked from Ivy to Oliver and back again. "If the pair of you are set on getting married, I will give the bride away."

Felicity flinched, as if Thorn had struck her. "You are all in league against me, I see. Very well, then. If you persist in this folly, Oliver, I shall have no choice but to cut you off without a penny. See if *that* does not change Miss Greenwood's inclination to marry you."

The notion of giving up full-time research to earn a living dismayed Oliver less than Ivy's crestfallen demeanor. Could Felicity be right, after all? Would Ivy be willing to wed a man with no prospects whatsoever?

Chapter Ten

Again, she'd made a muddle of everything. From the giddy heights to which they'd risen, Ivy's spirits plummeted.

One thing she would not spoil, whatever the cost to herself—Oliver's future.

"May we have a few moments' privacy to talk this over?" she begged Thorn and Felicity.

"Take as long as you like." Lady Lyte stalked toward the door. "I shall wait in my barouche for ten minutes. If Oliver does not join me by then, I will return to Bath without him and instruct my solicitor to write him out of my will."

When she had gone, Thorn looked from Ivy to Oliver. He seemed on the point of saying something, then he shook his head and left the room.

The door had barely closed behind him when Oliver spoke. "What do you say, Miss Greenwood? Would you consider marrying a man with only his brains to recommend him?"

He wasn't going to make this easy for her, but Ivy knew what she had to do, no matter how distasteful. "You have far more to recommend you than just your brains, Oliver Armitage, and if I had only myself to consider, I'd be happier than ever to marry you without a penny to your name. That way, you would know for certain it's *you* I care for.''

He made a move to gather her in his arms. ''That's settled then. You've made me the happiest pauper in the world. Let's go round up your brother and head for Gretna.''

''No.'' Ivy had never done anything harder in her life than speak that word and step out of Oliver's embrace. ''I won't be the cause of you losing your inheritance and perhaps having to give up your research. Your work is important, to you and to the world. Who knows what you might discover or invent? I'm not used to putting anyone else's interests above my own, and it isn't very pleasant, I can tell you. But I care for you in a way I've never cared for anyone else.''

She turned to the room's single tiny window, fearing the plea in Oliver's eyes might demolish her resolve. ''I'm not saying we must part forever, just for a while, until your aunt comes to realize that we are right for each other. You must see, this is the sensible thing to do. For once—for *you*—I want to be sensible.''

Not hearing his footsteps behind her, Ivy started when his arms closed around her and Oliver spun her into his embrace. Had she ever thought him a cold, dispassionate fellow? His kiss shattered that foolish notion.

''Your proposal is entirely rational,'' he agreed, ''but you have shown me that the most rational course is not always the wisest. I can and will find a way to continue my research without Aunt Felicity's support. What I cannot and will not do is postpone my happiness a moment longer. I have waited for it far too long. So long, I almost didn't recognize it when it finally barreled into my study and hauled me off on the adventure of a lifetime.''

"Please don't gainsay me in this." Ivy pushed him toward the door. "It's hard enough to do the right thing when half of me doesn't want to."

"One last kiss and I'll do whatever you bid me."

"One kiss," Ivy wailed, "and I may not have the will to bid you do anything but marry me."

"That's what I'm counting on," whispered Oliver as he lifted her off the floor. His lips brushed across hers with the lightest of touches, gradually increasing in pressure and heat until they seared her memory of everything but pleasure.

When he set her on her feet again, light-headed and breathless, her body on fire, it was everything Ivy could do to gasp, "Go with Lady Lyte."

A look of boyish mischief crossed Oliver's angular features. "Too late for that, I'm afraid." He picked Ivy up again and danced her across the room to the window. "That's her barouche just rounding the market cross. You are stuck with me now, Miss Greenwood."

"Monster!" Ivy planted a kiss on the tip of his nose. "Darling monster, you played me for time."

"So I did. I don't repent it for a minute and you must not, either. It's only what you would have done if our positions had been reversed."

How could she deny it? "I shall be obliged to make you a very dutiful wife, to compensate for all you've given up on my account. Fortunately, I can't think of a task I'd rather undertake. Now let's go find my brother and fetch him to Gretna Green with us."

Oliver and Ivy Armitage were married later that day by the local vicar, for Thorn Greenwood refused to countenance any ceremony performed by Gretna's notorious *anvil priests.*

As he stood beside his bride in the little Scottish church, speaking the vows by which lovers had sealed their union for hundreds of years, Oliver thought back over the precipitous tide of events that had borne him there. Reason could scarcely grasp, let alone explain, the sudden radical shift in direction his life had taken. Perhaps there was something to that fanciful nonsense about Cupid and his arrows, after all.

"With this ring, I thee wed..." He slipped his own signet ring onto Ivy's finger, privately vowing to replace it with something suitably precious and delicate as soon as he could afford to.

As the vicar intoned the final benediction, Oliver had to gnaw on his lower lip to keep from exploding with laughter. How had he ever convinced himself of the preposterous notion that a trip to Gretna would purge Ivy from his system?

They signed the marriage register with Thorn and the vicar's wife as their witnesses, then Ivy's brother drew Oliver aside for a few private words. "Be patient with her tonight, Armitage, and treat her gently."

Apparently satisfied with Oliver's assurances, Thorn softened his gruff manner. "The two of you are welcome to make your home at Barnhill for as long as you need or wish."

Barnhill—that name made Oliver's expressions of gratitude catch in his throat. Not only did marriage with Ivy promise to color his black-and-white world, it would make him a part of a family. And what could he give her in return?

"I promise you..." He found his voice again, and with every word it rang stronger and more sure. "I will do everything in my power to make certain Ivy never regrets her decision to wed me.''

Thorn held out his hand. ''Do that, and I will be proud to call you my brother. Now, I must go. Ivy insists I pursue Felicity and see that she doesn't come to any harm on the journey south…even if I'm obliged to watch over her from a distance.''

Ivy appeared at Oliver's side. ''You had better get on your way if you're to have any hope of overtaking Lady Lyte.'' She embraced her brother and kissed him soundly on the cheek. ''Take care of yourself, Thorn, and don't worry your head about me. I'm in capable hands.''

Oliver wished he felt as confident as his ever-hopeful bride appeared to be. He looked forward to their wedding night with a degree of fevered eagerness matched only by his gut-wrenching apprehension.

They dined at a nearby inn, recommended by the vicar as a respectable establishment. Though gratified to eat his first proper meal in days, and half inclined to linger over their supper to postpone their bridal rites, Oliver found himself with scant appetite. Besides, he did not trust an overindulgence of food and wine on his dubious stomach. What fellow wanted to spend his wedding night casting up his accounts?

Their sleeping chamber was a vast improvement over the musty little cupboard in Newport—modest but snug and clean.

Before his doubts had an opportunity to steal through the door behind them, Ivy slammed it shut and hurled herself into Oliver's arms. The soft pressure of her lips against his and the sweet, familiar taste of her kiss whetted his anticipation and banished any crumbs of misgiving.

''You aren't having second thoughts or cold feet, or

any awful regrets, are you?'' she asked. ''This is absolutely your last chance to back out. If we don't do all the things Rosemary told me about, I'm pretty certain you could have our marriage annulled. Then, after a little groveling, Lady Lyte would surely reinstate you as her heir.'' A small wistful cloud threatened Ivy's perpetual sunshine.

''Get one fact through your copper-curled head, Mrs. Armitage.'' Oliver hoisted her into his arms and strode to the bed. ''You are worth more to me than all Aunt Felicity's millions. Furthermore, I suspect that value to increase manyfold upon longer and...closer acquaintance.''

Settling her on the bed, he showered every inch of her face and neck with kisses, prompting a trill of silvery giggles.

''If I have any misgivings,'' he assured her, ''they are on your account, not my own. Wouldn't you rather pass your wedding night with some dashing rogue who knows his way around a woman's body as well as he knows the green baize tables?''

''On the contrary, Mr. Armitage.'' She set to untying his neck linen with nimble fingers. ''I much prefer the prospect of a lover inclined to *experiment* in the science of pleasure.''

Put that way, it did sound rather intriguing. For the first time he could recall, Oliver crowed with laughter. ''I'll own, I have a more than intellectual curiosity to explore that field of study.''

He pried off his boots and flung his coat on the floor. ''That is, if I can induce you to assist me in my research.''

His bride proved a most eager partner as they shed

their clothes, turnabout, and commenced to explore the intriguing differences in male and female anatomy.

Their avid curiosity led them to investigate the effects of friction. Her fingertips over his thigh. His tongue, moist and hot, over the sensitive tip of her breast. All the while a sensation of heat and urgency intensified within and between them, like the pressure of steam in an engine boiler.

When Ivy whispered her sister's instructions for the coupling that would consummate their union, Oliver chuckled. "Precisely like a piston and cylinder. I shall blush whenever I see a steam engine after—oh, my!"

Science and intellect dropped to the floor with his discarded clothes. Oliver gave himself up, body, mind and heart to the primitive enchantment that drummed in his veins with a cadence of surging fire. Even as it heightened all his senses, it seemed to waft his consciousness out of his body.

Now he understood the need for Thorn's warning to treat his bride with patience and gentleness. His tender feelings for her bolstered his waning self-control, until she gasped his name and squirmed beneath him. The slick, fiery grip of her body on his detonated an explosion of pleasure that hurtled him blazing into the stratosphere.

That violent convulsion of ecstasy gave way to an echo of downy, buoyant bliss. His arms wrapped around Ivy in a protective embrace, he rested his cheek against her moist, tousled curls and drifted toward sleep.

Ivy grazed her knuckles over his chest hair. "Any regrets, now that it's too late to back out?" she teased.

Contorting himself to reach the sensitive flesh of her neck just below her ear, Oliver flicked his tongue over it. "If you can even ask such a question, you can't have been paying very close attention."

She wriggled as laughter bubbled out of her. "I'll admit I was rather preoccupied with my own enjoyment."

"Then, to answer your question, I haven't a single regret in the world for us. It grieves me though that we didn't accomplish our original purpose in coming here—to reunite Thorn and Aunt Felicity. Like you, when I first saw them together, I believed we'd been successful."

Ivy nodded. "There is something ailing Felicity's spirit that has nothing to do with my brother, or very little at least. Never fear, though, I am not done matchmaking for those two yet."

With a fond chuckle, Oliver kissed her again. Though he only meant it for a brief benediction, the delightful interplay of their mouths threatened to rekindle his desire.

"Now that I have an intimate grasp of what they are missing," he murmured, "you may count on me to be your willing accomplice in matchmaking, Mistress Cupid."

* * * * *

NICOLA CORNICK

is passionate about many things: her country cottage and its garden, her two small cats, her husband and her writing, though not necessarily in that order! She has always been fascinated by history, both as her chosen subject at university and subsequently as an engrossing hobby. She works as a university administrator and finds her writing the perfect antidote to the demands of life in a busy office.

THE RAKE'S BRIDE
Nicola Cornick

Chapter One

The April sunlight was as blinding as a flash of gunpowder and the rattle of the bed curtains sounded like distant artillery fire. For a moment Jack, Marquis of Merlin, wondered if he had gone to hell and ended back in the Peninsula War. He rolled onto his back and flung an arm up to shield his eyes.

"Hodges?"

"Yes, my lord?"

The Marquis opened his eyes and looked at his valet. His gaze was dark blue and very unfriendly and his voice held a dangerous undertone. "Hodges, what is the time?"

The valet remained impassive. "A little after nine, my lord."

"That would be nine in the morning?"

"Indeed, my lord."

The Marquis stretched, with a ripple of honed muscles. "As I recall, I asked you to wake me at twelve of the clock and not before. No doubt you can account for the discrepancy?"

"Yes, my lord." Hodges opened the wardrobe and took out a coat of blue superfine. Truth to tell, he had been relieved to find that the Marquis was at home—and alone—for neither circumstance was a foregone conclusion. There had been plenty of occasions on which the Marquis had spent twenty-four hours in one sitting at White's, wandering home only to change his clothes before another spell at the faro tables. There had been many other mornings when Hodges had come to wake his lordship only to discover one of his *chères amies* sprawled naked in bed beside him. It was a sight that would have shocked a valet of less hardened constitution and a circumstance that would have been decidedly awkward that particular morning.

"Well, Hodges? I am awaiting your explanation."

"If I could encourage your lordship to rise?" Hodges said expressionlessly. "The Duke and Duchess of Merlin are awaiting you in the green salon—"

Jack gave an oath and sat up, clapping his hand to his head as a wave of brandy-induced pain threatened to lay him low again. "Damnation! My parents, you say? Here? What in God's name could induce them to call at such a confoundedly unsocial hour? Surely they are not about to parade some other unfortunate candidate for my affections in front of me?"

"His Grace, your father, did not share such information with me, my lord," Hodges said, allowing himself a tight smile. "However, the Duchess mentioned something about your cousin, Mr. Pershore, finding himself in a difficult position—"

Jack paused, running a hand through his disheveled black hair and making it even more disordered. "What, again?"

"Yes, my lord. The matter involves a designing female and a hasty marriage, as I understand it. The country was mentioned, my lord."

Jack swore. It was hardly the first time that his feck-less cousin Bertie Pershore had fallen into a scrape. "Damn it, that's too much! Why could Pershore not con-tract his ill-conceived marriage in Town? If I have to go chasing off to Oxfordshire again just to act as nursemaid to my cousin—"

"Quite so, my lord." Hodges finished brushing down the blue coat. "His Grace the Duke did mention one thing, my lord."

"Yes?"

"He said that if you had not joined them within the half hour he would come up here himself."

Jack swung his legs over the side of the bed and reached for his shirt. He glanced across at the clock. "How long ago was that, Hodges?"

The valet gave another small smile. "A little over five and twenty minutes, my lord. I tried to wake you before but you did not stir. I was about to resort to an ewer of water—most efficacious, my lord."

"Thank God you did not," Jack said feelingly. He looked from the valet's face to the coat in his hand and gave a sigh.

"Devil take it! I suppose I must..."

"Yes, my lord," the valet said.

"Thea," Miss Clementine Shaw said, fixing her elder sister with an earnest look, "are you marrying Mr. Per-shore for his money? He is very rich—is he not?—and it seems to me most unlikely that you could be marrying for love!"

Theodosia Shaw let her needlework fall to her lap. She was trimming the bodice of her bridal gown, adding the scraps of Brussels lace that she had garnered from her mother's old dresses that were still stored in lavender in the chest upstairs. The lace was fine but a little yellow with age now and the village gossips in church tomorrow would quickly divine that the entire dress was second-hand. Thea gave a little shrug; there was no point in pretending, for everyone in the village of Oakmantle knew their parlous financial state.

"Clemmie, you really must learn not to ask questions like that," she said severely. Her sister had never understood the art of polite conversation and at nineteen possessed an outspokenness that would deter even the most persistent of suitors. "The Honorable Mr. Pershore is everything that one would wish in a husband. He is…" Here she paused, desperately trying to think of some positive attributes. "He is gentlemanly and kind and good-natured…" she floundered. "And kind…"

"You said that already," Clementine observed critically. Her perceptive blue eyes, identical to those of her older sister, scanned Thea's face. "I cannot dispute that he is kind, for has he not offered to marry you and take all of us on, as well?" She ticked them all off on her fingers. "Ned will go to Oxford and Harry to Eton, and I may have my come-out and Clara her harp lessons and Daisy—"

"Pray stop at once!" Thea said, more sharply than she had intended. To hear her sister itemize the material benefits of the match made her feel intolerably guilty, for she *was* marrying Bertie Pershore for his money and could scarcely deny it. She wished that it was not so; somehow she felt that Bertie deserved better than that she take advantage of him. Yet she was in desperate straits and he was chivalrous enough to come to her rescue. For a moment she thought back to the day when he had made his unexpected declaration and a smile, half rueful, half sad, crossed her features.

"You know I'm dashed fond of you, Thea, old girl," Bertie had said that day in the drawing room. His kindly brown gaze, so reminiscent of Theodosia's favorite spaniel, had rested on her with sympathetic concern. "Can't bear to see you struggle on in this moldering old place any longer! I'll need a suitable wife one day and you're well up to snuff—we would deal well together! So what do you say?"

Thea had not replied at once. She had got to her feet and strolled over to the drawing room window. It was early spring. The trees were still bare but beneath them the ground was starred with snowdrops and yellow aconites. It was a pretty scene but it failed to distract the eye completely from the general air of shabby neglect that hung over Oakmantle Hall.

Thea had turned back to her suitor, unsure whether to laugh or to cry. There were those who held that the Honorable Mr. Pershore, a Pink of the Ton, cared for little beyond the set of his neck cloth or the polish of his Hessians. Yet Thea had known him since they had been children together and knew him to be good-hearted and kind. She had just had the proof of it in his generous, if unromantic, proposal.

She had given him a rueful smile. "Oh, Bertie, you are most chivalrous, but I know perfectly well that you can have as little desire to marry as I! If it weren't for the rest of my family I would not even countenance it! Besides, that odious guardian of yours will surely kick up a fuss if you marry a penniless prospect such as myself, a woman older than you are, with so many dependents—"

Bertie had tried to shake his head and almost impaled himself on his shirt points. He'd frowned as mutinously as someone of his mournful expression was able.

"Don't see what business it is of Merlin's! I'm of age and may marry whom I choose."

Thea had sighed with all the wisdom of her two and twenty years. "Bertie, only conceive of the trouble it would cause! The Duke of Merlin would never tolerate so imprudent a match, not even for a distant cousin! Can you imagine what he would do?"

"Probably send Jack down," Bertie had said, his face breaking into a sudden grin. "Jack is forever pulling me out of scrapes! Did I tell you about the time he found me at Madam Annet's when I was on *exeat* from Eton—"

"Yes!" Thea had said sharply, wincing more at the reference to their potential marriage as a "scrape" than the indelicate story of Bertie's foray into one of London's most notorious bawdy houses. From the age of five, Bertie had tired her ears with his hero-worshiping references to Jack Merlin, his cousin and idol, and as a result Thea had taken the Marquis in extreme dislike. She had never met him in person but had formed an impression of an arrogant nobleman who had been granted all of life's privileges and took them lightly, until they bored him. Bertie's assurances that Jack was a great gun and a devil with the ladies did him no favors in Thea's eyes. She knew that Jack Merlin was a rake— even in the village of Oakmantle they had heard something of his reputation.

Bertie had looked abashed. "Sorry, Thea. Dashed improper of me to mention it."

Thea had sighed. It was impossible to feel anything other than a faint exasperation for one whom she had always considered as a rather tiresome younger brother, which made the proposed marriage even more ridiculous. She already had five siblings and scarcely needed a husband who would constitute a sixth child. Yet did she have any choice? Her father had left her with a mountain of debts, a crumbling manor house and her brothers and sisters to care for. And there was scarcely a queue of eager suitors hammering on the door of Oakmantle Hall...

Thea came back to the present and cut her thread with a sharp snap. There was no point in dwelling on that now. She had made her choice and tomorrow the knot would be tied.

"Clemmie, you must understand that one cannot always marry for love." She tried to explain.

"Why not?" her sister said immediately. "Mama was most insistent that we should not compromise our principles."

Thea sighed again. Their mother had been a bluestocking in her day, one of Mrs. Montagu's circle, and had held strong views on women's education and independence. She had brought all her children up to view romantic love as the ideal, which was all very well, Thea thought crossly, but when she had no money and a family to support, high-minded principles were a luxury she could ill afford.

The true extent of their poverty had only become apparent when their father had died some six months previously. Mr. Shaw had been a scholar and a gentleman, but he had had no concept of the importance of more worldly matters such as money. They had lived in the old house at Oakmantle for more years than Thea could remember but on her father's death she had discovered that it was not their own, and now the landlord was threatening to increase the rents or repossess the house. They had no source of income. Thea could never earn enough as a governess or schoolteacher to keep a family of six and though her brother Ned talked wildly of finding work as a clerk in the city of London, he was only seventeen and had no one to sponsor him. They had subsisted on the generosity of friends and distant relatives up to this point but now funds were running short and a more permanent answer had to be found. Bertie Pershore was that solution.

Thea shook the wedding dress out and held it at arm's length for critical inspection. Her pride had rebelled at the thought of Bertie paying for her trousseau, so as a result she would have to go to him in these faded threads.

"There, that will have to do."

Thea sighed again, repressing the urge to bundle the dress up and thrust it to the back of a cupboard, or even into the fire. "I never was much of a hand at needlework but I have done my best. It requires a hot iron."

Clementine closed her book and bent to blow out the single stand of candles. "It requires more than that! Never mind, Thea, you may have no skill with the needle but you will be able to discuss philosophy and poetry and ancient history with Mr. Pershore over the teacups…"

Thea winced but did not reprove her sister. Clementine was a sharp observer but seldom intended malice and it was not her fault that her words conjured up so ridiculous an image. For no matter how amiable Mr. Pershore was, he was no scholar. The thought of making trivial conversation with Bertie day in, day out, for the next forty years was purgatory, but Thea knew she was being ungrateful. There was a price to financial security, and if this was all she had to pay then she had escaped lightly.

The wedding service had barely begun when Thea realized that she simply could not go through with it. The omens had been bad that morning but she had tried to ignore them. A light drizzle had been falling as she made the short journey from Oakmantle Hall to the church, dampening her veil and making the embroidered roses in her circlet droop miserably. At her side, Ned glowered in silence, still smarting over the fact that she was sacrificing herself because he, the head of the family, could not support them. The church felt cold and smelled of dust, and Thea shivered convulsively in her thin silk dress. Clementine, Harry, Clara and Daisy were lined up in the front pew looking scrubbed and subdued. They were a good-looking family—all possessed the cornflower-blue eyes and fair hair of the Shaw family and all were huddling in old clothes that had been sponged down for the occasion by Mrs. Skeffington, the cook housekeeper. Thea thought that Harry looked like an undertaker's boy in his best black coat and Clara and Daisy were clutching each other's hands and looking as though they were about to cry.

Bertie Pershore was standing before the altar, looking terrified. Thea wondered if he was having second thoughts but was too honorable to say anything. Her heart sank lower than her soaking satin slippers and right down to the gravestones beneath her feet.

"Dearly beloved…" the rector intoned, fixing Thea with a severe look. He had baptized her and all her siblings and had buried her father six months before. The same villagers who had come to pay their respects to the late Mr. Shaw now bobbed and whispered in the pews behind Thea's family, noting the secondhand wedding dress and the groom's terrified demeanor. None of Bertie's family was present and Thea did not know whether she was glad or sorry.

The rector had moved on to the reasons for which marriage had been ordained and was speaking of the procreation of children. Thea, who had managed to avoid all thoughts of her wedding night, was suddenly confronted by a picture of herself and Bertie lying side by side in the ancient tester bed at Oakmantle. Under the circumstances the knowledge of Bertie's experiences at Madam Annet's hands might have been reassuring, since Thea had no experience of her own to draw on. Instead the thought was decidedly off-putting, providing as it did too much information for comfort. Bertie was kind, but Thea did not find him in the least attractive, and whilst she was not naive enough to imagine that one had to enjoy submitting to one's husband's desires, she had once hoped that she would marry a man who stirred her feelings....

"Secondly, it was ordained for a remedy against sin, and to avoid fornication..." the rector said, glaring ferociously at the congregation, who shifted uncomfortably in the pews. Bertie stared at his highly polished boots and cleared his throat nervously.

Oh, dear... Thea thought.

"I am sorry," she heard herself say politely, "but I am afraid that there has been a dreadful mistake and I have to go now."

There was a moment of absolute silence that felt to Thea as though it went on for hours. The vicar opened and closed his mouth like a landed fish, Bertie went white then red and the congregation started to flutter and whisper as they realized that something was wrong. Then Thea found herself hurrying back down the aisle, holding her skirts up in one hand, the slap of her slippers sounding unnaturally loud on the stone floor. She looked neither left nor right, ignoring the avid faces of the villagers as they craned to see what was going on. Behind her she could hear a swell of voices like the roar of the sea, but she had already reached the door and was fumbling with the latch. Her hands were shaking so much that they slipped on the cold metal. She felt faint and light-headed but she knew that she had to escape.

The door swung open suddenly with a gust of cool spring air. Thea rushed forward, almost tripping over the threshold in her haste, blinded by her veil and the tears that were now threatening her. She stumbled a few paces down the path toward the gate, realized that she would fall if she did not steady herself, and put out a hand. She recoiled in shock as it was caught and held. Strong arms went around her, holding her close.

"What the devil—" a masculine voice ejaculated, then the veil was pushed roughly back from her face and she found herself staring up at the man who held her.

His face was heart-stoppingly close to hers. As though in a dream Thea noted the dark blue eyes with their ridiculously thick black lashes, the harsh angles and planes of his tanned face, the square chin and uncompromising line of the mouth. She could smell lemon cologne mixed with cold air and leather and it made her feel faint but in an entirely different way from before. Her knees buckled and his arms tightened about her.

A lock of black hair had fallen across his forehead and it looked soft and silky. Thea had a sudden urge to smooth it back, to let her hand linger against his cheek where the stubble already darkened his skin. Her fingers were already halfway to their destination when she shivered convulsively and snapped out of the dream that held her, stepping back and freeing herself.

The man made an instinctive gesture toward her. "Wait!"

Thea ignored him. With no thought to the rain or the slippery stones of the churchyard or the damp, clinging lace of her wedding dress, she ran from him as though her life depended on it.

Jack had seen her as soon as he came through the lych-gate and started up the path toward the church. She was hurrying toward him but he could tell that she had not seen him—there was an air of intense concentration about her that suggested she was completely wrapped up in her feelings. Then she had stumbled on the wet path and he had caught her hand, instinctively pulling her into his arms, as she seemed about to fall.

She had eyes of cornflower-blue, stricken and bright with tears now, but direct and uncompromising still. They widened as she looked up into his face and focused on him for the first time. He felt a jolt of something go through him, something like pain, deeper than desire.

Her fair hair was so soft it looked like spun gold as it escaped the confines of the wedding veil, and he had the near irresistible urge to loosen it and bury his face in the silken mass. Her mouth was tempting and voluptuous, as unconsciously sensuous as the rest of the yielding body that was pressed so intimately against his. She smelled of lavender and spring meadows and sunshine, and he found that all he wanted was to hold her closer still. Jack Merlin had never experienced so strong a reaction to a woman in his whole life. It was no surprise to find that he wanted her but it was a surprise to find himself so shaken.

"Wait!" The word burst from him instinctively as she freed herself violently from his arms. She took no notice. He saw that her hands were trembling as she scooped up the yellowing lace skirts of the old wedding gown, then she was running from him down the path and disappearing through the lych-gate. The whole encounter had taken less than a minute.

Jack let his breath out in a long sigh and felt the tension drain slowly from his body. Behind him in the church he could hear an excited babble of voices rising to a crescendo. He cast one look in the direction the girl had gone. Unless he missed his guess, he had just met his cousin's runaway bride. But whether she was running away before or after the knot had been tied was as yet uncertain. Jack found himself hoping fervently for the former, then sighed again. When he had set off from London the last thing he had expected was to find himself envying his cousin. The whole matter of Bertie's wedding was becoming a lot more complicated than he had envisaged.

Chapter Two

"At least I was able to hold my peace!" Jack said wryly. "I'd have felt a damned fool intervening in the service at the point where the parson asks if anyone has just cause to stop the proceedings."

"Never got that far." Bertie Pershore said gloomily, passing his cousin a glass of brandy. He joined Jack by the fire. "Devil take it, Jack, if Thea didn't want to go through with it she could have told me before that! Making a cake of myself in front of the entire village... Jilting me at the altar—"

They were in the private parlor of the Lamb and Rabbit hostelry, where Jack had abandoned his carriage and his valet an hour previously. Hodges had spent the intervening time bespeaking rooms and making sure that everything was comfortable. Sampling the brandy, Jack observed that he did indeed employ a prince amongst valets.

After the debacle at the wedding, Jack had simply strolled up the aisle, ushered his shocked cousin out a side door, pressed a large financial contribution into the startled rector's hand and suggested that the jilted groom be left in peace to recover. No one had dared to gainsay him.

Jack shrugged, settling himself deeper in the armchair. "Maybe Miss Shaw suddenly realized she could do better for herself, old chap! A title *and* a fortune, perhaps..."

"Thea isn't like that!" Bertie said hotly. He saw Jack's sardonic glance and added, "Oh, I know you think I'm besotted with an adventuress, but you couldn't be further from the truth. Thea and I have been friends for years and I was only trying to help her out—"

"Keep your chivalric instincts under control in future!" his cousin advised dryly. "Not that I can blame you, Bertie. Miss Thea Shaw is devilish attractive and I can quite see why you fell for her charms, but to make her an offer—"

He broke off at his cousin's blank stare. "Attractive? Thea? I'll concede she's not a bad-looking girl, and she's game as a pebble, of course, but she's no diamond of the first water! Sure we're talking about the same girl, Jack?"

Jack raised his eyebrows. He had never felt that Bertie's taste in women was either well developed or particularly subtle and here he had the proof. His cousin had evidently been in the ridiculous position of being blind to the considerable charms of the woman he was about to marry. Jack shrugged philosophically. He was not going to point out the error of his ways to Bertie for this way he could kill two birds with one stone. He could ensure that the marriage would not be revived and he could map out a very different future for Miss Theodosia Shaw. He already had in mind exactly what it entailed.

In the hour since he had met Thea outside the church, Jack had successfully managed to master the surprising and wholly unexpected feelings that she had aroused in him. Clearly Thea Shaw was a fortune hunter, no matter what Bertie said to defend her. That being the case, she might be receptive to an offer from him, which, whilst different from Bertie's chivalrous proposal, might still be as financially rewarding. Jack smiled, a little cynically. He was certain that he could satisfy both his own desires and those of Miss Shaw one way or another.

"I assume you have no intention of renewing your suit to Miss Shaw?" he inquired casually and was relieved when Bertie flushed angrily.

"Damned if I will! I have my pride, you know, Jack! All I ever wanted to do was help Thea out—a favor because of our long friendship, you know, and I think she could at least have been honest with me." He stared gloomily into the fire. "Think I'll eschew all women! Better off without them! No idea what makes them tick."

Jack grinned at that. "You and the rest of the male population, old chap! Well—" he stood up and stretched "—I am going to pay a call on Miss Shaw. Wouldn't want her stirring up any trouble in future."

Bertie shook his head. He looked up. "Barking up the wrong tree there, Jack! Thea won't take kindly to your interference. Why not let it lie, old fellow? Wedding's off—you can be sure that I won't be making any rash offers again. Fingers burned and all that!"

"All the same, I will be happier when I have made a few matters clear to Miss Shaw," Jack murmured. "It will not take long."

"Suppose you mean to pay her off," Bertie said, adding with gloomy relish, "Big mistake! Asking for trouble, old fellow! You'll see!"

"I have various offers to put to Miss Shaw," Jack

said lazily, reaching for his coat. "We shall see which one suits her best."

"I cannot believe that I have behaved so badly!" Thea was curled up in an armchair in the blue drawing room. She had changed out of the soaking wedding dress into a plain gown of gray-spotted muslin and her hair was loose, drying in corkscrew curls about her face.

"Poor Bertie! He will never forgive me. I cannot forgive myself. Jilting him at the altar! How could I do such a thing?"

"Well, it was very bad of you," Clementine confirmed with a judicious purse of the lips, "but far better than to marry Mr. Pershore today and change your mind tomorrow. It will only be a nine days' wonder until the next scandal comes along!" She pressed a glass of Madeira into her sister's hand. "Here, drink this. I always think it the best way to ward off a chill."

"I cannot see what you can know of such strong cures at your age!" Thea said severely, forgetting her dejection for a moment. Sometimes she felt she was a poor substitute for a mother to Clementine. It was impossible to control her sister's waywardness. She took a sip of the drink and sat back in her chair.

"What happened in the church after I left, Clemmie?"

"Not a great deal," her sister said, kneeling to add a couple of applewood logs to the fire. "The rector appealed to the congregation to keep calm." She snorted. "As well try to dam the river Oak! They were chattering and gossiping when you were barely through the door." She caught Thea's eye and said hurriedly, "It will all die down before you can say 'jilt'!"

Thea glared at her. "Thank you! And in the meantime

we are in as poor and parlous a situation as before. I cannot think what came over me.''

''You did the correct thing.'' Clementine stood up and dusted her palms together to remove the wood chippings. ''No matter how rich Mr. Pershore, it makes him not one whit more attractive as a husband.''

Thea turned her face away. She felt restless and on edge but she knew it had nothing to do with what had happened in the church and all to do with what had happened afterward. She had not even seen the stranger in the churchyard until she had stumbled into his arms and once she was there she had wanted him to hold her forever. It was extraordinary, it was deeply unsettling, but it was true.

''Did a gentleman come into the church just after I left?'' she asked casually. ''I thought I saw someone on the path.''

Clementine brightened. ''Oh, yes! I forgot to tell you! Apparently it was Mr. Pershore's cousin, but I had no chance to meet him as he whisked Bertie away in an instant. He was most prodigiously handsome, though. That I do remember.''

Thea sat upright, her heart pounding uncomfortably. ''Bertie's cousin, did you say? Oh, no, I do believe that must have been the Marquis of Merlin come to stop the marriage, just as Bertie predicted…'' Against her will she felt a blush rising. So it was Jack Merlin in whose arms she had taken refuge! Thea put her glass down with a snap, damning the confoundedly bad luck of the whole situation.

Clementine was sitting back on her heels and eyeing her suspiciously.

''That was the Marquis of Merlin? Is he not the one with the terrible reputation? The rake? The one who ran off with Lady Spence, then decided he preferred her younger sister who had just wed Lord Raistrick?''

''Yes!'' Thea said quickly, wondering where on earth her younger sister had picked up such scurrilous gossip. There was no denying that Jack Merlin was rakish and dangerous—she had assimilated that in less than ten seconds in his arms. Compellingly attractive was another matter, and one she did not wish to admit to her sister.

''And divinely handsome, as well!'' Clementine sighed. ''Oh, I do so wish I had had the chance to make his acquaintance.''

Thea was just reflecting that Clementine had absorbed a great deal of romance along with her mother's more stringent philosophies on life, when her eye was caught by a figure strolling around the corner of the house. There was no mistaking him, for all that she had met him so briefly. This was definitely the Marquis of Merlin come to call. Thea recoiled, stifling an urge to run away and hide upstairs. The doorbell pealed.

''I do believe that you may rectify your omission now,'' she said faintly, ''for that is the Marquis at the door. Though what he can be wanting with us—'' She broke off and smoothed her dress down with nervous fingers. Oh, to be wearing her old gray muslin at such a time! This would be the second occasion on which the Marquis would see her in her frumpish clothes, just when she needed the confidence that a really modish dress would give her. But then, she possessed no such thing, so bewailing the fact was immaterial...

''Excuse me, ma'am,'' Mrs. Skeffington, the housekeeper, arrived at the drawing room door looking flustered and disapproving. Thea squashed the ridiculous suspicion that the Marquis had been flirting with her.

''The Marquis of Merlin is asking if you are at home, ma'am—''

''Oh, show him in!'' Clementine said, almost hopping with excitement.

Thea sent her a quelling look. ''Thank you, Skeffie. I will see Lord Merlin in here. Clementine—'' she turned to her sister ''—it would perhaps be better if you were to leave us to talk in private.''

''Oh, no!'' Clementine said, adopting the severe tone her elder sister always used with her, ''that would not be at all proper!''

''Lord Merlin, ma'am!'' Mrs. Skeffington murmured, frowning sternly. She dropped a curtsy and moved away with a stately tread that managed to imply even greater disapproval.

The Marquis of Merlin came into the room.

Thea took a deep, steadying breath. Her heart was racing and not simply with nervousness. She had the time to study the Marquis properly now as he came forward to greet her, and she was disconcerted to discover that she had the inclination to carry on looking at him indefinitely. It was not simply that he was, as Clementine had said, prodigiously handsome, although this was not in dispute. There was something else, something more compelling than mere good looks. Here was a man who was everything that Bertie Pershore was not. In an instant Thea recognized that she had accepted Bertie because he was straightforward and safe and unthreatening. And even on so short, albeit eventful, an acquaintance, she could tell that Jack Merlin was the exact opposite—complicated, dangerous, a challenge she was unsure she wanted to accept. Such thoughts did nothing to quell the uneasy excitement that was coursing through her body.

Clementine was staring and Thea could hardly blame

her. The Marquis was tall, with a strong physique and a nonchalant grace that compelled the eye. His thick, dark hair was disheveled in the kind of style that poor Bertie could not have achieved even with the ministrations of the best valet. He bowed with ineffable elegance.

"Miss Shaw?"

His voice was low and warm, sending a curious shiver down Thea's spine. She nodded starchily. "Lord Merlin."

She saw a smile touch that firm mouth. "How do you do, ma'am? It is…most agreeable to meet you again."

Thea ignored the intimate implication of his words and gestured to Clementine. "Lord Merlin, may I introduce my sister, Miss Clementine Shaw."

Jack inclined his head. "Your servant, Miss Clementine."

Thea watched with exasperation as Clementine dropped a demure curtsy and smiled enchantingly at the Marquis. She had never behaved as such a pattern card of female perfection with any of their other male acquaintance. Such contrariness was enough to tempt Thea to shake her sister—until she realized that the Marquis was skillfully disposing of Clementine's company and suddenly she was tempted to cling to her as a safeguard.

"I hope you will excuse me if I beg a private word with your sister, Miss Clementine," Jack was saying, holding the drawing room door open. "It was indeed a pleasure to meet you."

Thea sent Clementine a look that was part beseeching, part commanding, but her sister seemed blind to her appeal. She tripped out without demur and Jack closed the door gently behind her.

Thea blinked. She cleared her throat hastily, searching for a diversion.

"Would you care for some refreshment, Lord Merlin?"

Jack's gaze fell on her half-finished glass. "Thank you. I will join you in a glass of Madeira, ma'am."

Thea poured the wine herself, trying to prevent her fingers from shaking. There was something unnerving about Jack Merlin, the direct, dark blue gaze that had barely wavered from her since he had entered the room, the instinctive authority that cloaked him. This was not a man Thea wanted to tangle with. And yet a part of her, a treacherous part, wanted it very much indeed...

She handed him the glass of wine, making sure that their fingers did not touch. The memory of their encounter outside the church was still in her mind and her equilibrium, already fragile, could not withstand another onslaught. She resumed her seat with what she hoped was an assumption of ease, gesturing Jack to take the chair opposite. He did so, his eyes never leaving her face.

"I hope that you are somewhat recovered from your ordeal, Miss Shaw?" Jack raised an eyebrow. "When we met outside the church I thought that you were a little...distressed? I would have assisted you had you given me the opportunity."

There was a warmth in his tone, an intimacy, that brought the color into Thea's cheeks. His words conjured up the memory of his arms about her, the comforting strength that had somehow been simultaneously protective and inexplicably exciting. Thea smoothed her skirts with a little nervous gesture. She did not—could not—meet his eyes.

"Thank you, my lord. I am much recovered now."

"Good." Jack's tone changed subtly, the gentleness gone. "Miss Shaw, forgive my abruptness, but I wished to speak to you of the wedding. Why did you abandon

Bertie at the altar? Having persuaded him to marry you, I cannot understand why you should throw away all your advantages! Unless, of course—'' there was a sardonic note in his voice now ''—you are contemplating a better offer?''

Thea looked up sharply. He had wasted little time on polite niceties. The gloves were off now, the contempt very clear.

''I fear that you are laboring under several misconceptions, sir,'' she said with cool haughtiness. ''In the first place I had no need to exert undue influence in order to persuade Mr. Pershore to propose! He did so because he is a true friend and most chivalrous—''

She broke off as Jack shifted slightly. ''And then you scorned his chivalry by jilting him at the altar?'' he queried gently. '' That was badly done, Miss Shaw.''

Thea bit her lip, all too aware that he was deliberately putting her in the wrong, but equally aware that her position was indefensible. It *had* been inexcusable to treat Bertie so, but she had no intention of accepting Jack's reproofs. She looked at him defiantly.

''Would you have preferred me to marry your cousin, Lord Merlin? Forgive me, but I thought your presence in Oakmantle indicated an intention to put a stop to the nuptials rather than to dance at the wedding! Am I then mistaken and you are here to persuade me to accept Bertie, after all?''

Jack laughed. ''Certainly not, Miss Shaw! My cousin has told me a little of your situation and I cannot but see it as a most undesirable match! No money, no connections, nothing to recommend you but...'' He paused, and his blue gaze slid over her with a mocking appraisal that made his meaning crystal-clear.

Thea was incensed. She stood up. ''You are imperti-

nent, sir! Since you evidently set great store by wealth
and connection, I am happy to tell you that my family
is at least as old and distinguished as your own—more
so! And we are far more honorable in our conduct!'' She
saw him smile and went on sharply. ''So have no fear,
I do not intend to importune Bertie to give me a second
chance! Your cousin is safe from my attentions!''

''I am happy to hear it,'' Jack murmured. He had also
risen to his feet and was standing disturbingly close to
her. For a wild moment Thea could almost imagine that
she could feel the warmth of his body, smell the faint
scent of lemon cologne she had detected when he had
held her before. Her senses went into a spin and she felt
herself tremble. It was deeply unnerving. She stepped
back hastily and almost overturned the table with her
wineglass upon it. Jack caught her elbow to steady her
and Thea shook him off, appalled at the tremor that slid
through her at his touch.

''I cannot believe that we have anything more to say
to each other, Lord Merlin,'' she said coldly, moving to
pull the bell for the housekeeper. ''I must bid you good
day.''

Jack put out a hand to stop her. ''On the contrary,''
he said, gently mocking, ''there are a number of points
I still wish to make. Please be seated, Miss Shaw.''

Their eyes met in a long moment of tension, then Thea
deliberately moved away to the stand by the window.
She was damned if she was going to do his bidding!

''I am sure that whatever you wish to say to me may
be adequately expressed with me standing here, Lord
Merlin,'' she said. ''Pray continue!''

Jack shrugged carelessly. ''As you wish, Miss Shaw.
My only concern was for your comfort.''

"Pray make your point!" Thea snapped, allowing the tension to overset her naturally good manners.

Jack was not in the least discomposed. "Very well. In recognition of your obliging nature, Miss Shaw, I would like to make you an offer. If you undertake not to see Bertie ever again I shall be happy to contribute something to recompense you for your loss." He looked around the shabby drawing room. "It will help to tide you over until you find another suitor, perhaps..."

Thea drew herself up. She had never previously considered that she had a bad temper, but then she had never been provoked by the Marquis of Merlin before.

"Do I understand you to be offering me a bribe, Lord Merlin?" she inquired icily. "You quite misunderstand me if you think I should be amenable to such a suggestion. I have *every* intention of seeing Bertie again, if only to apologize to him! We have been friends these twenty years past."

"My dear, you are the one who is deluding herself," Jack said, sounding to Thea's infuriated ears both bored and amused. "It may salve your conscience to pretend that the arrangement between yourself and Bertie was based on chivalry, or friendship, or however you wish to dress it up, but the truth is that it was a business transaction no different in essence from the offer I am making you now."

There was another sharp silence. "I do not accept bribes!" Thea said through stiff lips. "You have my word and that should be sufficient."

Jack shrugged gracefully. "The word of a woman of principle?" There was cold cynicism in his eyes. "I wish I could believe it, Miss Shaw."

He was unfurling a roll of banknotes from his pocket and casually placing them on the mantelpiece, stacking a column of golden guineas on top to keep them in place. Thea stared, transfixed. So much money... More than she could earn in a lifetime as a schoolteacher, enough to keep a family of six in comfort for years and years....

"You see, Miss Shaw—" Jack's voice was very soft "—principles are for fools! Take it. It is yours..."

With a violent sweep of the hand, Thea scattered the guineas to the four corners of the room. They spun across the floor, clattering against the skirting board and rolling under the furniture. One of them bounced off a particularly ugly sculpture that had belonged to Thea's father and chipped its nose.

Jack picked up the banknotes, folded them and put them back in his pocket.

He grinned. "I take it that that is a refusal?"

Thea was shaking but she managed to keep her voice steady. "You are most perspicacious, sir!"

Jack was laughing at her. "A woman of principle indeed! If you wish to save my father the expense of paying you off I shall not argue with you!" He took a step closer to her. "Do not think to come begging for money in future and threatening scandal, however!"

It took all of Thea's will to respond with cool disdain when she wanted to slap him. She glared at him with the angry intensity of a cornered cat. "I have no intention of acting so! That may be *your* preferred mode of behavior, my lord—"

Jack's eyes lit suddenly with wicked amusement. Thea took an unconscious step back, warned by the predatory brightness she saw there.

"Since you ask, *this* is my preferred mode of behavior, Miss Shaw."

His arms went around her, hard and fast, and his mouth had captured hers before she even had time to think. Thea's immediate feelings of outrage died a swift death, banished by the warm pressure of his lips on hers. Her lips parted, instinctively obeying the unspoken command; she felt his tongue touch hers and a seductive weakness swept through her, leaving her breathless with shocked desire.

There was no reprieve. Even as Thea's mind reeled under the onslaught of her feelings he deepened the kiss, his mouth skillful, demanding, making no concessions. Thea swayed a little, half astonished to find herself pressing closer to him, half wanton in her need to be closer still.

She moved slightly and her foot struck something against the softness of her kid slipper. A golden guinea. Thea's mind cleared abruptly and she pushed hard against Jack's chest, pulling away from him, utterly appalled. He released her at once.

Thea stepped back. Her voice was shaky. "That was—"

"Exceptional." Thea saw a heat in Jack's eyes that mirrored the desire still shimmering through her own body. His voice was rough. She repressed a shiver. What was it about this man that turned her bones to water? She was no foolish scullery maid to have her head turned by a handsome marquis!

"My dear Miss Shaw," Jack was saying gently, taking her hand in his and reawakening all the latent feelings that Thea was trying so hard to suppress, "might I suggest an alternative future based on the...surprising...harmony we seem to have achieved? In return for your favor I should be glad to help with your financial difficulties..."

It took a second for Thea to understand, but then the shock hit her with what felt like physical force and she found it difficult to breathe. She turned away and moved a few ornaments at random on the mantelpiece.

"I collect that you mean to set me up as your mistress, Lord Merlin?" She was amazed at her own mild tone. "Or do I mistake and you intend only a short but sweet liaison? Not that it matters." She spun 'round to face him with such sudden violence that one of the ornaments, a pretty little shepherdess, clattered to the floor. "The answer to either suggestion is no—thank you! First you try to bribe me and then you offer me *carte blanche!* Your arrogance, insensitivity and conceit are truly breathtaking! Now leave this house before I throw you out myself!"

Jack raised his eyebrows, seemingly unmoved. "Your indignation is magnificent, my dear, but is it justified? Did you not respond to me just now?" His gaze, suddenly insolent, swept over her and lingered on the curve of her breast. "How many times have you used your undeniable charms to aid you in a difficult situation? When it is the only card to play?"

Thea did not answer. She brushed past him and opened the drawing room door. Then she marched out into the hall, past the startled housekeeper, and flung open the main door of Oakmantle Hall. It crashed back on its hinges, the echo reverberating through the entire house.

Jack had followed her into the hall and was now receiving his coat from Mrs. Skeffington, whose mouth had turned down so far with disapproval that it looked as though the ends would meet. Thea was grudgingly forced to admit that Jack appeared to be taking his eviction with a good grace. He even bowed to her, a twinkle of very definite admiration in those dark blue eyes.

"Your point is taken, Miss Shaw!"

Thea still did not reply. She watched in stony silence as he went down the broad stone steps, then she slammed the door so hard that the crash raised the wood pigeons from the oak trees all along the drive.

Jack strode across the gravel sweep toward the drive, his mind still focused on Miss Theodosia Shaw. *Arrogance, insensitivity and conceit...* He winced. It was a long time since anyone—except perhaps his father—had dared accuse him of any such thing. Perhaps that was half the trouble.

Jack knew that he had mishandled the situation and he also knew that in part he had done it deliberately. He had wanted to test Miss Shaw, to see if she was the woman of principle that she claimed. And yet Jack realized that as soon as they had spoken, he had known instinctively that Thea would accept neither his money nor his amorous attentions. There was an innocence about her, a straightforward honesty that made such transactions seem grubby and demeaning. Which they were, of course. It served him right to have his offers thrown back in his face.

Jack smiled a little. He had ignored his intuition and put her to the test, but Thea had triumphantly proved his instincts to be right and this pleased him more than a little. He frowned whilst he grappled with the implications of this. It would have been so much easier to have either paid her off and forgotten about her, or to have set her up as his mistress until his surprising desire for her had waned. Instead he found that he wanted her to be innocent of deceit. In fact he wanted her to be innocent, full stop. Jack whistled soundlessly to himself. Purity had never particularly appealed to him before—he had enjoyed the attentions of plenty of experienced women and had never wanted it to be any other way. This, however, was different. For a moment Jack allowed himself the luxury of imagining what it would be like to introduce Thea to physical pleasure. She had responded to his kiss with an untutored passion that was wholly arousing. Multiply that effect ten times and it gave some indication of the conflagration that would surely follow…

Arrogant, conceited… Jack acknowledged that he was being both of those things in wanting Theodosia Shaw all to himself. Further, he was certain that given the time and the opportunity he could persuade her to his point of view, convert her to his way of thinking. He did not have the time, however, and there were any number of pressing reasons why he should return to Town at once, not least because he detested country life. Miss Theodosia Shaw would simply have to remain the one lady who had escaped him…

Jack shrugged his shoulders uncomfortably, frustrated in more ways than one. He was not sure why he was hesitating when Miss Shaw had made her aversion to him crystal-clear. If he had not found himself in actual physical discomfort, he would have laughed at the irony. Jack Merlin, the ruthless rake, was aching for a woman he could not have.

To distract himself, Jack looked around at Oakmantle Hall and the neglected gardens that surrounded it. He was surprised to find that they were rather charming. The house was a low building of golden stone, with higgledy-piggledy chimneys and a pale slate roof. It was surrounded by a moat of green water, almost full after the earlier rain, and beyond that the lawn stretched to the deer park, where clumps of daffodils were showing beneath the trees. The air was mild and soft. It was a tranquil scene.

Jack paused on the edge of the moat. He could see paddocks over to the right, where a fat pony grazed undisturbed. It would make the most excellent place to keep stables. Jack told himself, jokingly of course, that if he ever lived in the country he would breed horses and set up racing stables to rival the finest.

He could hear the distant sound of children's voices and wondered whether Thea's younger siblings were close at hand. He thought that he would like to meet them, then paused, frowning. Those were two uncharacteristic thoughts that he had had in the space of a minute. Perhaps there was something in the Oakmantle air that was turning his mind. He had better get back to the inn, and from there to London. Quickly.

There was a shout much closer at hand, and he turned abruptly, but it was too late. He was struck hard on the shoulder, a blow that knocked him to the ground. He felt something sharp hit him on the head and he went out like a blown candle.

Chapter Three

"Thea, come quickly! I've shot him! I've shot the Marquis of Merlin!"

Thea was in the drawing room, tidying her ornaments, picking up the guineas and trying to put Jack Merlin from her mind. So far her mode of doing so had involved going over every part of their conversation and feeling utterly outraged, then moving on to the kiss, and feeling deeply disturbed. The fact that she had spent ten minutes thinking of nothing but Jack Merlin was something that exasperated her even more, but she did not seem at liberty to prevent it.

"Thea!"

Clementine's voice broke through Thea's preoccupation and she hurried toward the door, colliding with her sister in the hall. Clemmie was pale, her hair in disarray, her eyes wild. She grabbed Thea's sleeve and almost dragged her to the front door.

" Thea, I've shot him—"

"I heard you the first time," Thea said soothingly, noting the bow propped in a corner of the hall. She gave Clementine a quick hug, feeling the tension in her sister's body and noticing that she was close to tears.

"Calm down, Clemmie, I'm sure it cannot be so bad! Now, show me where he is!"

It was a mild afternoon outside and the threat of rain was back in the air. As they came 'round onto the carriage sweep, a horrid sight met Thea's eyes. Jack Merlin was lying on the gravel by the moat, his head resting on one of the large white stones that marked the edge of the drive. The shaft of an arrow was sticking out of his shoulder, his face was parchment-white and he was quite unconscious.

Thea took a deep breath and knelt down beside him, feeling for his pulse. The gravel felt sharp through the material of her dress. She knew it must be uncomfortable for Jack to lie on, but she also knew that she should not move him until she could ascertain his injuries.

"Clemmie, send Ned for Dr. Ryland," she said over her shoulder, "then go to the kitchens and ask Mrs. Skeffington to heat some water and find some bandages."

Clementine peered at Jack's recumbent form. "Is he dead, Thea?"

"Certainly not!" Thea gave her sister an encouraging smile. "You are not such a good shot, you know! The arrow is not in very deep but I think he hit his head when he fell."

"He wandered straight across my sights."

Thea squeezed her hand. "Never mind that now. The best way for you to help him is to fetch the doctor. Hurry!"

She watched her sister run off a little shakily toward the shrubbery where Ned and Harry could still be heard playing at cricket. The archery target was visible on the drive fifty yards away. Thea sighed. Ever since Clementine had skewered the delivery boy's hat with an arrow a few months back, she had been afraid that a worse accident would happen and now she had been proved right. That it had happened to the arrogant Marquis of Merlin was only a small consolation, for Thea found that when she looked at Jack's lifeless body it was concern that she felt rather than triumph.

She turned her attention back to him. His face was still pale, chill and clammy to the touch, but she was a little reassured that his pulse was strong and his breathing regular. She moved his head onto her lap, taking care not to jolt his shoulder. He did not stir. Thea felt a surprisingly strong impulse to brush the hair back from his forehead, and after a second she did so. It was as soft and silky as she had imagined earlier and she lingered over the feel of it before recalling herself and snatching her hand away guiltily. Then she just sat and studied the sweep of his lashes against the hard line of his cheek. It gave her a strange feeling inside, breathless, warm and protective all at the same time. She shifted uncomfortably, then hastily stilled her movements as Jack groaned a little. She held her breath, but he did not open his eyes.

It was starting to rain, the drops pattering down on the drive and dampening Thea's gray muslin dress and wetting her hair all over again. A drop fell on Jack's face and Thea wiped it away gently. She saw him wrinkle up his nose as the cool water roused him. Then he opened his eyes and looked at her. For a moment his gaze was cloudy with pain and puzzlement, then Thea saw him focus on her face, and he tried to sit up.

"What the hell—" Jack broke off with a groan as the movement jarred his shoulder and made him wince. He closed his eyes again momentarily, then opened them and frowned.

"What in God's name is going on? Miss Shaw—"

Thea laid a restraining hand on his sound shoulder. "Please lie still, Lord Merlin. You have had an accident but I have sent my brother for the doctor and we shall have you inside the house in no time."

Jack raised his right hand to his shoulder, twisting awkwardly as he tried to discover the source of his discomfort. "What is this—an arrow?" There was stark incredulity in his voice, overlying the pain. "Good God, ma'am, have you shot me to protect your virtue? I assure you there was no such need."

"Don't be so absurd." Thea said crisply. "You wandered across the target where my sister was practicing her archery. It was the veriest accident! Then you hit your head when you fell."

"A veritable chapter of accidents, in fact!" Jack gave a sigh and rubbed his hand across his forehead. "Damnation, I feel as weak as a kitten and my head aches to boot." He shifted again. "This arrow in my shoulder—"

"Dr. Ryland will remove it as soon as he gets here, I am sure!" Thea looked around a little desperately, wondering where the good doctor had got to. It seemed like hours since Clementine had run to fetch help but perhaps it was only a matter of minutes. The rain was falling harder now and she knew she had no way of getting Jack to shelter. There was sweat on his face now but he had started to shiver. Thea felt the worry clutch at her.

"If I could reach it properly I would pull it out myself!" Jack was muttering, sitting up with an effort and straining to reach the shaft of the arrow. He struggled, a groan escaping his lips. "Devil take it."

"Please keep still," Thea besought him. "You will only make yourself worse! If you are strong enough we could attempt to walk to the house."

Jack looked at her, squinting with the effort of concentration. "I would gladly try but I cannot walk anywhere with an arrow stuck in my shoulder, Miss Shaw. It is damnably dangerous and could easily injure you, too, if I were to fall." He shook his head in an attempt to clear the pain. "Perhaps if you were to take it out for me—"

"Oh, I do not think so!" Thea recoiled. "Besides, surely it is too much of a risk."

Jack's eyes, bright with fever now, mocked her. "What, rejecting an opportunity to cause me pain, Miss Shaw? Do you faint at the sight of blood? I assure you, there will not be much and you would be doing me the utmost favor."

There was a silence. Thea looked at him, her face pale. He gave a slight nod, holding her gaze steadily with his. She gritted her teeth, trying to ignore the sickness inside her at the thought of hurting him. She knew she had to do it, but it was so very difficult to screw her courage up. She took a deep breath and set her hand to the arrow shaft, giving it a sharp tug. She heard the breath hiss between Jack's teeth as it came out in her hand, but he made no further sound. The blood spread from the tear across the coat of green superfine, not in a huge rush, as Thea had feared, but in a steady stream.

"One of Weston's best creations ruined," Jack observed dispassionately. "He will never forgive me! Miss Shaw, might I trouble you to lend your petticoat to stem the flow? It is likely the only opportunity I shall get to encourage you to voluntarily remove a garment..."

Thea smothered a smile. For some obscure reason his teasing made her feel much better, as though it was a sign that he was not at death's door.

"I am pleased to see you so much recovered that you can make fun of me, my lord!" she said. "I will gladly donate a strip of my petticoat, although I cannot afford to give you the whole as it is the only one I possess!''

"I will buy another one for you, if you will accept so personal a gift.'' Jack gave her a faint glimmer of a smile as he watched her pull up her skirts a little and hastily tear a strip from the material.

"Make it into a pad,'' he instructed, "then tie it in place with the loose ends…''

"You are very resourceful, my lord,'' Thea said, following his directions and trying to keep the surprise out of her voice. Such commonsense practicality did not seem to fit her image of the society rake at all.

Jack shrugged, then winced. "I learned to make shift as I could when I was in the Peninsula. Your petticoat is a very superior sort of bandage, Miss Shaw, compared with some of the dressings I was forced to apply then.''

"You were in the Peninsula?'' Thea asked, this time failing to hide her surprise. "I did not realize… That is, Bertie did not mention…''

Once again Jack's smile contained a flicker of mockery. He turned his head to watch her hands as she hesitantly wrapped the bandage about his shoulder. A lock of his hair brushed her wrist and Thea nearly jumped away, then schooled herself to carry on. She did not want him to see her vulnerability.

"A little tighter, if you please, Miss Shaw…'' Fortunately Jack did not appear to have noticed her discomfort although his gaze was disturbingly observant for a sick man. It returned to her face and stayed there, thoughtful, disconcerting.

"Perhaps there is much you have to learn about me, Miss Shaw. Does Bertie speak of me often?''

"Incessantly!'' Thea said briskly, tying the bandage with a little tug just to put him in his place. "He is quite boring on the subject. Now can you manage to struggle to the house by leaning on my arm, my lord? I regret that we do not have any servants who can carry you indoors…''

''No need, Miss Shaw,'' the Marquis murmured, ''though I appreciate your offer. I believe that must be the good doctor now, and bringing Hodges, my valet, with him.''

Thea looked up. Ned was hurrying across the drive, leading Dr. Ryland and a portly man who was carrying a traveling bag and wearing a long-suffering expression. Thea had the impression that the valet was accustomed to finding his master in such unusual circumstances and was wearily weighing up exactly what was required this time.

Thea accepted Ned's hand and struggled a little stiffly to her feet, then hung back as Dr. Ryland and Hodges between them managed to help the Marquis across the gravel sweep and back into Oakmantle Hall. It felt decidedly strange to see Jack Merlin escorted back into the house she had thrown him out of only twenty minutes before and Thea could not be sure if she was glad or sorry that he had not been so easy to dismiss. One thing she was certain of, however, was that she had to get rid of him again, and fast. She had no wish for Jack to realize just how much the whole experience had shaken her and how protective of him she had felt. Pulling out the arrow had taken all her courage and she had admired Jack for the stoical way in which he had accepted her fumbling ministrations. Clearly he was no mere society rake. There was indeed a lot that she did not know about him. She was not certain if it was safe to know any more.

Once inside the house, Thea was confronted by a new dilemma. Dr. Ryland was insistent that the Marquis should be put to bed and Thea saw no alternative than to donate her own room for the time being. She saw them safely upstairs then went to check that Clementine was feeling somewhat improved. Her sister was in the kitchen regaling Mrs. Skeffington with the tale of how she had shot the Marquis, but she broke off, looking guilty when Thea entered.

"A cup of tea, ma'am?" Mrs. Skeffington suggested quickly, pushing the pot toward her, and Thea sat down gratefully whilst the housekeeper poured her a cup. She let Clementine's chatter flow over her, aware that most of it was prompted by relief, and unwilling to give her sister the scolding she so clearly deserved.

Thea leaned her chin on her hands, feeling tired and out of sorts. The whole incident had left her feeling curiously vulnerable and prey to all manner of conflicting emotions. She did not want Jack Merlin in the house, but it was not because she disliked him. She knew she *ought* to dislike him intensely after what had happened between them and it was all the more disconcerting to discover that the reverse was true. Jack was too disturbingly attractive, his presence too unsettling for her peace of mind. So he had to go. She would insist that, as soon as Dr. Ryland had seen him, the Marquis be taken straight back to the Lamb and Rabbit, or to London, or to hell for all she cared. For the one thing that she did know was that even in his weakened state, if she gave Jack an inch, he would take a mile.

"Not much harm done!" Dr. Ryland said reassuringly half an hour later as he joined Thea in the library. "The Marquis has a lump on his head but his vision is unaffected and the arrow wound is slight. It may be that he has taken a fever but—" the doctor shrugged philosophically ''—with your excellent care, Miss Shaw, I am certain he will be up and about within a se'nnight!''

Thea stared. She had not thought of this, had not really thought beyond the necessity to get Jack out of the rain and seen by the doctor. But for him to have to remain in bed, and for it to be her bed…

''But he cannot stay here!'' she said, appalled. ''My dear Dr. Ryland, that is quite improper! You know that there is no one here but my family and Mrs. Skeffington. Surely you could arrange to move him to the Lamb and Rabbit.''

Dr. Ryland drained his glass of wine and put it down on the drawing room table. He was shaking his head. ''Lord Merlin cannot be moved at present, my dear. Leaving aside his injury, which would be aggravated by movement, there is the blow to the head. Besides, it is raining and that may encourage the fever. There are many ways that Lord Merlin's condition could deteriorate!''

Thea pressed her hands together. ''Then what is to be done?''

''We can only watch his progress over the next few days and see how soon he is recovered,'' the doctor said. ''Besides, would you condemn Lord Merlin to Mrs. Prosper's somewhat…hit-and-miss nursing, my dear Miss Shaw? The poor fellow would certainly perish within the week!''

Thea gave a rueful smile. Mrs. Prosper's brand of brusqueness was admirable in the landlady of the local inn, but she had little time for invalids and her cooking was desperately bad. Even so, Thea felt most awkward. She did not wish to appear inhospitable but she could not explain to Dr. Ryland that what she dreaded about having Jack Merlin in the house was nothing to do with the expense or the propriety of the arrangement and everything to do with Jack himself and the way he made her feel.

"Besides," Dr. Ryland said cheerfully, picking up his bag and heading toward the door, "you have the valet, Hodges, to help with the nursing. He seems a most accomplished fellow—has been in the Marquis's service some ten years, I understand." His shoulders shook slightly. "By George, the things he must have seen—"

Thea waved the doctor off, having extracted a promise from him that he would call the next day, and went slowly up the stairs and along the landing to visit her unwanted guest. Her hand was raised to knock on the bedroom door when she heard voices from within and instinctively froze, listening.

"So what do you think of the place then, Hodges?" That was Jack, sounding none the worse for his adventure. "Somewhat picturesque, eh? I feel my opinion of the country undergoing a change, you know!"

"It is most charming, my lord," the valet returned.

"As is Miss Shaw," Jack added lazily. "She is quite an original, you know, Hodges, with her quaint notions and her fancy dress!"

Thea looked down. It was just conceivable that the ancient wedding gown could have been mistaken for fancy dress but her old gray muslin certainly could not. She bristled.

"She seems a most pleasant and accomplished lady," Hodges replied woodenly.

Thea heard Jack yawn. "Damned pretty, too, though I understand from Bertie that the situation is not precisely as my father imagined."

"Just so, my lord." There was distinct disapproval in

the valet's tone now. "One can scarce imagine a lady such as Miss Shaw trapping a gentleman into marriage."

Thea drew a sharp breath, the color flaming to her face. So that was what the Duke of Merlin had thought when he had heard of her wedding to Bertie! She blushed all the harder to think that he had not been far out in his assessment.

There was a noise close at hand and Thea came to her senses and knocked loudly and hastily on the bedroom door. The voices within stopped immediately and Hodges opened the door to her. She thought that she detected a shade of embarrassment in his manner.

"Good afternoon, madam." He slipped past her. "Excuse me. I shall leave you to speak with his lordship alone."

This was not precisely what Thea had intended, but it was too late to stop Hodges, who was already halfway down the stairs. Thea went into the room and made sure to leave the door open.

Jack was sitting up against the pillows, looking faintly comical in one of her father's old nightshirts. Evidently his traveling bag had contained nothing so practical as night attire, and Thea wondered faintly if he actually wore anything when he was asleep, then hastily tried to think of something else. Unfortunately the ancient linen of the late Mr. Shaw's shirt concealed little and only served to emphasize Jack's muscled physique and superb form. Thea hastily averted her eyes, telling herself primly that she should be more concerned about whether or not Jack was running a fever rather than giving herself a temperature simply through looking at him. He gave her a faint smile that only served to make her feel warmer still and she just managed to prevent herself from turning tail and rushing from the room.

''I am sorry to be an additional burden on your household, Miss Shaw,'' he said politely. ''I shall try to be as little trouble as possible.''

Thea doubted it. ''I am sorry that my sister shot you, my lord,'' she replied equally formally. ''It is all most unfortunate.''

Jack smiled. ''Well, I suppose it was a little unorthodox of her, but then yours is hardly an ordinary family!'' His smile faded and Thea thought that he actually looked slightly discomfited. ''I meant what I said, Miss Shaw. I do not intend to be a…a financial burden to you.'' He met her eyes, and looked away. ''Forgive me for broaching such a confoundedly delicate subject.''

''I see no need for apologies, my lord,'' Thea said sharply. ''It is but a few hours since you offered me plenty of money and your guineas are more than enough to bespeak the best medical care and hospitality for the next few days!''

Jack winced. ''*Touché,* Miss Shaw! I can only beg your pardon once again for assuming in so unsubtle a manner that I knew your price.''

Thea's eyes narrowed. She did not like the implication of that. ''I thought that I had made it clear that I could not be bought, my lord.''

There was a cynical light in Jack's eyes. He pulled a face. ''Come now, Miss Shaw. Your price may be above rubies but any commodity can be bought—even innocence! It is a question of finding the right currency.''

Thea's eyes turned a stormy blue. ''And am I to understand that you think you will find my…currency, my lord?''

Jack laughed. ''It should not be so difficult! Bertie has told me something of your circumstances and how much you would do for your family. There is your brother…Ned, is it? The one who wishes to be a soldier... A commission for him in a good regiment would be a fine thing, and such matters take influence as well as money. With my connections I could arrange such a thing as easily as breathing!" His blue eyes mocked her. "You see, Miss Shaw, it is not very hard to find a weakness to exploit..."

Thea found that she was shaking. She pressed her hands together, then put them behind her back to ensure that she did not hit an injured man.

"That is just bribery by another name, Lord Merlin! It does not impress me. Nor do I believe that you will find breathing so easy when I smother you with a pillow!"

Jack's wicked grin deepened. He leaned forward. "Very well then, Miss Shaw. How about an old-fashioned wager? No bribery or blackmail involved. Just my...expertise...against your virtue. What do you say?"

Thea gave him a scornful look. "That will be easy, my lord. You are scarce irresistible!"

Jack inclined his head. "I am willing to believe that you will prove that," he said easily. "How piquant, to pit goodness against—"

"Wickedness!" Thea finished for him. "I cannot believe you so devoid of any sense of morality, my lord! It is most disturbing!"

Jack laughed. "Perhaps you can redeem me, my sweet Theodosia."

"You need not start immediately!" Thea said sharply. "I should warn you that I am on my guard, my lord."

"That's good..." Somehow Jack had taken her hand and his warm touch was already undermining her defenses. She snatched her hand away and straightened the already straight bedclothes in an attempt to cover her confusion. She hoped that Jack would feel too weary to continue the conversation, but unfortunately he did not appear in the least bit affected by his injury.

"This is quite an unusual establishment, is it not?" he continued. "Do you have no older relatives living with you, Miss Shaw?"

Thea pursed her lips. "No, my lord. I am quite old enough to run an establishment on my own."

Jack raised his brows. "In the light of our conversation, I was thinking more of the propriety of such a situation—"

"Oh, I am well known in the neighborhood as a respectable spinster!" Thea said with spirit.

Jack gave a derisive laugh. "I do not doubt it, my dear Miss Shaw, but wearing a lace cap scarcely convinces me that you are in your dotage. Surely you are forever fending off the advances of unsuitable men."

"Not at all, my lord," Thea said, plumping his pillows with unnecessary force. "At the least, not before you arrived here. Such things seldom happen in the country and as I said, my reputation is of the most respectable. Besides, I have Mrs. Skeffington to lend me countenance."

"Oh, the hatchet-faced female who acts as your housekeeper? She doesn't approve of me, you know."

"One can scarcely blame her," Thea said hotly. "And anyway, Skeffie is the dearest creature imaginable. She has taken care of us all since our father died."

"Yes—" the laughter left Jack's eyes briefly "—I heard that Mr. Shaw died only six months ago. I am very sorry."

There was unmistakable sincerity in his tone. Thea swallowed hard, wishing that she had not raised the subject in the first place. Jack was confusing her, one moment so infuriatingly arrogant and the next so perceptive. She suspected darkly that it was all part of his planned seduction. He would lull her into thinking that he was not so bad after all, undermine her already-shaky defenses, destroy her resolution and seduce her ruthlessly. Thea shivered at the prospect, and not entirely from horror. She started to tidy the bedside table with a certain fierce energy.

"Thank you, my lord."

"A shotgun accident, I understand," Jack pursued gently. "I am sorry if my own accident raised any difficult memories."

Thea looked at him swiftly, then away. The last thing she wanted to explain to him was that pulling the arrow out of his shoulder had been so difficult because she still remembered trying to staunch the flow of blood from her father's injuries. That would make her just too vulnerable. She changed the subject rather abruptly. "Are you quite comfortable here, my lord?"

Jack accepted the change in the conversation gracefully, although Thea had the unnerving feeling that he also understood the reason for it. That blue gaze was very searching and she knew she had to defend herself better against it. Then she saw a wicked glint come into Jack's eyes, which was more unsettling still.

"Yes, I thank you, I am most comfortable. This is a very pleasant room. Yours, I imagine? If you wish to share it with me..."

Thea compressed her lips. Dealing with his flirtation was as difficult as coping with his insight.

"I shall just remove some of my possessions, my lord," she said pointedly, "and leave you to sleep."

She was very conscious of Jack's gaze resting on her as she moved about the room, collecting her bottles from the top of the dressing table and her clothes from out of the cupboard. She hesitated before going to the armada chest to take out her underwear but she had little choice. With her hands full of chemises and stockings she skirted the bed and edged toward the door.

"You need not be shy of my seeing your underwear, Miss Shaw," Jack said softly. "I am sure I have seen items far more shocking."

"I am sure you have!" Thea snapped, trying to hide them behind her skirts and only succeeding in scattering her stockings across the bedside rug.

"Your practical clothing is far more respectable than the apparel I am accustomed to seeing," Jack continued. "Though I can imagine what you would look like in something more…provocative…."

"Pray do not exercise your imagination so!" Thea glared at him. "You are outrageous, my lord."

"And you are so charming to tease! I feel such a slow convalescence coming on, by which time I am convinced that I will have persuaded you to share more than just the secrets of your underwear…."

"You are more likely to find yourself sharing the moat with the swans than my bed!"

Thea vented her feelings by going out and slamming the bedroom door behind her. It was becoming a habit and a very damaging one, since the whole house was so old and neglected that it might fall down around her ears. She could still hear Jack laughing as she made her way down the corridor. The sound was disturbing and her heart sank to think of him occupying her bedroom for another week. Something told her that he was going to be a very difficult patient indeed, and then there was the matter of the wager. Thea paused, leaning against the paneled wall of the corridor for a moment and closing her eyes. It mattered not one whit whether or not she had accepted Jack Merlin's challenge, for he would try to seduce her, anyway. Just for the fun of it, just for the thrill of the chase, just because he was a rake. Thea's shoulders slumped. She was not at all sure that she could resist.

Chapter Four

"You will not be able to keep Lord Merlin in bed for much longer, you know, Thea."

Thea jumped, her book sliding off her knee. Had Clementine but known it, her words summoned up all kinds of visions in her sister's overactive mind. Tending to Jack over the past three days had been absolute purgatory, not because he had been a troublesome patient but because of the sheer overwhelming effect of his presence. It had been exactly as she had feared—only worse.

Jack had developed a fever initially but after it had subsided, he had grown bored of his own company and had wanted to talk. It had been difficult, for Thea found that he asked all manner of perceptive questions and challenged her assumptions on a variety of topics in a manner that no one had done since her father had died. In a strange way it was very similar to the sparring matches she had had with Mr. Shaw, but in another way it had been far more stimulating—and exciting. She would become engrossed in their discussion, then would look up and find Jack watching her steadily. In an instant she would lose the thread of her thoughts and feel herself blushing whilst that lazy, dark blue gaze swept over her so searchingly that she was sure he could read her thoughts.

Their discussions had also been a revelation of Jack himself, for Thea knew that many of her greatest assumptions had been made about him and his lifestyle, and not one of them had survived. Well, she had dismissed all but one. She was still utterly convinced that he was a dangerous rake and that given the right circumstances, he would prove it. The wager was always at the back of her mind, an unspoken thought, troubling her, and the fact that Jack made no overt move to seduce her simply added to her concern. She could not afford to trust him.

Then there were the difficulties engendered by Jack's physical presence. Thea had been happy—relieved, even—to leave the practical nursing to Hodges, who had tended his master with exemplary skill and was fast becoming one of the household to boot.

Then, two nights previously, Thea had heard a sound on the landing and, thinking it was Daisy sleepwalking, had got up to investigate. She had found Jack, his fever returned, about to tumble down the staircase. There had been no time to call Hodges—she had had to catch Jack and support him back to bed, whereupon he had fallen in a heap on the covers and had pulled her down with him. It had taken her some time to extricate herself from his embrace, particularly since her efforts were so halfhearted because the weight of his body on hers was so peculiarly exciting. The whole experience had been deeply disturbing, and if Thea had not known that Jack was ill, she would have been convinced that he had done it on purpose. As it was, he had seemed unconscious throughout and after she had gently bathed his face, she went back to bed and lay awake for hours, tormented by the memory of his touch, the scent of his skin and the warmth of his body.

After that she had not been to visit his room for two days. She dared not.

Thea bent to retrieve her book and looked over the top of her glasses at her sister. "Whatever can you mean, Clemmie? I am not deliberately confining the Marquis of Merlin to his bed—"

"Pshaw!" Clementine snorted. Thea did not even trouble to admonish her. "You know you persuaded Hodges to keep the Marquis in his chamber today when Dr. Ryland said that he was quite well enough to get up! I do believe that you would lock him in if you could. You are afraid of what will happen once he is loose about the house."

"That is a most unfortunate turn of phrase to apply to a man of Lord Merlin's reputation," Thea said, trying not to giggle. "Besides, you make him sound like a wild animal, Clemmie, dangerous to the rest of us."

"Dangerous only to you, I believe," her sister said calmly. "You know he has you in his sights."

"I know no such thing!" Thea said hastily, wondering how Clementine could possibly have guessed. "I am only concerned that Lord Merlin should not overtax his strength, and once he is recovered he will be gone from here anyway. It is quite straightforward."

Clementine muttered something that sounded considerably ruder than "fustian," but Thea chose to ignore it and read on in a dignified silence. After a few moments she gave a sigh and cast her book down again.

"Oh, this is ridiculous! No matter how many moneymaking schemes I read about I can see a flaw in every one! At this rate Harry will have to become a climbing boy and Clara and Daisy can sell flowers in the street, whilst you and I will be teaching spoiled brats their letters and Ned will be apprenticed to some backstreet lawyer!''

Clementine put down her own book on the pedestal next to another of the sculptures that the late Mr. Shaw had delighted in. Thea was intrigued to see that the book was Mrs. Kitty Cuthbertson's *Santo Sebastiano* rather than her sister's favorite, Mary Wollstonecraft's *A Vindication of the Rights of Women.* She wondered why her sister had suddenly taken to reading romance and hoped that it was not because Clementine was developing a *tendre* for the Marquis. That would become too intolerably complicated. Thea could cope with her own foolish feelings but not Clementine's, as well.

''Well, it might not be so terrible to work for a living,'' Clementine said slowly. ''Only Harry is too big to be a sweep's boy now for he would get stuck up the chimney, and Clara suffers from sneezing fits when she is near flowers—''

''There is no need to be so literal,'' Thea snapped. ''I am sure I shall come up with something, even if it is only to sell lavender pillows or royal jelly! Oh, if only we possessed something valuable to sell.'' She took a deep breath, anxious not to add further credence to her sister's view that she was on edge about Jack's presence in the house. Her eye fell on the book again.

''What do you think of Mrs. Cuthbertson's writing, Clemmie? It is much lighter than your usual read, is it not?''

''It is all very well.'' Clementine wrinkled up her nose. ''Hodges recommended it to me, you know. He is a great reader of contemporary romances, but I find there are a little too many sentimental parts for my liking.'' She laughed. ''The hero is forever swooning at the lady's feet, you know, and how impractical is that? I fear romance is vastly overrated, Thea! Perhaps you would have done better to marry Mr. Pershore, after all!''

Jack woke suddenly, wondering where he was. For a moment he lay still, taking in the pale candlelight and the worn bed hangings, the daylight fading beyond the windows. Then he remembered. He was at Oakmantle Hall—had been there for almost seven days now—and though the fever had not yet carried him off, the starvation diet certainly would. And soon.

On the first evening after his accident, Thea had sent Hodges up with a bowl of gruel, which Jack had immediately sent back with a demand for a bottle of port and a side of beef. Ten minutes later the gruel had reappeared in Thea's own hands and she had made it abundantly clear that unless he ate it he would receive nothing else at all. Jack had submitted with an ill grace but the starvation diet had continued with a thin soup the following day and bread and cheese the day after, until Jack had wondered if it was simply that Thea's household budget could not afford anything better, the golden guineas notwithstanding. When Hodges had explained that this was Mrs. Skeffington's view of a healthy diet for a convalescent, Jack had been unimpressed, and whether it was the effect of his illness or the unaccustomed frugality of his meals, he had been unable to drag himself from the bed and had been disgusted at his weakness.

He had also been bitterly disappointed that Thea had not been in to see him for the past two days. She had accompanied the doctor upstairs on his visits—Jack had heard her voice outside the door—but she had not been into the room since the third night, the night when she had rescued him from falling down the stairs. Despite his fever, Jack could remember the details of that encounter in vivid detail, the softness of her body beneath his on the bed, the sweet scent of lavender in her clothes and hair, and the way she had extricated herself with what seemed regretful slowness from his embrace... He smiled a little. He had been too ill to take advantage, which was a shame in a way, but he would have needed to be near death not to have appreciated the experience.

Except that Thea had not been to see him since. Perhaps she was only acting out of propriety, or perhaps she was embarrassed at what had happened between them, but whatever the cause, it was deeply frustrating. He wanted to see her, to talk to her. It was a troubling realization for a rake, but he was forced to admit that he missed their discussions, which had broached topics from the London Season to the writings of Shakespeare. He had never crossed swords with a bluestocking before and he had found it a stimulating experience, almost as stimulating as holding her in his arms. But perhaps she would bring his food that night...

On the thought of food, he rolled over and sat up. And blinked.

There was a vision sitting on the end of his bed, a tiny angel. For a second Jack wondered whether he had died in his sleep and whether this was as a direct result of requesting that Hodges smuggle him in an illicit bottle of brandy. When he considered the angel more carefully, however, he realized that she was clutching a ragged toy sheep in one hand and looked about five years old. She also looked a lot like Thea, a miniature version, with tiny fair corkscrew curls and huge blue eyes. Perhaps Thea had looked like this as a child, or perhaps this was what a child of Thea's would look like. Jack felt something twist inside him at the thought. A child with fair curls and a cherubic smile… He grimaced. His illness was turning him quite ludicrously maudlin.

"Hello!" the angel said.

"Hello," Jack replied.

"Thea says that you're trouble," the angel announced, fixing him with a stern blue stare. "She says that we're not to see you."

Jack felt hurt at this apparent treachery. Did Miss Shaw really consider him a monster with whom her younger siblings were not safe? His own sisters had always praised him as a most indulgent uncle even though he had had no thoughts of setting up his own nursery— until now.

He smiled at the angel. "I think that you must be Daisy."

A nod was his only reply. Daisy was still weighing him up.

"So if your sister told you not to come here, Daisy, what are you doing?"

There was a pause. "Seeing for myself," Daisy said solemnly.

Jack grinned. It seemed that Clementine was not the only one who had absorbed Mrs. Shaw's philosophy of independence! If Thea thought that she had problems with her sisters already it seemed that her troubles were only beginning. He raised his eyebrows.

"And what do you think?"

Daisy was in no hurry to commit herself. Her corn-flower-blue eyes appraised him thoroughly and Jack found himself holding his breath.

"You look very nice," Daisy said. Her rosebud mouth curved into a smile and she crawled toward him across the bedcover. When she reached his side she simply held her arms out.

"Cuddle," she said.

After a moment of frozen incomprehension, Jack shifted obligingly so that she was curved into the circle of his good arm, her golden curls brushing his shoulder, the toy sheep clutched against his chest. Now that he could see it more closely, he realized that it was moth-eaten and more than a little chewed. No doubt toys in the Shaw household had to last from one child to the next and were never thrown away. He watched as Daisy yawned suddenly and her eyelids flickered closed.

"Story," she said.

Jack's mind was suddenly, frighteningly blank. Although he was indeed a generous uncle, his indulgence had never stretched to telling his nephews and nieces bedtime stories. After all, it was hardly his place. There were nursemaids aplenty to do such a thing. He looked down at Daisy and after a moment she opened her eyes again and frowned at him.

"Story!" she said again, slightly more querulous this time.

Jack felt panic rise in him. He glanced toward the door, but there was no sound from the landing, no rescue at hand.

"Er...does Thea tell you stories?" he asked, playing for time.

Daisy nodded. Her hair tickled his nose. "Stories 'bout the fairies in the garden."

Fairies. Jack took a deep breath, trusting to magic himself. "They live in the garden but you can't see them, can you?"

"S'right." Daisy snuggled down again. "Cos it's magic."

Jack relaxed slightly. He seemed to be on the right track. He dredged his memory for anything that he could recall about the Oakmantle gardens. It was a shame that he had not seen them properly. There were the trees, of course, and there was also the moat...

"Has Thea told you about the water sprites who live in the moat?" he asked.

Daisy shook her head a little. "No..." She sounded sleepy but willing to give him a chance. "Tell..."

Jack started cautiously on a tale about the water sprites who shared the moat with the swans and ducks. He invented a castle for them under the water and a feud with the goblins in the oak trees that had led to much magic and mayhem. He was about to launch into the story of the fairy princess who had been kidnapped and rescued by the sprites, when he felt Daisy shift and relax further into his arms, her breathing soft, deeply asleep.

Jack stopped speaking and looked down at her. Her cheeks were flushed pink, her rosebud lips parted. His arm felt warm and damp and he was tolerably sure that she was dribbling slightly as she slept.

Jack sat still, afraid to move in case he woke her. He wondered why his sisters never told their children bedtime stories when surely it was one of the best bits of having a child. That led him to wondering why the fashionable farmed their children out at every available opportunity and if they knew what they were missing. The warm weight of the child in his arms seemed to load him down with love. He almost decided that he wanted one of his own, but his mind shied away from the implications of that particular thought.

Daisy and Clara and Harry and Ned and Clementine. His heart ached suddenly for Thea, trying to do the best she could as a substitute mother for her siblings. If he could help her... Jack shook his head, as if to dispel the thought forcibly. That was the trouble with the country—

he had always sworn that it addled the brain and here was the proof.

There was a step on the landing and the door was pushed wider. Thea herself stood in the doorway, a white apron over her dress, her face flushed, the hair escaping from her cap, as it always seemed wont to do.

"Oh!" She saw the sleeping child in Jack's arms and lowered her voice to a whisper, "I am so sorry! I have been looking everywhere for her! It's just that she sleep-walks sometimes—"

"She just wanted a bedtime story," Jack said softly.

Thea's eyes met his. Hers were very dark and unreadable. "Did you tell her one?"

"I did indeed. Fairies and sprites and kidnapped princesses..."

He saw her smile. "I should have liked to hear that."

Jack grinned at her. "I would gladly tell you a bedtime story anytime you wish, Miss Shaw!"

He saw the blush that came into her cheek, but she did not answer. She leant down to take Daisy from him. Her sleeve brushed his cheek. He could smell her scent, lavender and roses, faint and elusive. Jack shifted, pretending that he was simply moving his arms now that the weight of the child was removed. Perhaps it was just hunger that was making him light-headed, or perhaps it was something more.

"You have not been to see me," he observed lightly, watching as Thea scooped Daisy expertly into the crook of her arm. "I could have died in here for all that you knew..."

"No doubt Hodges would have told me if that had happened," Thea said calmly. She smiled at him suddenly and Jack felt his pulse rate increase. This fever was proving damnably stubborn to shift, or perhaps that was something else, too.

"However," she continued, "I am happy to see that you are far from death's door."

"Are you?" Jack quirked one dark brow. "Then why have you been avoiding me, Miss Shaw?"

"I must go," she said hurriedly. "Daisy will wake—"

"But you have not answered my question!" Jack protested. "Surely you are not afraid to be alone with me, Miss Shaw!"

There was a pause. "Not afraid, precisely, my lord," Thea said slowly, "but I have not forgotten your reputation. Now if you will excuse me—"

"A moment." Jack touched the back of her hand and she paused by the side of the bed. His tone was unwontedly serious. "Why did you tell the children that they were not to see me? Am I then *so* disreputable that you think I am not fit company for them?"

"Oh!" He heard Thea catch her breath. "It was not that, Lord Merlin. I simply wished you to have undisturbed rest and I thought that if the children pestered you…"

"You have permitted Bertie to visit me," Jack pointed out.

"That was different. Besides, I wished to make my peace with Bertie myself."

Jack raised an eyebrow. "So that is why he has had the best of your attention and I have had nothing myself."

Daisy stirred then, murmuring in her sleep. "I must go," Thea said again. Jack let his hand fall to his side and watched as she walked slowly to the door.

"Miss Shaw?"

She paused in the doorway. "Yes, Lord Merlin?"

Jack grinned. "Is there gruel for dinner tonight?"

He saw the answering smile gleam in Thea's eyes before she wiped it clean away. "No. Mrs. Skeffington has prepared a nourishing mutton stew for you. Oh, and Lord Merlin…"

"Miss Shaw?"

"I have confiscated the bottle of brandy that you asked your valet to bring up. It is not healthy. But if you are very good I shall allow you one glass of homemade elderberry wine." And she closed the door very softly behind her.

Jack lay back on the pillows, a smile curling his mouth. Theodosia Shaw. She might have the upper hand at the moment whilst he was laid low in so inconvenient a manner, but tomorrow he was determined to leave his bed and then she would not find it so easy to avoid him. Then he would progress his acquaintance with Miss Shaw. He was looking forward to it immensely.

"It is plain as a pikestaff that you are still avoiding Lord Merlin!" Clementine said bluntly, helping Thea to gather up the bunches of daffodils that they had just cut for the house. "You denied it before, but you know that it is true and you *know* it is because you like him!"

Thea paused, her flower basket over one arm. It was a beautiful morning and she had decided at once to go out into the fresh air for she found that being cooped up in the house only seemed to encourage the feelings of restlessness that she had suffered of late. And Clementine, with her usual sharp observation, had immediately identified the reason why her sister was feeling so on edge—the Marquis of Merlin.

In truth Thea could find very little to dispute in Clementine's words, for she *had* been avoiding Jack, particularly since he had become active again and was wont to pop up in all sorts of unexpected places. She knew he was deliberately seeking her out, and it was all very strange and disconcerting, all the more so since she could not ignore the speculative intensity of that dark blue gaze when it rested on her so warmly, nor the enjoyment she derived from his company. She felt as though she were being hunted—gently, patiently but relentlessly, and the feeling engendered a mixture of fascination and excitement. She knew she was being drawn into a trap, and it was one that she had to avoid, though she had little desire to do so.

"I think Lord Merlin likes you very much, too," Clementine added slyly, and Thea knew she was blushing and felt vexed.

"Lord Merlin is most amiable to everyone," she said, trying to sound indifferent. They started to walk back toward the house, their skirts swishing through the long grass. "He has been giving Harry some coaching on his cricket."

"And talking to Clara about music."

"And telling Daisy bedtime stories." Despite herself, Thea felt a smile starting.

"And chatting to Skeffie about recipes!" Clementine finished with a giggle. "She has quite altered her opinion of him, you know, and praises him to the heavens!"

Thea laughed, as well. "That, at least, is self-interest on Lord Merlin's part! I believe he finds our diet sadly circumscribed and is longing for a side of sirloin and several bottles of port!"

They had reached the edge of the park and paused to look across the moat to the house. The golden stones of Oakmantle Hall glowed warm in the sunlight. The ducks were quacking on the water and the swans stretched their wings in the sun.

"Lord Merlin has also been speaking to Ned…" Thea spoke hesitantly. "About joining the army, you know."

"Capital!" Clementine gave a little skip. "Ned has always wanted to be a soldier and if Lord Merlin can help."

"Ned should be going to university!" Thea said shortly. "And don't say 'capital,' Clemmie—it should not form part of a lady's vocabulary!"

"Stuff!" her sister said, clearly unimpressed. "You know that Ned has no time for book learning and has set his heart on following the drum! If Papa had not died so untimely—"

"I will not allow Lord Merlin to buy a commission for Ned!" Thea's words came out in a rush. "I could not bear to be so beholden to him." It was impossible to explain to Clementine the conversation she had had with Jack that first day, when he had spoken of there being a price for everything and used Ned's example to make his point. It only served to prove that he could not be sincere now.

Clementine was looking at her curiously. "Why not? He is influential and you would not think twice if there were another sponsor for Ned!"

Thea's hand tightened on the basket. "Lord Merlin is different. He…I… He might expect…"

"Something in return for his generosity?"

"Clemmie!"

Clementine took off her bonnet and swung it by the ribbons in a casual manner that Thea considered deplorable. Not for the first time she felt hopelessly incapable of controlling her sister.

"Has Lord Merlin made such a suggestion to you, Thea?"

"Yes!" Thea said, goaded. "Several times!"

Clementine's eyes widened. "Glory! Oh, lucky you!"

"Clementine Shaw!"

Clementine did a little skip. "Well, I must leave you to fight the matter out with Lord Merlin himself, for I see him coming this way! I am sorry that I cannot stay to protect you!" She took the basket of daffodils from her sister and sped off toward the house before Thea could say a word.

Thea turned her head. Jack was indeed walking toward her, one of the spaniels panting at his heels. In Thea's father's day there had been a whole pack of dogs at Oakmantle but there were only three left now and this was the oldest and most arthritic of them all. Thea was certain that Jack had slowed his pace to allow the ancient creature to keep up and she smiled. Really he was very kind and, confusingly, that made him far more dangerous to her.

She thought that Jack was still looking a little pale, but he was immaculately elegant in gleaming black top boots, pristine white linen and a green hunting jacket that was the epitome of good taste. He was bare-headed and the morning sunshine made his dark hair gleam with tawny and gold. Feeling a certain shortness of breath that she knew was nothing to do with her exertions out walking, Thea decided that she had to be firm with him before he undermined her defenses completely.

"Good morning, my lord," she murmured as he reached her side, "did you come equipped for a long stay in the country, or do you always come accompanied by a baggage train?"

Jack smiled and Thea's heart did a little leap. He took

her hand and her pulse rate increased still further. She tried to tug her hand away; he retained it, tucking it through his arm as he fell into step beside her.

"To tell the truth, it is only Hodges's ingenuity that has kept me so well turned out," he said ruefully. "I shall soon be reduced to asking Bertie for a loan of his linen. And one of his coats."

"I doubt that it would fit you—" Thea began thoughtlessly, then flushed scarlet as she realized she was expressing a view on a matter a lady should not even have considered let alone articulated. It was all very well for her to notice Jack's impressive physique—how could she avoid it?—but to give away the fact that she had been studying him... She saw him smile, felt the warmth of that midnight-blue gaze trap and hold hers, and cursed herself.

"I am flattered that you should have been observing me so closely, Miss Shaw," he drawled, proving to Thea that any opportunity she gave him would be exploited to the full. "Should you wish to continue your inspection, I am at your service."

Thea was determined to not be easy game for his teasing. "Indeed, my lord? But will I have the chance? Surely you will be leaving us now that you are so well recovered."

Jack gave her a limpid look. "Alas, Miss Shaw, traveling could be very dangerous to one of my enfeebled constitution."

To Thea's mind, feeble was the very last thing that he looked. Rakish, perhaps. Dangerous, definitely. But feeble—the idea was ridiculous.

"I am sorry that your lordship is not in better health by now," she said politely. "Perhaps you should go inside and rest? Further exercise might prove fatal to one of so weak a disposition."

"Oh, I believe in exerting myself a little more each day, Miss Shaw," Jack said with a devastating smile, "and I have not yet reached my target for this morning. Speaking of which, is your sister planning further archery practice today? If so, perhaps I might prevail on you to show me the herb garden, where we will be safe?"

Thea gave him a suspicious look, wondering what had engendered in him this newfound interest in gardening. She was certain that it was a pretense, but on the other hand it seemed churlish to refuse him, particularly as Clementine had taken the basket of flowers, and with it any excuse Thea might have had for going back inside.

They crossed the moat by a little wooden footbridge that led straight into the remains of the Oakmantle formal gardens, where Thea had only recently pruned the rosebushes for the coming season. Jack opened the gate at the end of the bridge for her, handing her through. His touch was light and warm and it filled Thea with an acute physical awareness. He was watching her, his gaze steady on her face, and she found she could not look away.

"We collect the rose petals from the bushes here in the summer," Thea said, a little at random, to cover her confusion. "We dry them to scent drawers and chests and…and things. And we grow herbs for eating and for perfume, as well, especially lavender…" She was rambling; she knew she was, and Jack's next words did nothing to calm her.

"So that explains why your bedclothes are scented with lavender," he said softly. His voice dropped. "And you are, too…"

Thea felt a rush of heat under her skin. The lavender scent was all around them, faint but disturbing.

"My lord, you should not say such things."

"Should I not?" Jack's voice had roughened. "I remember from the time I held you...after the wedding. And later..."

Thea moved away, along the path where the line of ragged lavender was starting to show its new spring growth. Her heart was racing, beating so loudly that she was surprised that Jack could not hear it. She could hear his steps behind her on the gravel; he was following her and she had a sudden and ridiculous urge to escape him, to run away. Unfortunately the path she was following led only to the fishpond and to flee she would have to scramble through the shrubbery on the far side. Common sense returned quickly. She was hardly in any danger and would simply walk back the way she had come. On this eminently sensible thought she turned to face Jack. And stopped.

He was a bare three steps away from her and there was something in the way he was standing—something cool, something watchful—that warned her exactly what would happen next. Jack was going to kiss her and she...

Thea felt the last vestige of sensible thought drift away from her as Jack's lips touched hers. He took immediate advantage with a long, exploratory kiss that sent a jolt of pure desire through her body from head to toes. His arms went around her. He tasted of fresh air and something indefinable and far more intoxicating, and his skin smelled of sandalwood. After a moment, Thea found herself raising her arms to encircle his neck and hold him to her.

The kiss was softer and more persuasive than the one in the drawing room, coaxing a response from her rather than demanding one. Yet underneath the gentle surface was something that made Thea shiver. It was both a threat and a promise. He was drawing closer to his goal all the time. And she knew exactly what that goal would be.

It was a long time before Jack let her go, steadying her with a hand on her arm as she stepped back—and came down to earth. Thea frowned, trying to gather her thoughts, which seemed to have scattered like straw in the wind. She looked at Jack. He looked expressionlessly back at her.

"It goes against the grain with me, but do you wish me to apologize for my behavior, Miss Shaw?"

"No…" Thea had been brought up to be truthful and just at that moment it was a severe trial to her. "It is not a matter of blame—"

Jack's hand tightened on her arm and for a moment she thought he was about to pull her to him again. "A matter of pleasure, then?"

"No!" Thea stepped back abruptly. "That is—yes, but—"

"But no one has kissed you like that before and you are startled at the results?" To Thea's ears Jack sounded odiously complacent even if what he was saying was true. She drew breath to give him a much belated set-down.

"Certainly it is true that I have not been kissed by a rake before! At least not before you kissed me the first time, sir!"

"And did you like it?"

Thea frowned stormily. "Pray stop asking difficult questions, my lord!"

"So you did. Would you like to do it again?"

"No!" Thea backed away. It was the first direct lie

that she had told in a very long time and she knew at once that he did not believe her. He caught first one hand and then the other, trapping them both in one of his and bringing them up against his chest.

"Oh, Miss Shaw!" That dazzling blue gaze caught and held hers. "I had formed the opinion that you were always truthful yet now I have forced you into falsehood. It seems I am closer to corrupting innocence than I had realized…"

Thea knew that it was absolutely imperative to break free. She did not move. This time Jack bent his head with agonizing slowness to capture her mouth with his own, the touch of his lips fierce and sweet, their demand explicit. Thea's fingers uncurled to spread against his chest. She could feel the thud of his heart against her hand. The warmth of the sun mingled with her body's heated response and she felt utterly intoxicated. And totally confused. She freed herself from his embrace and felt the reluctance with which Jack let her go. He was breathing hard and his gaze, as it rested on her face, held the same concentrated desire that Thea had seen there before. She caught her breath.

"I am going inside now, my lord. I…I need to think and I cannot do so with you near me!"

"Thinking is a vastly overrated pastime in comparison to some others," Jack drawled. He followed her up the path. "My dear Miss Shaw, is there really any necessity to think at all? Can we not try something else?"

Thea warded him off with her hands. She did not want to speak since just at the moment she had lost all her *savoir faire* and knew she would only make matters worse for herself. She certainly did not want to linger here in the scented garden, where Jack's very presence was too much temptation. Besides, she knew it was all a game to him. He was simply following the dictates of the wager, proving to her just how easy it would be for him to win... The thought hardened her resolve. She would be the greatest fool in Christendom to fall into the arms of a rake who was only looking for a little entertainment.

"Pray excuse me, my lord," she said frostily, turning on her heel. "I have many household duties to attend to."

This time Jack made no move to follow her. Everything that Thea knew about him was conflicting in her head, the good, the bad and the downright wicked. She took four steps away and stopped. There was something she had been meaning to ask him for a long time.

"Lord Merlin," she said slowly, "will you answer something for me?"

Jack made a slight gesture. "If I can."

Thea's cornflower-blue eyes were troubled. "The first day we met—when you offered me the money and told me that principles were for fools—did you really mean that?"

Their gazes held for a moment and Thea had the oddest feeling that she was trembling on the edge of some precipice she did not understand. Then Jack let out his breath on a long sigh.

"Miss Shaw, you have the most damnable way of putting a fellow on the spot!" he said ruefully. "If you will have the truth, it was one of the most foolish things that I have ever said—no, I do not believe that."

Thea's expression lightened and the pretty color came into her face. "Oh, thank you!" she said.

Jack watched her until her upright figure disappeared around the side of the house, then he drove his hands into his jacket pockets and followed the way that she had gone. He whistled softly under his breath as he walked. Good God, how had that happened? He had been utterly in control, within an ace of winning his wager, yet Miss Theodosia Shaw had almost brought him to his knees with her devastating combination of honesty and innocence. He had no notion how it had happened but he could deny it no longer. He could fight it, perhaps, but the outcome was uncertain. Suddenly he was a rake who felt dangerously close to reform.

He shook his head slightly. If anyone had suggested such a thing to him a few days before he would have laughed them out of court. His parents had been nagging him to marry these five years past and he had always rejected the idea with scorn, preferring the transient enjoyment of a series of *affaires* with women who played by the same rules as he. Yet now his rules appeared to have changed when he had not been paying attention. Jack sighed. If he had learned one thing in life it was not to fight against fate. And he had a feeling that his fate was just about to catch up with him.

Chapter Five

"Sorry, Thea old thing, but it's dashed difficult!" Bertie avoided Thea's eyes and fidgeted on the rose brocade sofa. "I'd love to help you but I've a previous engagement, don't you know. In—" he closed his eyes briefly "—in Yorkshire! I'll be away above two weeks!"

Thea raised her eyebrows in patent disbelief. Bertie had always been a desperately poor liar and it was clear now that he was spinning her a tale. Now that the difficult matter of the wedding was behind them they had become friends again, but she knew there was something he was hiding from her. She decided to test him a little.

"But, Bertie, Lord Merlin is your cousin! Surely a little family feeling prompts you to offer him hospitality at Wickham…"

"Naturally I should be delighted were I to be at home," Bertie muttered, squirming, "but I've already told you I'm to go away—"

"Still trying to be rid of me, Miss Shaw?" a languid voice drawled from the doorway. Thea jumped. She had not heard Jack come in and now she blushed with vexation that he had overheard her.

She watched Jack stroll over to the carved marble

chimney piece and rest one arm negligently along the top. He was standing at the precise angle where he could most easily fix her with that penetrating blue gaze. Thea shifted uncomfortably in her chair, acutely conscious of his scrutiny and aware of the blush that stained her cheeks.

Whilst Bertie and Clementine had been with them over dinner it had been relatively easy to avoid looking at Jack too much, although it was another matter to avoid thinking about him. Thea knew that she had been tiresomely absentminded for the whole meal, aware that Jack was watching her with a mixture of amusement and speculation that was deeply disturbing. When she remembered the kisses they had shared that very afternoon… But here she abruptly dragged her thoughts away. She would not remember them, for that way led inevitably to her downfall. Accustomed to ruling her heart as much as taking care of her home and family, Thea found her inexplicable attraction to Jack Merlin excessively disturbing.

"I am sorry that I cannot oblige you with my absence sooner, Miss Shaw," Jack said smoothly. "Dr. Ryland assures me that it would be foolhardy to travel before the weekend and I am anxious to take his advice. I will, however, make myself scarce just as soon as I am able."

"Forgot to mention that we are all invited to a ball at Pendle Hall on Friday," Bertie said, brightening now that Thea's attention was diverted away from him. "Lady Pendle was most insistent, even when I explained you are still an invalid, Jack! It would crown her house party to be able to boast of your attendance."

Jack grimaced. "Well, if we must! I suppose it would be bad manners to refuse when the good lady has been sending hothouse flowers over every day to aid my recovery.''

Thea made a business of finishing her cup of tea. In her opinion Lady Pendle was an ill-bred harridan whose motive in cultivating Jack's acquaintance was all too clear. Thea had suffered the Pendles' disdain for several years. The only occasion on which she had attended a ball at Pendle Hall had been marred for her by the patronizing way in which the Pendle sons and daughters had treated her. It had quite taken the pleasure out of her evening and since then she had refused all invitations.

''I shall not be attending,'' she said forthrightly, ''and surely neither shall you, Bertie, since you will be away?''

Bertie flushed. ''Oh, of course! I shall be in Lancashire—''

''Yorkshire!'' Thea corrected gently. She got to her feet and Bertie politely followed suit. ''Good night, Bertie, and thank you for dining with us tonight. I hope that you enjoy your trip!''

Jack moved to hold the door open for her. ''I am sorry that my cousin could not help you with your problem, Miss Shaw.''

Thea looked up at him. There was a dangerously wicked twinkle in his eye that suggested that he was not sorry at all.

''On the contrary, my lord,'' she said sweetly, ''I am the one commiserating with you. You will get your just deserts at Pendle Hall! I am sure that you will find the Misses Pendle most attentive to you! Either of them would be overjoyed to attach a Marquis.''

Jack gave her a speaking look. ''Thank you, Miss Shaw. Might I not prevail upon you to accompany me then, for protection?''

Thea smiled. "Do rakes need protection from respectable ladies? I am sure you are well able to take care of yourself!"

Jack caught her hand, drawing her out into the candlelit shadows of the hall. The drawing room door swung shut behind them. "Do not be so certain of that, Miss Shaw." He squared his shoulders. "All jesting aside, do you really want me to leave Oakmantle?"

Thea flushed. "I am sorry that you heard me say that, my lord. I had not wished to sound inhospitable—" She broke off. Here was exactly the situation that she had not wished to explain, for how did she persuade Jack to go whilst keeping a secret her growing feelings for him? She could hardly tell him the truth.

"A matter of propriety, I collect, Miss Shaw?" Jack queried gently. "I realize that my presence here must seem most irregular."

"Yes!" Thea grasped gratefully at the proffered excuse. "For my own part I think the gossips to be idle troublemakers, but..."

"But you would not wish to give them fuel for speculation."

Thea frowned a little. Jack seemed to be making this a little too easy for her. "Well, no, of course..."

"Despite your respectable spinster's reputation, as confirmed by that ridiculous lace cap and the monstrous apron you have taken to wearing."

Thea, aware that he was still holding her hand, tried to snatch it away. Jack held on to it.

"My lord, if you seek only to make fun of me—"

"On the contrary." Jack smiled at her. "I am trying to do the right thing—for once. It is not a matter that has exercised my mind very often before."

"That I can well believe!" Thea said sharply. She gave her hand another experimental tug, to no avail.

"How about a bargain, then, Miss Shaw?" Jack pursued. "I shall leave Oakmantle tomorrow and move to Wickham for a short time—if you will allow me to escort you to the ball on Friday."

Thea frowned. "But if you are leaving Oakmantle you might as well leave the county altogether, my lord! Why delay?"

She could not read Jack's expression for his face was in shadow. His voice was cool. "Perhaps I do not wish to leave, Miss Shaw. Come, your answer?"

"And if I refuse to go to the ball, you will refuse to leave Oakmantle?"

"Precisely."

"How very difficult you can be, my lord! It seems a strange, quixotic idea and I told you before that I do not take kindly to blackmail."

"Call it persuasion, Miss Shaw, and you may feel more kindly disposed toward me!"

Thea shook her head. "It seems most irregular, my lord, but I suppose it can do no harm. I accept—for the sake of my reputation…"

"Of course." Jack pressed a kiss on her palm and released her. "Thank you. I will speak to Bertie about making the necessary arrangements." He passed her a candle from the stand at the bottom of the stairs.

"Good night then, my lord."

"A moment, Miss Shaw."

"Yes?" Thea's voice was a little husky. She looked into Jack's eyes, realized that he was really very close to her indeed, and moved reluctantly away from him. Jack smiled.

"I thought to mention that if you have not yet come

up with a better moneymaking scheme, you could always sell the drawing room sculptures. There are at least two by John Edward Carew that would fetch several thousand pounds in town, although the one with the chipped nose has obviously gone down in value because of the damage.'' He gave her a slight mocking bow and sauntered back to the drawing room door.

''Good night, Miss Shaw.''

Back in the drawing room, Bertie was finishing his port and preparing to leave.

''Have to go and pack for Yorkshire,'' he said gloomily as Jack reappeared, ''though why the devil I had to go and choose such a far-flung place I can't imagine! Must be touched in the attic even to think of getting involved in such a scheme!''

Jack grinned at his cousin. ''My thanks, Bertie! I owe you a favor!''

Bertie's shoulders slumped. ''Pretending to go away just so that you could stay at Oakmantle. Devil take it, Jack, I'm no hand at deception. Thea knows there's something up, you mark my words! Sharp as a needle, that girl!''

Jack laughed. ''There's no deception needed after all, Bertie. Miss Shaw and I have made a bargain. I have promised that I will remove to Wickham on the morrow in return for her agreement to accompany me to the Pendle ball.''

Bertie frowned ferociously. ''What, have I just pledged myself to a trip to Yorkshire all for nothing?''

''You can always cancel your fictitious invitation,'' his cousin said soothingly. ''And it is scarcely nothing, Bertie, unless my future happiness counts as nothing to you.''

"What exactly does constitute your future happiness, Jack? That's what worries me! Dash it, you had better be aboveboard with this. Don't mind helping you out, but if any harm comes to Thea—"

The laughter died out of Jack's eyes. He met his cousin's gaze soberly. "You can trust me, Bertie. I would do nothing to harm her."

Bertie shifted uncomfortably. "Better not. I'd call you out myself. You may be a damn fine shot, but principles are more important than…"

"Than self-preservation?" Jack laughed. "Acquit me, Bertie! I know my reputation tells against me but I plan to ask Miss Shaw to marry me."

Bertie swallowed convulsively. "Marry! You? Now I know you're in jest!"

"On my honor I swear it's true!" Jack passed his cousin the brandy bottle. "Here, take a glass before you go. You look as though you need a restorative."

Bertie sat down again. "Marry!" he said again. "Of all the mad starts—"

"I know," Jack said apologetically. "A vast comedown for a rake. But I fear I love her. It is inescapable!"

Bertie swallowed half the brandy in one go. "She'll never take you."

Jack went very still. An arrested look came into his eyes. "Why do you say that, Bertie?"

"Because she knows you're a rake!" Bertie pointed out. "She doesn't trust you. What's more," he added incontrovertibly, "she won't marry for money. I should know."

Jack sighed. Since he had just presented Thea with the reason why she need never marry for money, he could not argue.

"I thought women liked to reform a rake," he said

ruefully. "Good God, I have spent years avoiding the lures of matrimonially minded maidens in favor of other pursuits and now you're telling me that the only woman I want will not have me? Where is the justice in that?"

Bertie grinned. "About time someone gave you a set-down, Jack," he said without malice. "I reckon you've met your match at last!"

Jack drained his brandy glass. "Now that," he said, "is where we do agree, Bertie. I have indeed."

"Oh, Miss Shaw, you look so beautiful!" Mrs. Skeffington, who had removed her cook's apron to double as ladies' maid for the evening, went quite misty-eyed at the sight of her mistress dressed for the ball. "The Marquis of Merlin is here, madam," she added. "He is waiting in the drawing room."

Thea hesitated before the mirror. It was not concern about her appearance that held her, for she had sought out her only serviceable ball gown and although it was not in the first stare of fashion, it was simple and elegant. No, she knew that what was delaying her was a sudden and cowardly desire to avoid Jack.

In the two days since he had left Oakmantle she had felt quite low in spirits. In fact, she had to admit to herself that she had missed him quite prodigiously. The children had remarked upon it and she knew that they were also feeling quite dejected. They had been difficult and noisy, withdrawn and silent by turn. Ned had got into a temper when she had spoken about him finding a job in London, and had stormed out and disappeared for several hours. Daisy had burst into tears when Thea had told her that Jack was no longer able to tell her a good-night story, and Clara had spent hours playing dirges on the old piano until Thea thought her head would burst and was fit to scream with frustration. They had all missed him, but she had missed him most of all. And now Jack was here, ready to take her to the ball, and she hardly dared to face him.

She picked up her black velvet cloak and her bag and made her way slowly down the staircase. In point of fact, Jack was not in the drawing room as Mrs. Skeffington had indicated; he might have started off there but now he was waiting for her at the bottom of the stairs. He looked up at her as she descended and Thea's heart contracted as his gaze raked her from carefully arranged curls to silk slippers, before returning slowly to her face. He smiled, the old devil-may-care, wicked smile that was so dangerously attractive and Thea feared she might melt into a puddle of longing where she stood. She steeled herself.

"Good evening, Lord Merlin."

Jack inclined his head. "Good evening, Miss Shaw. It is a great pleasure to see you again. You look quite… ravishing."

There was a look in his eye that suggested that ravishment would be high on his list of preferred entertainments for that evening. With a shiver, Thea admitted to herself that the idea held considerable appeal. But this was no good. She reminded herself sternly that she had worked hard to rid Oakmantle of Jack's troublesome presence and it was her own foolish fault if she was now languishing after him like a green girl.

She accepted Jack's proffered arm and went out with him to the carriage.

Pendle Hall was a bare ten-minute journey time away, but Thea had previously given little thought to being in a closed carriage with Jack for that time. After all, ten minutes to a rake was surely plenty of time to effect a seduction. She held her breath, but Jack behaved with impeccable and frustrating courtesy for the whole journey, handing her into and out of the carriage politely, sitting as far away from her as possible and speaking only on totally uncontroversial subjects such as his improved health and the welfare of her brothers and sisters. Thea found it perversely disappointing.

The ballroom at Pendle Hall was already crowded when they arrived, for Lady Pendle had lost no time in informing all her friends and neighbors of the remarkable coup she had achieved in tempting the Marquis of Merlin to the ball. Jack's welcome was overly warm; Thea's considerably less so. At first she thought that she was imagining the slightly barbed remarks, the exaggerated withdrawing of skirts. Soon she realized she had not. Whilst Jack was forcibly dragged from her side and marched over to dance with the Misses Pendle, Thea found herself besieged.

"It must have been *such* a pleasure to have the Marquis of Merlin as a guest for an entire week, Miss Shaw," Lady Pendle, resplendent in puce velvet, was positively purring with malice. "Such a charming man but such a shocking accident! One scarce knows whether to me more alarmed at your sister's wildness in shooting the poor man in the first place, or at the thought of you entertaining a bachelor at Oakmantle quite unchaperoned!"

Thea took a deep breath. "We were scarcely entertaining the Marquis, Lady Pendle, for he was much too ill to be seeking diversion!"

Another matron pushed forward into the group. "Lord Merlin looks much recovered now, does he not, Miss Shaw? No doubt as a result of your nursing!"

Someone tittered, hiding behind their fan. Thea looked

'round the sea of faces. Some were avid, some openly disdainful. None was friendly. There was nowhere for her to seek refuge.

"My family and I were happy to be of assistance to the Marquis," she said colorlessly. "We all did what we could to help his recovery."

"And does Lord Merlin intend to stay long in Oxfordshire?" Lady Pendle pursued.

"I am not party to Lord Merlin's plans, ma'am," Thea said. She spoke coldly although she was feeling increasingly heated. "However, I believe he is soon for London."

"No doubt having exhausted the pleasures Oakmantle has to offer," another dowager said meaningfully. "I believe he tires easily—"

"One often does after an illness, ma'am," Thea said. Her temper had quite frayed away. She gathered her skirts up in one hand, about to flee the gossips but with no clear destination in mind. "If you will excuse me—"

"Care to dance, Miss Shaw?" The drawling tones of the Honorable Simon Pendle stopped her in her tracks. He was a well set-up young man who had often looked down his nose at her, but just now Thea grasped him as a lifeline.

"Thank you, Mr. Pendle!"

They moved onto the dance floor and away from the circling harpies. Thea breathed a sigh of relief. It was short-lived, however, as Simon Pendle drew closer to her than the dance steps dictated.

"So how have you got on with Merlin, Miss Shaw? Is he not a splendid fellow? Generous, too, I hear!"

Thea's eyes narrowed. Her nerves already on edge, she was still willing to believe that she had misread the freedom of his words and his tone—but only just.

"Lord Merlin has certainly been generous to my family, sir," she said coolly.

Pendle guffawed. "No need for false modesty, ma'am! I was hoping you and I might have a little chat later—sort out a few things…" He squeezed her shoulder in a disgustingly familiar manner.

"I do not believe that we have anything to discuss, Mr. Pendle," Thea said frigidly, moving away.

"Oh, come now…" As the dance drew them together again, Simon Pendle deliberately let his hand brush intimately against the side of her breast and Thea recoiled, the color flaming to her face. "I hear Merlin is to return to Town on the morrow. Then you may be more inclined to talk to me—"

Thea itched to slap him rather than speak to him. She kept her voice low but her tone was arctic.

"You mistake, sir. I have nothing to say to you!"

Pendle leered at her. "Hoity-toity miss! You won't be so quick to refuse when Merlin's money runs out—"

"Servant, Pendle. Miss Shaw, may I beg this dance?" Jack's voice cut smoothly through Simon Pendle's insults and through the angry words clamoring for release in Thea's head. She had not even noticed that the music had ceased, nor that Jack had approached them.

Simon Pendle bowed slightly. For the first time Thea realized that he was more than a little drunk.

"Evening, Merlin. I was just telling your charming *inamorata* here that—"

He broke off, gulping, as Jack stepped intimidatingly close. "I think you mistake, Pendle, as no doubt Miss Shaw has told you already." Jack's voice was dangerous, suggestive of an inclination to take Simon Pendle by the throat and choke the life out of him. "If we were anywhere other than in your parents' ballroom I would show you the error of your ways. As it is—'' Jack stepped back ''—if I hear you speaking at all for the rest of the evening, I shall call you out!''

He offered his arm to Thea and they moved away.

''That should ensure a little peace for the rest of us,'' he said dryly. He glanced down at Thea. ''Are you quite well, Miss Shaw?''

Thea knew that her hand was shaking and was sure that Jack could feel it, too, for after a moment he pressed her fingers comfortingly with his. She could see the Pendles' guests whispering and gossiping behind their hands. The words burst from her.

''I wish to go home now. At once!''

''You cannot run away.'' Jack seized her arm in a hard grip. ''Do you wish the scandalmongers to say that they drove you out? I did not think you so poor-spirited, Miss Shaw.''

Thea's eyes flashed. ''It is all very well for you, Lord Merlin! I am just another of your conquests—''

Jack's face was tight with anger, but Thea sensed it was not directed at her. ''Thea, you know that is not true—''

''I know that it is not true, but these people—'' Thea gestured wildly ''—they will only believe the worst!''

The music struck up again. Before Thea could move away, Jack had pulled her into the dance.

It was a shrewd move. Thea realized at once that it was almost impossible to quarrel whilst performing a minuet, for the stately music and the movement of the dance demanded a show of perfect decorum. It was the slowest and most mannered dance and it was the exact opposite of the wild, ungovernable feelings that were pent up inside her. Yet every time she opened her mouth to launch a blistering attack on Jack the dance steps forced them to part.

"It is all very well for you," she began as they came together, "coming to Oakmantle and causing all this trouble—"

They stepped apart. And together again.

"That is a little unfair," Jack murmured. "You were the one who started it all by planning to marry Bertie. And a more hen-witted scheme could not be imagined."

They moved away, joined hands and circled the other couples.

"Pray do not blame me!" Thea whispered crossly. "You came to Oakmantle to prevent the marriage!"

"Indeed. And a good thing, too. And it was your sister who obliged me to stay here by shooting me..."

Thea ignored this undeniable truth and swept on. "And now you are trying to distract attention when it is *your* behavior that has been disgraceful—"

They moved apart. And together. Jack grinned down at her.

"I protest! I was an exemplary invalid!"

"Do you deny that you offered me *carte blanche?*" Thea hissed. "*And* tried to seduce me?"

They executed a complicated twirl.

"I do not deny your first accusation, but the second?" Jack raised his brows. "That is scarcely fair. I most certainly did *not* attempt to seduce you!"

"Yes you did! You even wagered that you would be successful, but I won *that* bet!"

They stepped apart, turned and linked hands again.

"I admit that I issued a challenge to that effect," Jack conceded, "but I abandoned the idea of the wager after I kissed you in the garden—"

"Hush!" Thea threw a scandalized glance over her shoulder at the other dancers. "Someone will hear you."

Jack shrugged. Thea hurried in to seize the moment.

"Am I then supposed to believe that I only won because you let me, Lord Merlin? And am I also supposed to accept that if you *had* tried to seduce me, I should have noticed the difference in your behavior?"

"Most definitely you would! And—"

"And?"

Jack raised his eyebrows. There was a twinkle in his eyes that made Thea even crosser. "My dear Miss Shaw, you would have succumbed! I would bet any money!"

"Oh!" Thea stamped her foot, and then tried to pretend it was one of the dance steps as others in the set looked at her curiously. It was infuriating, particularly as he was right. She sighed angrily, caught Jack's eye and the gleam of speculative amusement in it, and almost squeaked with annoyance. "Lord Merlin, you are the most provoking man! I am trying to quarrel with you but you persist in funning me! Yet it is *not* amusing. You are here being feted by these obsequious people whilst I am suffering their censure!"

Jack bowed. "I acknowledge that. It was foolish of me not to anticipate it."

"You have ruined my reputation!" Thea said wildly, feeling her self-control slipping perilously yet seeming powerless to stop it. "Worse, you have wormed your way into the affections of my family, making them unhappy! Now Ned wants to join the army and Harry wants to be a Corinthian just like you when he grows up and…and Daisy wants a new father! You have turned our heads when you should have left well alone!"

She broke off, realizing that her words had struck a sudden chill. She saw the amusement leave Jack's eyes.

He still spoke softly, but there was an undertone of something in his voice that froze her and made all her anger shrivel away.

"If you truly believe that I have deliberately upset your family then you are right to reproach me, Miss Shaw. And if you have a concern for your reputation, I suggest you think hard, for you are contributing to your own downfall even now with your intemperate behavior!"

It was only then that Thea became aware of every eye upon them, every ear flapping for the next snippet of scandal. She could not believe that she had handed it to them on a plate. She wanted the earth to open up and swallow her whole, but worse than her humiliation was the coldness she now saw in Jack's demeanor, the formality with which he offered her his arm to move off the dance floor. Thea knew that he would not abandon her to the gossips but she also knew that he was performing his duty with no sense of pleasure anymore. She could not be certain how those undeniably bitter words had spilled out. Yes, she had been worried about her siblings—oh, yes, Jack had turned their heads, it was true, but more importantly he had turned hers. *That* was what had made her so miserable. She had fallen in love with him and she had no one to blame but herself.

Thea closed her eyes briefly and reopened them, hoping that the sea of curious faces might somehow have disappeared, that the clock would be put back, that she could have another chance. The unyielding hardness of Jack's face, the rigidity with which he kept his distance, told another tale. Around her the sea of tittle-tattle rose and fell and she felt like a cork tossed on its surface. Thea was just wondering in despair whether matters could possibly get any worse when the ballroom door swung open.

There was a silence. Then there was a commotion. Thea saw Lord and Lady Pendle detach themselves from the couple they were speaking with and rush forward with undignified haste. She saw Jack turn, and heard him swear under his breath, but before she could even wonder who had arrived so late in the proceedings, and why they were causing such a fuss, the butler cleared his throat to announce portentously, ''The Duke and Duchess of Merlin!''

Chapter Six

Thea drew in a sharp breath.

The Duchess was a tall, patrician *grande dame* in pale gold, with an ice-cool countenance. The Duke, who looked startlingly like an older version of Jack, was equally tall and austere.

Beside them, looking shifty and ill at ease, stood Bertie Pershore.

Thea experienced an almost overwhelming urge to turn and run away, but it was too late. The Duke and Duchess were already disentangling themselves from the Pendles' eager overtures and were coming toward them. Thea made an instinctive movement and Jack's hand closed around her arm like a vise, holding her by his side.

"Jack, darling!" To Thea's amazement the Duchess's face broke into a smile of startling sweetness. She came up and kissed her son on the cheek, then turned the full warmth of her smile on Thea, taking both her hands.

"Miss Shaw. Bertie has told us all about you. We are so pleased that you are going to marry Jack!"

"I…" Thea shot Bertie a look of confusion and dire retribution. Her former friend seemed to shrivel beneath her glare. "I am very pleased to make your acquaintance, Your Grace, but I fear—"

She broke off as Jack's hand tightened on her arm almost murderously. He moved smoothly into the gap.

"Pray do not put Miss Shaw to the blush, Mama! We had not announced our betrothal yet."

Thea shot him a glance of mingled horror and confusion. Jack smiled back at her blandly.

"No doubt you were wishing for us to meet your fiancée, Jack, before making a formal announcement!" The Duke of Merlin now stepped forward to shake his son by the hand. Thea felt his gaze on her face, as direct and searching as Jack's own. He smiled at her. "I fear the Duchess is precipitate, my dear Miss Shaw, but it is only because she is so pleased to welcome you into the family!"

"Of course!" The Duchess enveloped Thea in a scented hug. Thea submitted, wilting with shock. "Miss Shaw—Thea—may I call you Thea as you are to be my daughter? I could scarce believe it when Bertie told me. But I am so pleased!" The Duchess turned to Jack with shining eyes. "It is high time you settled down, dear boy, as we have been telling you this age past—"

"Yes, Mama!" Jack said hastily. "Perhaps we could continue this conversation later?"

"By all means," the Duke murmured. He turned to Thea, his eyes twinkling. "Will you grant me a dance, my dear, to grace the Pendles' Ball? They will be *aux anges* to be first with the news and to be able to boast that the Duke led out his future daughter-in-law!"

Thea realized that this was not so much an invitation as a direct order. Jack clearly did, too. He gave her a rueful smile, kissed her fingers in a way that sent Thea's feelings into even more of a spin, and offered his arm to his mother.

"May I offer you some refreshments, Mama? You may then tell me how you come to be here, for I am all agog—"

Thea was desperate to know, as well, but the Duke was waiting. She took his arm gingerly, almost as though she were afraid he would explode on touch. She was convinced that this extraordinary masquerade must come to an end very soon. The Duke covered her fingers very briefly with his own in a gesture that Thea was surprised to find gave her immense reassurance.

"No need to look so terrified, my dear!" the Duke murmured. "I am the gentlest of fellows, despite my reputation!"

Thea laughed a little shakily. "I do not doubt it, Your Grace, but if you were to find that your good nature had been abused by a misunderstanding—"

Merlin's dark blue gaze, so like his son's, fixed upon her. He spoke with emphasis. "But I shall not do so, shall I, my dear Miss Shaw? I am persuaded that you are the ideal wife for my son, and further, I am delighted to see that it is a love match!"

Thea was silent. Indeed, she was not certain what she could say. The Duke of Merlin was clearly too intelligent a man not to have read the situation correctly, but she realized that for reasons of his own he had chosen to interpret it differently. Indeed, the warning in his tone as he led her into the dance told her not to pursue the subject, least of all in public. She would be a fool to do so—the arrival of the Duke and Duchess had transformed her situation from one of scandalous misfortune to blazing triumph. All around her Thea could hear the buzz of censure transformed into pure envy.

"Betrothed to the Marquis of Merlin!... Why did she not say so before... Dear Thea has so much natural delicacy... Indeed, the Duke seems much taken with his future daughter..."

It was true that the Duke did seem most attentive to her, Thea thought, feeling more than a little dazed. His conversation was light but he complimented her sincerely on her dancing and at the end said, just loud enough for the gossips to hear, "Thank you, my dear. I suppose I must hand you back to my son now before he starts looking daggers at me! He is to be envied such a charming bride..."

Jack was indeed watching them and his expression was quite different from the coldness he had shown Thea a brief half hour before. His gaze fixed on her face with an intensity that made her feel strangely self-conscious. She knew that he was only playing up to the situation, but it added to her confusion. As the Duke escorted her from the floor, Jack took her arm proprietorially in his.

"If you are not too fatigued, my love, will you grant me one waltz before we retire? Now that our secret is out, there can be no need to dissemble..."

Thea narrowed her eyes. Jack seemed to have moved from the formality of addressing her as "Miss Shaw" to the intimacy of "my love" rather too swiftly. There was a spark of amusement in his eyes that suggested he was about to play the situation to the full, and she itched to give him the set-down he so richly deserved. But the Duke and Duchess were smiling indulgently and as she hesitated, Jack slid an arm about her waist and steered her back onto the dance floor.

"My lord," she began, as soon as they were out of earshot.

"Jack," the Marquis murmured, his lips twitching.

"You really must address me by my given name now that we are betrothed…Thea!"

"We are *not* betrothed." Thea hissed. "I have no notion how this occurred but I have no wish to be married to you—"

"Hush!" Jack touched her lips fleetingly with one finger and the contact silenced her more effectively than any words could. "Is it your wish to reverse your good fortune? Half an hour ago you were berating me for ruining your reputation. Now you are triumphantly restored and about to throw it all away."

The music struck up and they started to circle the floor. Thea pinned a bright smile on her face, one that she hoped successfully portrayed the happy sentiments of a young lady in love.

"Yes, my lord."

"Jack."

"I perfectly understand that, but the price of such a situation—"

"Is too high?"

Jack's hands moved against her back, drawing her closer to him, and Thea was suddenly and devastatingly aware of him. All coherent thoughts flew straight out of her head. She looked up into Jack's face and felt herself tremble at the look of unabashed sensuality in his eyes.

"Are you sure, Thea?" Jack's breath brushed her cheek, sending the shivers down her spine. His lips just grazed the corner of her mouth. Thea tried to think straight, tried to cut through the web of desire that threatened to envelop her. It was no easy matter.

"Surely this is all a pretense, my lord," she said breathlessly. "You cannot wish for a wife! You are temperamentally unsuited to such an enterprise as marriage."

"I assure you I am becoming more inclined to it by the moment."

Jack's hands slid into the small of her back, holding her hard against his body so that their legs almost tangled. The sensation of the hard length of him pressed against her softness was almost her undoing. Thea gasped.

"Jack!"

"Well, that's an improvement!" There was a note in Jack's voice that threatened to undermine her completely. He was making no secret of the fact that he wanted her. It was in his voice, in his touch.

"You must accept what has happened, Thea," he continued softly. "My parents have trapped us both—so neatly I have to applaud their strategy! They have wanted me to marry for a long time. Finally I have presented them with the opportunity to enforce that wish and I cannot find it in my heart to regret it."

"But surely we are to call off this fictitious betrothal?" Thea searched his face unhappily. It seemed extraordinary to her that Jack might be prepared to go through with it. "Surely you cannot wish to marry me!"

Jack looked down at her and she saw his gaze soften. "Why not? You are delightful and entirely suitable."

"But..." Thea made a despairing gesture, "I know you are putting a good face on this, my lord, but I do not expect that you even like me very much, let alone wish to marry me! After what I said to you earlier—"

Jack's smile faded. "Did you mean it, Thea?"

Thea looked away. His gaze was too penetrating. It made her feel vulnerable. But even so she was aware that she had treated him badly and owed him an apology.

"No. I am sorry. It is true that you have turned our heads, my lord, but I acquit you any deliberate intent."

"Thank you!" Jack flashed her a grin. "Then we are reconciled...and betrothed—my love."

Thea blushed at the warmth of his tone. She was aware that he had skated very adroitly over her objections, but she could be as stubborn as Clementine when she chose. She frowned. "But—"

Jack's arms tightened about her again. "Thea, If you make one more objection I shall kiss you here and now."

Thea felt a shaky smile start. "Oh, Jack—"

"Well, perhaps I shall kiss you anyway..."

"Pray be serious!" Thea tried to focus her mind. "You have been trapped into this—"

"Yes, and I do not object at all!" Jack's tone became more serious. "Do you?"

Thea looked away from that searching blue gaze. "I do not know." What she did know was that she loved Jack but she was afraid. Afraid that whilst there was an undeniable attraction between them, that was not sufficient to sustain a marriage. Afraid because his society lifestyle was so different from her own that she was not sure she could adapt. Afraid because suddenly she felt that she did not know him well at all. She knew that she loved him, but she did not dare to tell him so.

"I do not know," she repeated softly.

She missed the fleeting expression that crossed Jack's face as he looked down on her bent head, the combination of disappointment and hurt, chased away by determination. His arms loosened about her. The dance was finishing, anyway.

"Come," he said, "I'll take you home now."

When Thea glanced at him his expression was quite blank, but she could tell from his voice that he had withdrawn from her. The excitement, the sensual pleasure, had drained away, leaving her feeling uncertain and cold, and suddenly she was not at all sure what she was going to do.

The Duchess talked for most of the journey back to Oakmantle, directing her conversation to Thea with an excitement that was both touching and disconcerting. Jack, who knew his mother of old, realized that now she had the bit between her teeth she would be as irresistible as a tidal wave. Yet when the Duchess started to speak about wedding dates and trousseau and Thea turned her away with slight answers, Jack felt his heart sink. Here was the confirmation of what Thea had said earlier—she was not at all sure that she wished to marry him.

Jack shifted a little on the carriage seat and maintained his silence, cursing himself for failing to declare his feelings before the Duke and Duchess had arrived. Now that they had been trapped into an engagement, Thea would never believe that he genuinely wished to marry her anyway. The only thing that had prevented his declaration before had been Bertie's assertion that Thea did not trust him. A rake's reputation, Jack thought bitterly, was a damned encumbrance when one wished to make the first honorable proposal of one's life.

She would not marry him for his money. Jack acknowledged that he had known that even before he had told her of the value of her father's sculptures. A smile curved his lips in the darkness. So he would have to persuade her of the genuineness of his feelings. He would have to court her with irreproachable decorum. The problem was that that would take time and he did not feel inclined to patience. And he might even fail to convince her. In which case he would have to seduce her.

Desire shot through him at the very thought. He

shifted again, concentrating fiercely on the intellectual side of his predicament rather than the physical. Just how persuadable would Thea prove to be? Surely a bluestocking should be susceptible to an approach through the intellect? Yet she was convinced that he had been obliged to offer for her against his inclinations and once she had an idea she could be very tenacious.

How persuadable did he want her to be, in truth? Jack watched the carriage lights flicker over Thea's bent head and smiled again. If the thought of wooing her was sweet, the thought of seducing her was even sweeter.

"Very sorry, Thea, old thing, but what could I do?" Bertie spread his hands apologetically. He looked like a whipped spaniel. "There was Merlin demanding to know what was going on, and there was I—"

"You were supposed to be in Yorkshire, not London!" Thea abandoned her seat beside him on the garden bench and leaped to her feet. "Really, Bertie, this is absurd! Whatever can you have said to the Duke and Duchess to send them down here with the harebrained notion that Jack wanted to marry me?"

Bertie looked acutely uncomfortable. "Anyone could see the way that matters were tending between you and Jack! Once I had told Merlin a little about you and explained that you had captured Jack's affections he became positively indulgent to me! Never seen the old man like that before!"

Thea glared. "Yes, because you handed him what he wanted on a plate! Oh, Bertie, you know that the Duke has been angling to marry Jack off for these five years past and now you have played right into his hands!"

"Nothing wrong in that," Bertie said virtuously. He ran a finger around his collar where his neck cloth was feeling particularly tight. "Don't see the problem myself. Thought you'd be glad to be rescued from that nest of vipers at Pendle Hall, Thea. Ripping your character to shreds—"

"That is beside the point!" Thea threw her hands up in the air. "Jack will not release me from this so-called engagement and my future mother-in-law is setting a wedding date—"

"Good thing, too!" Bertie got to his feet. "Just the thing for you to marry Jack. All your brothers and sisters are delighted—Ned was telling me only yesterday how pleased he was—"

"Well of course he is! Now he has someone to sponsor him through the army!"

Bertie looked at her mildly. "Tell you what, Thea, I'm glad you didn't marry me. You used to be such a sweet-natured girl and now you've turned into a shrew! Perhaps Jack should change his mind before it's too late."

Thea stopped pacing and stared at him. Bertie's words had somehow hit home. He was right. She could remember a time when few matters had ruffled the smooth calm of her temperament. Certainly she had never been as cross-grained and shrewish as she was now. That had been…three weeks ago. It felt like a lifetime, and it was Jack Merlin who had effected the change by stirring up her life until it could never be the same again. She sat down a little heavily.

"Oh, dear. I have become so very cross about everything, have I not!"

Bertie patted her hand. "Never mind. Perhaps you can make up for it, old girl. Especially to Jack, for he does care about you, you know. He told me so."

To hear that was the final straw. Thea burst into tears.

Bertie backed away hastily, a look of horror on his lugubrious features.

"I say, there's no need for that, Thea!"

"Sorry, Bertie!" Thea sniffed, groping for her handkerchief, grasping after her self-control. She gave a hiccuping sob. "I shall be better directly."

She blew her nose hard, trying not to give in to the abject misery that threatened her. She felt wretched. She had quarreled with Jack from the night of the ball until that very morning, six days later. During that time he had called every day, taken her driving, courted her in exactly the conventional way that her parents would have approved. He had been the epitome of good behavior, he had gently rebuffed all her attempts to break the engagement and his baffling good humor and steadfast persistence had made Thea want to cry.

Only that morning he had pressed her gently about a wedding date and she had snapped at him that she would not marry him, would never marry him. She had seen an expression cross his face so quickly she had wondered if she had imagined seeing the hurt there, and then he had turned on his heel and gone out. Thea had gone up to her room and cried, without really understanding why, and then she had kept herself very busy until Bertie had arrived. Now, despite herself, another small sob escaped her.

Bertie gave a hunted look around. "Shall I call your sister?" he asked hopefully. "Needs a woman's touch, and all that!"

Thea shook her head. "Everyone is out today. Ned and Harry are playing for the village side at cricket, Skeffie has taken Daisy and Clara to watch, and Clementine is visiting with the Duchess." She brightened a little, scrubbing her eyes. "Do you know, Bertie, the

Duchess believes that she might even make Clemmie presentable! Can you believe that? She was talking about giving her a Season next year.'' She slumped again. ''But, of course, if I do not marry Jack…''

Bertie snorted. ''Marry or not, you're going a step too far there, Thea! Clementine presentable? I'll wager a monkey against it!''

Thea gave a watery giggle. ''Maybe you are right and it is too much to hope for! Oh, Bertie—'' she gave him an impulsive hug ''—you are the very best of good friends and I am sorry that I have been so horrible to you!''

After Bertie had left, Thea donned an apron over her old blue muslin and walked listlessly to the herb garden. It was a beautiful spring day and the clumps of mint, parsley and thyme were flourishing in the warmth by the old brick garden wall. Thea walked on, past the hyssop and rosemary, until she reached the lavender bed. She took a small knife from the pocket in her apron and cut some new sprigs before going back inside the house.

Oakmantle Hall was very quiet. Thea went softly up the stairs and into her own bedchamber, where she busied herself folding the clean bed linen and storing it away in the armada chest. She folded the sheets, put the sprigs of lavender between them and closed the lid. The scent of lavender was on her fingers, reminding her of that day in the garden, the way that Jack had held her. Perhaps he would not come back now that she had been so horrible to him. Thea blinked the tears back. She seemed to be turning into a watering pot these days and it was most infuriating.

She did not hear the front door open or the tread on the stairs, did not even realize anyone was there until she heard a step in the bedroom doorway and turned to see

Jack lounging against the doorpost. He did not speak, simply stood there watching her. There was a look in his eyes that made Thea catch her breath. The words dried on the tip of her tongue.

"Jack."

"Thea?" Jack straightened up and came toward her, moving with what seemed to Thea's unnerved eyes to be the predatory concentration of a cat. Two thoughts occurred to her simultaneously. One was that they had never been completely alone together in the house. The second was that Jack was a rake. And even as she thought it she realized his intention and her heart started to race. She took a step back, crushing one of the sprigs of lavender that had fallen to the floor. The lavender smell entwined itself around them. Jack stepped closer, his eyes darkening as he inhaled the scent.

Thea's words came out in a rush. "Jack, I must speak to you."

Jack barely paused. "We'll talk later."

"But—"

A second more and Thea realized that he was not going to waste his breath arguing with her. Not when he could kiss her. He leaned forward, closing the distance between them slowly, sliding one arm about her gently. His lips barely brushed hers, the merest touch, yet Thea felt the echo of that contact all the way through her body. Her hand came up to rest on his chest and she made one last effort, leaning back a little.

"Jack…" She found she had to clear her throat. "What are you doing?"

The danger and gentleness in his eyes made her feel weaker still.

"I am going to seduce you, Thea." His voice was as husky as hers. "I have courted you with decorum, I have tried to reason with you, but if this is what I have to do to persuade you of my genuine desire to marry you...."

Thea's eyes were huge. "Oh! I am persuaded!"

Jack shook his head. "Too late. If I let you go now you will think of another reason to refuse me. This is the only thing that I can do to claim you for my own..."

To claim you for my own... Thea gave a little gasp that was lost as his mouth took hers again, this time holding nothing back. The kiss was hot and hungry, spiraling down into desire. Thea felt the passion flood through her like a riptide, huge, powerful, too urgent to resist. She did not even try—at last her mind was telling her that there was no need to hold back, for Jack wanted her for herself alone, not to rescue her reputation nor to help her family but because he wanted to claim her as his, body and soul.

She was trembling as Jack drew her down onto the yielding softness of the bed, and she lay back gratefully for she was not certain that she could stand any longer. The kiss had softened into sweetness now, long and lingering but no less breathless. Finally Jack propped himself up on one elbow, pulled the lace mobcap off her curls and tossed it across the room.

"I have wanted to do that for a long time," he murmured. "And as for this monstrosity of an apron—" His fingers had found the ties and were tugging hard.

Thea murmured a faint protest and Jack bent his head and kissed her again. And again, until she could scarcely speak.

"Thea..." When Jack let her go this time, Thea simply looked at him in mute silence. "I wanted to tell you that when you ran into my arms that day at the church I felt something far stronger for you than I had ever felt for any woman before."

His fingers were undoing the buttons of her gown with deft skill. Thea smiled a little as she watched him. "Was that not desire, Jack?" she whispered.

"Perhaps," Jack conceded. "Yes, definitely. But it was not just that…"

He opened her gown and slid his hand inside, baring her small, gently rounded breasts. Thea gasped and arched against him. She was filled with the most sublime ache and when Jack bent his head to her breast and captured one rosy peak in his mouth, she felt a simultaneous rush of exquisite relief and an even deeper need, awoken by the roughness of his cheek against her skin, the teasing of his tongue.

"It was much more than that," Jack continued, his lips against her skin. "My feelings did not take long to deepen into admiration and…love. So you must be gentle with me, sweetheart, for it hasn't happened to me before…"

Thea's heart seemed to do a somersault. "Do you really love me?"

"Yes…" Jack's hands were drifting over her skin in distracting circles, stroking, soothing, making her melt again with love and desire. He leaned over to kiss her long and hard. She could feel her body softening again, aching for him, opening as Jack moved across her, one leg sliding between hers.

"I think you have done this before, though," she murmured.

"It's different…" Jack's words were a breath against her bare skin. He bent his head to her breasts again, teasing her until she dug her fingers into his back in exquisite agony. Her whole body was slipping and sliding down into delicious pleasure. She never wanted it to stop.

Jack sat up reluctantly and tugged off his boots, tossed them aside, and dealt summarily with the rest of his clothes. Neither of them spoke as he rejoined her on the bed and removed the rest of her garments with equal ruthlessness. The touch of his skin against hers made Thea gasp in shock and pleasure. She shivered as he started to kiss her again, long, slow kisses that drugged the senses until she was desperate for him.

Urgency caught them both then, sweet and strong, and Jack shifted again, drawing her to him, parting her thighs, sliding into her gently.

Thea gave a soft gasp and Jack lowered his head, brushing his lips across hers.

''Thea?''

She opened her eyes, dazzling blue, bright with desire. She did not speak, simply raised a hand to tangle in his hair and bring his head down to hers so that she could kiss him again. All the love and triumphant possessiveness fused within him then, and slowly, with infinite gentleness, he made her his.

When Jack awoke the sun had moved across the room and was lying in a bright bar across the tangled bed linens. Thea was kneeling at the end of the bed, craning her neck to see the clock on the mantelpiece, the sunlight turning her hair into a web of bright gold, light and insubstantial like a fairy net. It was a net that had trapped him firmly and would never let him go. Jack examined the thought, the strange but satisfying rightness of it, and felt a smile start to curl his lips. He stretched luxuriously.

At his slight movement, Thea turned her head toward him. She was in shadow, every curve outlined in black like a silhouette. Jack felt his body stir. He told himself that he had a lifetime in which to watch Thea, to memorize her face, to explore all those tantalizing lines and curves. However, when she almost lost her balance on the tangled bedclothes and leaned over the foot of the bed to steady herself, the need suddenly seemed urgent.

Jack moved swiftly, catching Thea around the waist and tumbling her back down beside him. She lay still looking up at him, her eyes widening as his desire communicated itself to her. Jack brushed the hair away from her face, bending to kiss her.

"I am thinking that whilst I have made a most humbling declaration of love to you, sweetheart, you have not actually told me that you love me…"

Thea looked at him. Her face was flushed pink, her lips parted. "Oh… I thought that you knew. Yes, of course I do…"

Jack kissed her softly again, his lips clinging to hers. She felt sweet and warm and wonderfully yielding.

"In that case I must go and get a special license. At once. There is not a moment to lose."

He felt Thea shift beneath him. Her hands caressed him tentatively and he drew in a sharp breath.

"Jack—" it was a whisper "—can it not wait a little?"

"Well…" He moved inside her again, gently, tantalizingly. Thea gasped. He bent his head to her breast. "Perhaps it can wait just a little longer…"

Whereas he knew that he could not. As he reached for her and she responded in full measure, all Jack's good resolutions fled. He had meant to be tender, to introduce her to the pleasures of making love gradually and with consideration, but her natural sensuality swept all of that aside. This was a wild lovemaking with none of the gentleness of their previous encounter and at the end they were both dazzled, sated with pleasure. Jack wrapped his arms about Thea as they slowly drifted down to earth.

"The children will be back soon," she murmured against his shoulder.

Jack made a sound of sleepy contentment.

"We must get up." Thea wriggled out of his embrace and groped around for her clothes, which seemed to be scattered to the four corners of the room. "Daisy will want her story, and Clara will want to play for you and the boys will want some more cricket coaching if the village team lost—"

Jack rolled over and looked at her. His midnight-blue gaze raked her lazily from head to foot. "And what do you want from me, my love?"

"Oh, just to marry you," Thea said airily. "That will suffice!" She looked at him and smiled. "I know those sculptures are worth a fortune but I could not bear to sell them for sentimental reasons! My father was prodigious fond of them! So I am sorry, Jack…" She bent over to kiss him, "I have to marry you for your money! It is the only solution!"

* * * * *

Lookin' for some spicy Westerns seasoned
with just the right amount of sizzling
romance and rollicking adventure? Then help
yourselves to these Harlequin Historicals novels

ON SALE MARCH 2002

A MARRIAGE BY CHANCE
by **Carolyn Davidson**
(Wyoming, 1894)

SHADES OF GRAY
by **Wendy Douglas**
(Texas, 1868)

ON SALE APRIL 2002

THE BRIDE FAIR
by **Cheryl Reavis**
(North Carolina, 1868)

THE DRIFTER
by **Lisa Plumley**
(Arizona, 1887)

(HHH) Harlequin Historicals®

Take a jaunt to Merry Old England
with these timeless stories from
Harlequin Historicals

On sale March 2002

THE LOVE MATCH
by Deborah Simmons
Deborah Hale
Nicola Cornick
Don't miss this captivating bridal collection
filled with three breathtaking Regency tales!

MARRYING MISCHIEF
by Lyn Stone
Will a quarantine spark romance between a
determined earl and his convenient bride?

On sale April 2002

MISS VEREY'S PROPOSAL
by Nicola Cornick
A matchmaking duke causes a smitten London
debutante to realize she's betrothed to the
wrong brother!

DRAGON'S KNIGHT
by Catherine Archer
When a powerful knight rushes to the aid of a
beautiful noblewoman, will he finally conquer
his darkest demons?

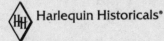

Harlequin Historicals®

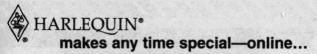